APATHY'S HERO

TRUTH'S HAREM BOOK 3

ALLYSON LINDT

ACELETTE PRESS

This book is a work of fiction.

While reference might be made to actual historical events or existing locations, the names, characters, places and incidents are either the product of the author's imagination or are used fictitiously, and any resemblance to actual persons, living or dead, business establishments, events, or locales is entirely coincidental.

Manufactured in the United States of America
Acelette Press

For my eternal dragon

ONE

ACTAEON DIDN'T WAKE UP WITH HEADACHES OFTEN.
After three thousand years, he could count the occur-
rences on one hand. All of them had happened after
huge fights—the kind that drained the spirit and body
equally.

Then again, the last thing he remembered was
fighting for his life against Hades. Arguably the most
powerful god in existence.

That would explain the hammering in Actaeon's
skull. The rest of his situation didn't make sense. All he
smelled were the blood and sweat that coated his clothes
and skin. The only sounds were his breathing and the
steady thrum of his heart. *Nothing* stretched in every
direction.

And then there was a new scent. Mountain air
tinged with exhaust.

"Morning, Sleeping Beauty." The voice came from
behind him.

Actaeon turned, taking in the vast stretches of noth-

1

ingness. Hermes stood in the middle of the blank space—was there a middle? Actaeon's head pounded at the attempt to grasp logic.

Hermes was the only thing in here with any color. He wore skinny jeans, Converse, and a neon green fitted T-shirt with the letters FTW across it.

"Where are we?" Actaeon asked. It didn't look like the underworld. "Where's Lexi? Icarus? Cerberus?"

"Nowhere. Everywhere. Earth. I don't know."

Everywhere? That sounded bad. "I have to get to her." He stood and stumbled. *Fuck*, he hated feeling weak. Why hadn't he recovered? It usually only took a few hours of rest for him to heal from even the gravest injury.

"Hold on, hero. We need to talk. Then I'll deliver you."

There were some things Actaeon rarely had patience for. The gods and their vague bullshit always made the top of the list. "Nope. I have to get back to Lexi. To Hades—"

"Whom you killed." Hermes' short mohawk matched his shirt, but it had been decades since he wore his natural hair color.

Actaeon backpedaled over the words. "Wait. Hades? I didn't kill Hades."

"Probably not alone. And if you did, don't let that shit get out. The last thing we need people knowing is that it only takes one of you to kill one of us."

He hadn't been alone. He was fighting side-by-side with Cerberus. Lexi was there. She did something. He remembered a siren's scream. Cassandra's pain.

He had to get to Lexi.

This time he managed to stand and started walking. "Which way is out?"

"No place you're going to find on foot. Traveling that way is only going to make you more exhausted, and you need a little time to heal." Hermes strolled next to him.

"It's better than sitting on my ass."

"Since when?"

Irritation spiked through Actaeon, and he clenched his fists. His annoyance was directed as much at himself as Hermes. Actaeon spent far too many years not meddling in the business of the gods, for all the wrong reasons.

"Are you going to answer my questions, instead of speaking in bullshit and riddles?" he asked. Right about now, it sure would be handy to have Lexi's gift for seeing when people were lying.

"I'm trying. If you'd chill the fuck out for about two minutes, I'd tell you everything I know about the situation. No cryptic twists. No holding back." Hermes sounded sincere. Almost somber. This wasn't like him.

Actaeon paused and faced the god again. "Why?"

"Why not?" Hermes' hair drooped, falling in straight curtains around his face, and the green wilted to something closer to the color of dead grass. "This is bad. That's why."

Actaeon tried to shrug off the serious tone, but *bad* sent goosebumps racing over him.

Hades recently took an interest in humanity, after being locked away for several decades. After being content for millennia to stay in the underworld. That interest meant killing millions, to grow his power—the dead dying in his name made him stronger—then resurrecting key figures, to spread the message of his greatness.

If the current situation was bad compared to that, Actaeon was almost sorry he'd asked.

Almost.

He sat on the nothing. If he was sticking around, he might as well use the chance to recover. "I'm listening."

"Where to start?" Hermes sighed. He crouched, forearms resting on his knees. "There was a fight. Hades died. According to Icarus, you played a big part in that."

"So you've talked to Icarus?" That was promising. Relief trickled in. Not for an old friend, but carried on a more intimate emotion. A desire Actaeon didn't have time to examine. He didn't care to, either, after their last conversation.

"I haven't. Aphrodite has. And since you're so concerned, she spoke with part of Lexi as well."

Fuck. He'd failed her. Failed *them*. "*Part of?* How's that supposed to ease my concern?" Aphrodite's involvement was the only bit that didn't have Actaeon concerned. Hermes was married to Eros, Aphrodite's son, and the family was close. For gods, they were almost well-adjusted. Still, how long had Actaeon been out, that the news had time to spread?

"*Shut up*, and I'll tell you." Hermes' shout rocked the nothingness.

Now was probably a bad time to mention that the whole shout-and-shake-the-room thing the gods did stopped being terrifying about twenty-five-hundred years ago. "I'm listening."

"Apparently, Hades wasn't just a god of death; he *was* every bit of the underworld. Nice of Zeus to let anyone know, right?"

Actaeon wanted to be surprised. "Lovely."

"You killed Hades. His realm crumbled with him. It threw the non-dead out—you, Lexi, Icarus, and I assume Cerberus—because it didn't exist anymore. I found you. You're more or less nowhere. Limbo? No one can find Cerberus. It should have thrown the dead free, too. But... something—someone—stopped it."

"Lexi." Actaeon wasn't sure how he knew that, but he had no doubt.

"Yeah. Turns out Persephone was keeping a very old secret. She was born without an aura—without any visible power—so everyone assumed she was mortal. She figured out she was a goddess and hid it."

"Why?"

Hermes shrugged. "Are you going to ask her?"

Unlikely, since she'd been destroyed, her soul wiped from existence by a vessel of Hades. Actaeon didn't want to dwell on the details of confrontation that killed her. If Persephone was a goddess, and Lexi wasn't mortal... a god and a goddess didn't have hero children. "So Lexi is a goddess?"

"The new goddess of the underworld, as far as we can tell. What she thinks of as her body is with Icarus. The rest of her..."

"Is where?" Actaeon wasn't letting him cut things off now, when they were to the information he wanted.

"Charon can explain it better than I can."

Actaeon should have guessed there was a catch. He stood and stretched. Muscles that should be healed by now protested. Why wasn't he better? "So much for telling me everything I want to know."

"I'm taking you to the source. It's more than you'd get from most of the gods."

Actaeon couldn't argue that. He didn't want to see Charon. He owned the ferryman a favor and had been promised he wouldn't leave the underworld the next time they crossed paths.

He'd deal with the problem when it presented itself. He needed to get back to Lexi.

"Off we go," Hermes said. The nothingness vanished, replaced by a river.

Trees lined the shore, and a dock stood a few feet away. A heavy enough haze covered the water that the other side was hidden. Was there still an *other side*? Actaeon smelled trees and dirt and mist.

This was Styx, and Charon ferried souls across it, to their afterlife.

Hermes ensured the dead made it here in the first place.

A boat rippled into view at the pier, and a cloaked figure stood at the bow. The oar clasped in his gnarled hand vanished into the water below. "Good." Charon's baritone rolled over the landscape. "I was hoping he'd find you."

"I'll leave you two to it." Hermes vanished.

Actaeon's headache was subsiding. "I'm not in the mood for theatrics."

"Fine. Take a guy's fun away." Charon pulled back his hood, revealing a nondescript, human-looking face.

"Hermes said you could explain why he thinks Lexi is in pieces."

"You want something from me? If I remember right, you still owe me a favor from the last time we talked. And you don't have anything new to offer in exchange for information."

It was tempting to punch a hole through the nearest tree. If Actaeon wasn't impressed with the displays of power, Charon wouldn't be either, so the poor tree would be the only thing to suffer.

"But since you're here, it seems like a good time for me to call in that favor," Charon said.

Moonlight with no source crackled over Actaeon's skin. "This is exactly the opposite of a good time for that." A growl rumbled from his chest. He'd been spending too much time around the hellhound.

"You don't have a choice." Without magic to make his voice boom, Charon might as well be the guy talking too loud on his phone while he waited for his coffee. "You offered a favor. I'm calling it in."

The sooner Actaeon got this over with... "Name your favor and your terms."

"Find Alexandria. Help her."

Actaeon barked out a laugh. "Are you kidding me with this drawn-out, melodramatic bullshit? That's what I'm trying to do. Tell me where she is, and I'll go get her."

"No."

Actaeon was going to yank his hair out over this.

And that tree was looking like a really tempting target. His fingertips twitched, begging for him to summon a weapon. *Something*, as an outlet for this frustration. "Why not?"

"It's not as simple as *here's a map. Go forth and find her.* Even for you, hunter." Charon stepped from the boat and onto the pier. His oar vanished, but his vessel stayed moored by an invisible line. Two wicker chairs materialized on the dock, looking too stark and ludicrous in this place. He sat in one and gestured to the other.

Actaeon moved closer but remained standing.

"I was there the day she was born," Charon said. "If you've never seen a god come into creation, it's literally miraculous. I was in the next room, but I felt her the moment she took her first breath. I knew she would become this. The details—the how and when—were a mystery, but there was no doubt in my mind she would replace her father."

This was a lot to process. Lexi wasn't even half a century old. Other heroes and gods born during the enlightenment were still securing their place in the world. *Tartarus*, so was she. Actaeon sank into the empty chair. "How many people who aren't her hold pieces of information about her fate?"

"I can't tell you. I don't get out much." Charon's chuckle was weak. "I can feel her. Everywhere. Hades was obliterated, and the underworld started to crumble. She took his place before it all fell apart. I don't think she knows how to handle it, though. Her body is with Icarus. I can't tell you where her mind is. He can't reach it. I believe her soul is down here, somewhere."

"That's appropriately vague." Actaeon was trying to be nonchalant, but his thoughts were racing.

Charon gave him a thin smile. "This setting molds to the person who inhabits it. You know that. I suspect, wherever that part of her is, she's created it to be hers. You know her. You have to find her and stay with her."

That hurt. "Do you think I'd do anything contrary to that?"

"Becoming the underworld pushed Hades past the edge of sanity he teetered on. He was never the same afterward. Lexi doesn't know what's happening to her, and I can't say what's out there. This transition could be as simple as walking down to the corner market for a pack of smokes, or she could encounter trials that would make Heracles cower."

It didn't matter. Actaeon would face it all for Lexi. "I'll find her, regardless. Point me in a direction."

"I can take you across the river. No toll today." Charon stood, and his robes swished around him. He returned to the boat.

The offer made Actaeon wary. Charon never broke the toll rule. "Why are you doing this?" Actaeon asked. He stepped into the craft and took a seat.

"For everyone else, Styx is a temporary layover. Heroes come to me when you need to prove your valor on the other side. People only stop by long enough to take the trip. For me, this is my home. It exists because the underworld exists. If she dies—or worse, goes insane—my world is impacted." Charon pushed away from the shore, steering them into a dense expanse of fog and darkness.

His answer was difficult to argue with.

The shore behind them vanished, and there was no wind rushing around Actaeon. It was impossible to tell how fast they moved or how far away their destination was.

"Where should I start my search?" Actaeon needed a direction.

"I can't say. Yes, *can't*, not *won't*. You love her. You must know her heart. Her mind. You have a better chance of finding her that almost anyone."

Cerberus would know exactly where to look. Icarus might have a better idea than Actaeon as well. Their last conversation—argument—echoed in Actaeon's thoughts. The accusations that he wanted to be a martyr. That he only wanted Lexi around because she was a lost soul with a tortured life.

All complete and utter shit.

They reached the far shore more quickly than he expected, and he found himself standing on solid ground.

"Good luck, hero. Don't fuck this up," Charon boomed and disappeared back into the mist.

"Thanks." Actaeon sneered at the empty space where the ferryman had been.

Where was he supposed to start?

Lexi was on this side of the river, so that was one direction eliminated. He walked toward the spot he'd most recently seen everyone—Persephone's old house.

Large cracks ran along the ground, vanishing into half-crumbled buildings and partially scorched fields. It looked like things deteriorated a little before Lexi claimed this place.

A sobbing woman appeared out of nowhere and bumped into him. "Help me. My home…" She gestured vaguely.

Before he could thing of a response, she vanished. In the distance, he saw other forms blinking into sight before disappearing again. Displaced souls.

Actaeon had no idea where to look. The landscape was eternally vast. What would Lexi call it? A Tardy? She liked those geek references. She, Cerberus, and even Icarus, swapped them without pause.

Actaeon didn't have a lot of use for pop culture. He knew other things about Lexi, though.

She was strong.

Tortured.

Lost.

A fantastic lay.

Fuck. Icarus was right. Actaeon didn't have any clue who she was. He'd meant to rectify that. They were supposed to go out. Have dinner a few times. Get to know each other. As soon as they dealt with Hades.

Actaeon knew more about the layout of the under-world than he did about Lexi, and this place was all but unrecognizable in its current condition.

But that didn't mean Actaeon was attracted to her because her fate bordered on hopeless. He truly cared about her.

Why?

He didn't need to explain it. He just did.

Which didn't him where to look for her.

TWO

"ARE YOU ALL RIGHT?" LEXI'S VOICE SEEPED INTO Cerberus' consciousness, and she brushed her fingers across his cheek.

He felt her aura. Smelled the lilacs and ozone. He didn't hear her in his thoughts, though. Was she keeping him out?

He forced his eyes open, then squeezed them shut again until he could adjust to the sunlight. More of his surroundings trickled in—grass and hard-packed dirt digging into his side, the sound of laughter and cars, and the tang of blood on his tongue.

Cerberus dared to look again, as he pushed himself into a sitting position. "I don't think I'm in Kansas anymore," he muttered.

"New Orleans." Lexi was kneeling next to him. She didn't look like herself, though. The starkest difference was the absence of a tattoo on her neck. She wore a black dress, and a streak of vibrant blue ran through her dark hair.

"Not the underworld?" The last thing he remembered was fighting Hades—the screams, the exhaustion… He didn't feel any pain, though. He must have slept long enough to heal.

Lexi furrowed her brow. "I'm not sure when the last time was you looked at a map, but Kansas borders Missouri, not Tartarus."

They were in a park, in a patch of grass surrounded by trees and set back from the path. This was so bizarre.

He leaned in closer, dipping his head near her neck for a better sniff, partly for comfort, but just as much to decipher what was different about her.

"Whoa, pushy McShifter Boy." She landed her palm on his chest and held him at arm's length. "Getting familiar much?"

"*What's up with you?*" He sent the mental question.

There was nothing. It wasn't as though she'd locked him out of her head, but the link between them didn't exist. He couldn't feel her heart. Her emotions. He and she didn't share a bond.

Hades wasn't in his head either, though. And he wasn't dying. What the actual fuck? "Do you know me?"

"I know you were lying unconscious in the grass. I know you're some kind of three-headed shapeshifting dog-man. I know I'm not comfortable with you slobbering on me."

"How old are you?"

She stood and brushed the grass from her knees. "Nope. You're alive. I'm glad to see it. Or I was until you broke out the presumption. We're done talking." She turned on her toe.

"Lexi, wait."

Her body went rigid, and a hint of fear wafted from her, mingling with her self-assurance. "That's not my name."

She was a terrible liar. The woman who could see truth. Go figure.

"Alexandra Leia Graham," he said. No one knew her full name, except her parents and Cerberus. She'd sworn that when she told him.

Sweat mingled with her familiar scent. Her heart beat faster. She clenched her fists.

On the path, a pair of women chatted while they pushed strollers.

Lexi reached in her purse. Before he could puzzle out what she was doing, she whirled back to face him and pressed a bloodstained gargoyle claw to this throat.

"Tell me who the fuck you are and how you know my name." Her voice was tight. Pink and purple flared around her, dancing like flames along her skin. "I don't know if you're one of those impossible to kill things, but I doubt it's pleasant to have one of these buried in your windpipe." A faint tremor ran through her hand, vibrating through the claw and against his skin.

Cerberus tried to scoot back, and she pressed the tip hard enough to nick him. "Answer me," she said. There was more than fear and command in her voice. Grief lay underneath. He hadn't noticed it before.

"We know each other." He needed to tell her the truth, but without knowing when or where he was, he didn't dare say too much.

"Try again. I'd remember that."

"You told me your full name. Said only your stepfather used it."

She clenched her jaw and searched his face.

Then vanished.

Fuck. When were they? Who was she? This couldn't be a younger Lexi. She hadn't known how to make herself invisible until a few weeks ago.

It was an illusion. Her scent wasn't fading. It sang to his heart and soothed his soul.

And the fact that she didn't know him left an empty pit beneath it all.

The only way through this was honesty. "You don't trust the gods, their servants, or other heroes. I don't blame you. Ninety-nine percent of them are selfish, lying assholes."

"Cynical much?" Her question came from empty air.

"This from a woman who carries a gargoyle claw in her purse. Who didn't hesitate to pull it on a stranger. Does Poseidon know you have that?"

She appeared again. She hadn't moved. "Some creepy-sexy guy I've never met pushes himself on me and knows my full name. You'd react differently?"

"I'd tear my throat out. In my defense, I know you."

"So you keep saying." She crossed her arms. The claw was still clenched in her fist, and she stood as straight as if she had a rod rammed up her spine.

"Why haven't you left?" he asked.

She clenched her jaw.

"Because you know I'm telling the truth."

"You *believe* you're telling the truth."

"Which means I'm not lying to you." He didn't want to spend the afternoon nitpicking the finer points of truth versus reality with her. "My name is Cerberus."

Her nostrils flared. "You served Hades."

"Past tense. Correct." He had to measure his response carefully. The wrong answer would send her running. "You and I met online. You were looking for more information about Hades. Your stepfather told you the history books lied and Hades was still alive. I don't know why you don't remember. There are things we've shared that mean more to me than most people can imagine."

"Like what?"

He *tsk*ed. "Trust goes both ways. There are some things I'm not willing to share with just anyone."

"Like how much you love someone who looks just like me."

She was observant. It had kept her alive for this long.

"She doesn't look like you. She *is* you." Cerberus didn't understand why he was certain, but he was.

"We're at an impasse, then. You won't open up to me. I'm sure as fuck not telling you anything."

There were only a few topics he was keeping off-limits. "Ask me another question."

"You know me, but now how old I am. How does that make sense? Is this a *Sliders* thing? *Quantum Leap*?"

Wow. Her stepdad had gone old school with her geek-education. Had Cerberus traveled in time? "Neither, as far as I'm aware. You're missing some of the scars my Lexi has, so I assume you're younger. My turn. Why do you have a gargoyle claw in your purse?"

Her laugh was bitter. "The police said I could keep it. Dad was sacrificed, not murdered, so it's a souvenir, not a murder weapon."

"That's fucked up." Like so much of what came with the enlightenment. "Are you dressed for a special occasion?"

"You don't get two questions in a row, but I'll give you a freebie. Yes. As horrifically special as this moment in any child's life is, when the gods have picked a loved one for sacrifice—my father's funeral."

That told him she was in her early twenties. Had he time traveled? It wasn't as though Hades and the world around them exploded, and threw him back a couple of decades. If Actaeon and Icarus were facing the opposite direction, did they go forward in time?

Another pair of women walked by, chatting and pushing strollers.

Or they were the same pair.

Having the same conversation?

Something wasn't right. He sniffed the air. The only scents were those of Lexi and the foliage.

"I get a question now," she said. "If you know me as well as you think, does this ache in my chest ever go away? Do I ever stop missing Dad?"

"No. It changes shape. There are some days when it doesn't hurt as much, but it never goes away." He'd felt it for himself—that quiet sadness that lived in her heart. There was a piece of her that had never moved past her stepfather's death.

That was important. Why?

Lexi settled onto the grass, tucked her legs to the side, and smoothed her skirt. "Maybe you do know me." Sadness dripped from her words.

The two women with the strollers walked by again, having the same conversation.

Were Cerberus and Lexi stuck in some part of her mind? The bit of her that had never escaped her past? That was almost as ridiculous as the time travel theory. He wouldn't smell her, if that were the case, because she didn't pick up her own scent the way he did.

A memory nudged his thoughts, then burst in uninvited.

He kissed along the back of Lexi's neck. Her groan danced over his skin and through the bond they shared. "I'll always know you. Your smell. Your taste. Your voice."

"What do I smell like?" she asked.

"Lilacs and ozone."

She giggled. "So poetic."

"You bring out my inner Vogon."

"I actually like *your poetry." Lexi snuggled into him. Her bare skin against his was one of his favorite sensations. "What would you do if you couldn't smell anymore?"*

"I'd know your voice anywhere. Recognize your aura from a mile away."

"And what if all your senses were gone?" It was a somber question, but her tone was light.

"My heart would still recognize you."

She sighed and pulled his arms tighter around her. "From anyone else, that would fall strictly in the cheesy as fuck column."

"Why is it different coming from me?" He already sensed the answer. It flowed between them, unvocalized but potent.

"Because you mean it."

Cerberus shook the thought aside. "Are you coming or going? From the funeral?"

"Going. I couldn't listen to them anymore. So many people lining up to lie about their feelings for Dad."

"Your stepfather was a good man. I'd expect people to adore him."

She gave him a twisted smile. "What was it you said? Ninety-nine percent of people are assholes? I suspect most of them liked him all right. But the platitudes and glowing praise? They're lying. I don't know why. Maybe they're bitter that he was a better man than any of them will ever be. Besides, one of them must have thrown his name in the *sacrifice* hat. Someone in that fucking church was the reason he was killed."

"I'm sorry."

"Don't be. It's not your fault." She plucked a strand of grass, shredded it into several smaller pieces, then discarded the remains and moved to the next blade. "Is it?"

"Not that I'm aware of. I didn't have any idea who or where you were at this point in your life. But I've met some of history's best and brightest, and from the things you've said about your stepdad, a lot of them couldn't hold a candle to him. I would have liked to have met him."

"See, that, I believe." She let out a frustrated groan and scrubbed her face. "This sucks."

Her pain echoed in his chest. Even without the bond that connected them, he felt for her. "It does."

"That's not comforting." She rolled onto her back, face to the sky.

"You'd rather I lied?"

She patted the ground next to her. "I'd rather you watched the clouds with me."

"When did we reach that point, where you decided to trust me rather than kill me?" Not that he was complaining.

"We're not there yet. But I'm exhausted. It's been a long week. I just want to feel the rain on my face."

Dark clouds appeared, blotting out the sun in a heartbeat.

A high-pitched whine split the air, threatening to do the same to his eardrums.

He pressed his palms to his ears, but the noise was in his skull. It was too loud. It gnawed at his brain, until the only thing he could think was *make it stop*.

THREE

ICARUS PACED HIS ROOM. AT THE END OF EACH CIRCUIT, he turned to look at Lexi. She lay on his bed, unmoving.

She was alive. It wasn't obvious from here, but when he was next to her, he saw her chest rise and fall.

He didn't have to be watching her to see how fucked up her aura was. The jagged shards of pink and purple faded to near invisible, before growing beyond the expanses of the room, then shrinking into her again.

What was he supposed to do? He knew electricity. How to weave it with magic. Lexi had plenty of both, especially right now.

But he didn't know how to make them work with a human body.

"Damn it, Jim. I'm an inventor, not a doctor," he muttered to his comatose audience.

He couldn't see into her thoughts. They'd only shared the bond for a few days that gave them an almost psychic connection. In that short amount of time, he'd gotten used to holding mental conversations with her and glimpsing pieces of her past, through her eyes.

He'd managed to meditate long enough to probe the edges of her mind, but when he prodded, he was thrown out.

Icarus wouldn't be surprised if the shock from the last attempt left his hair standing on end.

The proximity alarm around his property went off. He'd tuned it so the high-pitched whine went off anytime an immortal other than himself or Lexi stepped inside.

A flicker of hope sparked in his chest. It could be Actaeon and Cerberus. Would their presence bring Lexi back where Icarus hadn't been able to? He wouldn't be surprised if Cerberus could. Actaeon… Icarus couldn't deal with that land mine from the past right now.

He snapped his fingers, and the screen on his wall flickered to life, showing a picture provided by the camera on the front of his shop. Disappointment flared inside at the sight of Aphrodite knocking. It was a beautifully polite gesture, considering all of the glass in the windows and the door was broken, and his shop had been trashed.

He didn't expect to see her again so soon. They'd left her less than an hour ago, when he and Lexi landed back on Earth, alone, after fighting side-by-side with Actaeon and Cerberus to kill Hades.

He squeezed Lexi's hand. "If you could wake up while I let our guest in, that would be swell."

With one more glance at her motionless form, he headed upstairs.

"Love what you've done with the place," Aphrodite called, when he stepped into the main room.

Icarus choked off a laugh. A pre-fight fight with Hades was responsible for some of the mess. The rest was courtesy of his neighbors. People he'd stood by for years. This was their *thanks*.

Then again, he'd brought destruction to their front door. They deserved a little leeway for their response. "If you'd like, I'll give you the name of my interior decorator. Come on in."

Aphrodite picked her way gingerly through the shattered remains of electronics. In her wispy, flowing, white dress, she looked Photoshopped on top of the mess. She paused in front of a Barbie doll nailed to the wall, and ripped it down—an effigy of Lexi that Icarus' *charming* neighbors left behind. The plastic and rubber burst into flames in her palm, and were ash a second later. "Charming." She looked at Icarus. "Where is she? Is she all right?"

"No." Icarus gestured toward the stairs. "She's unconscious. Talk to me. Why did you come back?"

Aphrodite followed him into the basement. "Hermes is seeking out Actaeon and has a message for you from Charon. Lexi is becoming the underworld, and she doesn't know how to handle being both a person and a place. She's fracturing."

Well, fuck. That sounded bad. He stepped into Aphrodite's path. "Why do you care?"

"Am I not supposed to?"

"Not like this." The gods did things that served their interests. Even the nobler ones. "You've taken a personal interest in Lexi since the day you met her. You brought Conner into her world, to introduce her to the gods. You've always kept her safe. Off everyone's radar. You're there at the right time, when she needs you. Why?" This might not be the right time to ask, but he wasn't letting her near an unconscious Lexi if she had ill intentions.

Could he stop a goddess?

He'd die trying, if it took that.

Fuck. Apparently Actaeon and Cerberus' martyrdom was contagious.

"Has she told you about the red strings of fate?" Aphrodite asked.

"You mean those cords only you and she see, that dictate whom she's supposed to love?"

"I'll take that as a *yes*. True love is rare. So many people never experience it once, and she'll fall three times over. I can't turn my back on that."

Icarus frowned. "That's it? You've done all of this for Lexi, because fate wants her to have extra feels?"

"And why are you doing it?" Aphrodite's smile was tight. "I don't expect you to understand. It's not something that can be logicked into existence." She sounded as if she was speaking to a child. "Love isn't this tiny, insignificant thing. Not to her and never to me. If you'd fallen, you'd see that. I'm the goddess of love. Lexi embodies the thing that gives me life and power. Of course I've gone out of my way to protect her."

"Can you help?" Changing the subject was easier than admitting he almost understood.

"I don't know. May I see her?"

He gestured to the bedroom. "Yes."

Aphrodite's frown grew as she approached the bed. She sat on the edge and took Lexi's hand. "Did anything unusual happen?"

"I don't know what you want. Nothing about her life is normal. She's a goddess, and fate is making her earn it." Icarus had learned the truth when he visited Lexi's past in her mind, and accessed a memory Aphrodite had hidden from her.

Aphrodite pursed her lips. "Put aside the typical trials. What's left?"

Typical trials was a wide spectrum. Lexi hadn't fought a hydra, but she had gone to the underworld and back for loved ones. "I don't know." Icarus had only spent a few days with her. They had a fascination that might become more, when she woke up. *Creation,* let her wake up soon. "I was able to share her thoughts. I can't now. As I understand it, the link between her and me wasn't the same as it is with Cerberus?"

"She's not completely here."

"Thanks. I got that far. Especially after your *she's becoming the underworld* explanation." Taking out his frustrations this way wouldn't help. Sarcasm wasn't even making him feel better.

"Is there anything else at all? Significant or otherwise?"

It was a long list for the short amount of time he'd know Lexi. "Lorelei tried to break her. Hades sicced a chimera on her. She's been to the underworld and back twice. She hears voices. All standard-trial stuff."

"Voices?"

"I don't know much about that. She said there were

hundreds, possibly thousands, of them. Whispering in her head. Screaming. Begging for help. Offering praise."

"That makes sense."

"It does?" Between Icarus, Actaeon, and Cerberus, none of them could offer any solutions.

Aphrodite looked up from Lexi. "They're prayers. It sounds like the dead were seeking her even before Hades was destroyed."

"Prayers." Icarus let the word fall flat between them. "That's anti-climactic."

"Sorry to spoil the plot." She stood.

"What do we do? How do we get her and the others back?" He'd been focused on Lexi, but she'd be upset to be pieced back together, only to discover Actaeon and Cerberus hadn't returned.

Icarus might be a hint upset too. Especially if he lost Actaeon for good.

He stashed the stray thought aside, with all the others like it from the centuries.

"We find her," Aphrodite said.

She was right here. "That's not as helpful as I hoped for."

"I wish I had better answers. I came here to fill you in and check on her. I don't know what else to tell you. I doubt you can build a machine to fix this."

"I'm not qualified to do much else." That lay at the root of his frustration. Icarus invented machines; he didn't have any idea how to help the woman on his bed.

If he could see… What? An idea hovered in the back of his head, out of reach. He frowned and grasped at it. "Wherever the rest of Lexi is, she's probably connected to herself still?" Icarus asked.

There weren't just red threads that indicated who a person loved. Those were fleeting. There were also cords that tethered a person's soul to their body. Immortals had different gifts. Most could see auras, no one but Lexi could see through illusions, and a handful could see that lifeline. If Icarus were one of them, he might be able to follow it to the other side.

Aphrodite held her hands out, palms up. "I assume. But if the lifeline hooking body to soul is like the threads of love I see, it may currently be impossible to see where the line goes."

The lines went somewhere, though. A place Aphrodite couldn't follow.

Icarus didn't have another lead. Who would be willing to help Hades' brat of a daughter? Who didn't have the hang-ups of most immortals? "I need to talk to Conner." He was already reaching for his phone.

Two great things about post-Enlightenment kids— they weren't put off by the idea of magic plus tech, and they didn't have the same prejudices as their parents.

"That's my cue to go." Aphrodite stepped toward the door. "You don't want me here when he's around."

That didn't make sense. Conner was her grandson. Eros and Hermes' son. "He get tired of you playing *glorified matchmaker* with his life?" Icarus laughed.

Aphrodite's scowl spoke volumes. "Perhaps." She held up her index and middle finger, and a piece of paper appeared between. "Skip the temple if you need me. This is faster." She handed him the phone number, written in flowing script.

"I will. Thank you." He let his gratitude show. The situation was frustrating, but not a lot of gods would climb off their pedestals for something like this.

He saw her to the front door. The gesture was as much decorum as her choosing to leave the property before vanishing was. It was rude to pop in and out of other people's homes, rather than using the door.

The gears in Icarus' head were turning smoothly and with minimal squeaks. He had the portal he set on a ley line, which allowed heroes and mortals to travel through invisible gates without assistance from a god. Could he build something similar that followed Lexi's ties to herself? To the others? He had no idea how to tap into that specific current, but he'd figured out more obscure solutions.

He dialed Conner, who answered on the second ring. "Hey. What's up?"

"Are you available for a little brainstorming?" Icarus asked.

Conner was a tenured professor at a nearby university. Growing up around the gods didn't wear on him as well as he'd implied to Lexi. He decided he preferred people and higher learning over sacrifices and empty prayers. He taught computer science and cyber security. "Always. When and where?"

"My place. The sooner the better." Icarus appreciated Conner's willingness to jump in without details. Part of the fun was in the discovery.

The knock on his basement door was lost in the sound of the proximity alarms blaring.

The kids didn't have any of the manners their parents did.

Icarus snapped the sirens off and let Conner in.

"You sure I'm not imposing?" Icarus tried to keep his tone light and teasing. "You didn't have to drop anything?" Though he appreciated it.

Conner shook his head. "I need something to occupy my mind. Hoping this is the solution."

"It's a blast from the past. Have you talked to your family recently?"

"Yeah. That's kind of what I'd like to distract myself from. Not much was said, though." He paused and sniffed the air. "Is that jasmine? My grandmother was here."

"She left. Didn't want to piss you off. I'm going to assume you don't know anything about what's going on, but stop me if what I say gets repetitive." Icarus led him toward the bedroom. "Really short version—Hades is dead, his daughter is taking his place, and she's not coping well."

"His daughter? Not…" Conner paused in the doorway, mouth agape. "Zee." He let out a long sigh. "This definitely fits my definition of *distraction*."

Icarus gave Conner a brief rundown of what he'd discussed with Aphrodite.

"She pulled that *fated mates* shit with you, too?" Conner's gaze never left Lexi.

"Yeah." Except Icarus was willing to accept there was something to it. "Who'd she pair you off with?"

Conner laughed. "It doesn't matter; it's not Zee. She's in a bad way, though. What do you need from me?"

"Can you see the tether to her soul?"

"Yeah. At least, this side of it." Conner squinted as he stepped closer to the bed. "The rest of it is twisted, like an ethereal knot. I can't tell where it goes."

Icarus allowed a sliver of hope to trickle in. "Can you point me toward it and help me connect to it, the way we did with the ley lines? I need to follow it, somehow."

"Yeah." Conner knelt next to Lexi, his face pinched. "I missed you after we parted ways, Zee. But you're lucky you didn't go with me." His voice was low. "I always hoped that, since you steered clear of our kind from the start, you got the better end of the deal. I guess not."

Icarus felt a little guilty, eavesdropping on the one-sided conversation. Lexi and Conner would probably be different people if they'd grown up together. There was no telling if that would have been better for them.

Conner cleared his throat and stood. "Sorry. The nostalgia slapped me in the balls. Let's get to work."

Lexi's aura flared vibrant and dense, filling the room to the point where it was impossible to see through.

Icarus struggled to draw breath through the weight of her energy.

Then the blinding light vanished. Purple and pink twisted faintly around her body, flickering out of sight before dancing into view again. Lexi let out a light laugh but didn't move.

This was as creepy as it was concerning. The cocktail of emotion swirled through Icarus. Whatever was happening, it couldn't be healthy. She'd deteriorated to this in just a few hours. "I don't think we have a lot of time."

FOUR

Actaeon followed a winding path of cobblestones. He had no idea where he was going. Experience told him answers never sat right on the trail. Instinct argued this was the best direction.

He was wary when it came to his instinct. It had led him good places—back to Lexi in a bar, to buy her a chocolate martini she didn't order.

Other times, it fucked him over in a serious way— sending him after Heracles for killing Cassandra.

Who did he need to offer a favor to, for this to be one of the good times?

The air was still, and heavy clouds of dust kicked up by the quakes hung in the air. The faint scent of death clung to everything.

To the uninitiated, that would be expected. The underworld took the shape of the people who occupied it, though, and those souls left the rotting corpses back on earth.

He stepped over another crack, this one running

several meters in both directions but fortunately only a few centimeters across.

Shapes faded in and out around him. Unanchored souls, he assumed. The place was eerily devoid of any dead who'd settled in and called it *home*.

A sharp breeze kicked up, shifting the dust and pelting him with dried leaves and twigs. He winced against the onslaught and pushed forward.

A gust slammed into his chest, knocking him back several feet.

He steeled himself and drew more energy, to stay stable. He was still weak from the fight with Hades, and that bothered him.

Then, as if he'd stepped from one room into another, the air was clear and pleasant.

An Old West town stretched in front of him. Not a historically accurate one, though. This was a single street, lined with about five buildings on each side. The facings were flat and wooden, like stage props or a Bugs Bunny cartoon.

The cobblestone path was gone, replaced with dirt packed so hard, it barely stirred as he strolled into town.

There were no people on the street.

Ghost town. Great. His bad pun both irritated and a him.

Music reached him. It spilled from the building with the big *Saloon* sign on top. The letters were carved in sturdy wood, but they looked as though they came from a digital display. Like what old calculators and clocks had.

He stepped through a set of double swinging doors.

Really? This was *cliché meets all sorts of wrong*. The music was a 2050's synth pop remake of *Hey, Jude*, and it spilled from an upright piano in the corner.

Being played by… a goblin?

The building was filled with people. A man in a vest and bowler hat stood behind the bar running along the far wall, a mirror reflecting his back.

"You made it." Lexi's happy squeal drew Actaeon's attention. Her voice was the most glorious thing he'd heard all day.

He turned, as she tossed her arms around her neck and buried her face against his shoulder.

He squeezed her tight and inhaled her familiar scent. This wasn't so bad. Trials. *Pshaw.*

He let go and stepped back to take her in. She wore a peasant blouse, cinched in place by a bustier, and cut low enough to show off her cleavage. Her slacks were dark-brown suede, and her boots were knee-high, polished black leather.

"You like it?" She gestured and spun. She looked like she'd taken her outfit from a video game character.

"It's not exactly period appropriate." Just like the rest of the place. "It's stunning, though. You look incredible. Are you all right?"

"Sure. Worried about all of you. Where are the others?"

She didn't sound like someone suffering the psychological trauma of being torn into pieces as she became a plane of existence.

"I don't know. We were tossed to the four corners of the earth, more or less. I woke up alone."

A frown whispered across her face, before vanishing again. "That's okay. I mean, it's not—it sucks—but I had a feeling finding the three of you was part of the quest. That means, since I have you now, the first task is complete."

"The quest?"

"That's probably not what it *actually* is, but it's the best term I could come up with. I'm starting to figure this out." She grasped his hand and led him to a table at the back of the room. "I built this place myself. Do you like it?"

This wasn't the Lexi he knew. There were similarities —not just her appearance, but also the way she held herself, the way she spoke. This woman was more carefree, though. Lighter.

"It's different," he said.

"That's what people say when something is ugly and they don't want to be mean." She didn't sound upset.

"I love it. I've never seen anything like it."

She grinned and dropped into a wooden chair. He took the one across from her. The table setup resembled the one in the bar where he'd bought her that drink. The wood grain was polished, with only a few rough spots against his arms.

"Thank you. These people needed a place, and I wanted a tavern, because questing, right?" she said. "But I've never seen an old-school tavern, and the sketches in Dad's books weren't really the kind of thing I could build from, so I went with what I know."

"So when you say you made all of this..." He looked

around. The details were mismatched, but the structure was sound overall. "You mean literally?"

"It's like what Icarus taught me, but it doesn't disappear."

Actaeon tried to make sense of the words and ignore the pang that came with her casual mention of Icarus. It wasn't jealousy. More, anger. Possibly the tiniest hint of longing. "What did he teach you?"

"How to make illusions real." The *duh* was implied in her tone. "So I've been thinking. The only reason we've been plopped in the middle of something like this must be to defeat a great beast."

He wasn't sure he followed her logic. "Is the beast coming here? Is that why you built it?"

She rolled her eyes. "It's a *quest*. We have to do it right. Go out there and find the monster. This place is for mood. And so everyone has somewhere to stay, even after we leave. I have a plus-one dagger of slaying, and I'm pretty sure I can cast magic missile, but I don't know what version of the rule set we're using, so I can't say yet how many times per day I can cast."

"Lexi." He covered her hand, and she focused on him. How to put this kindly? "You know this isn't a game, right?"

If she'd already stepped off the deep end of sanity, he didn't know if he could pull her back from that.

She pursed her lips and narrowed her eyes. "Spoil sport. *Yes*. I know we're not playing a game. But we actually do have to go on a quest, and we might as well enjoy it while we're out there. Sprinkle a little magic on top."

He wanted to argue that he'd had enough of *a little magic* sprinkled on his life, but her request wasn't a taxing one. He gave her a tight smile. "We'll try it your way."

She kissed him on the cheek. "Better. We have a long journey ahead of us, and you look a little beat up. We should rest before we head out. But there's only one room left, so we have to share."

"How are there not more rooms?" He was missing a big part of where she was going with this, and was unsure how to ask.

"Most of the people go home when they want. But Bob is the manager. That's him behind the bar. He needs a place to sleep. Greg is in back, washing dishes. Jim"—she nodded at a table next to them—"is the house blackjack dealer. They all need beds."

"And is that a goblin on the piano?" Actaeon was getting distracted.

Her smile grew. "Stair troll. I didn't even know those were a thing, but she wandered in here and needed a place to stay. She's good, isn't she?"

He'd never seen Lexi so carefree. And he wasn't sure stair trolls existed. Was that the troll a creation of Lexi's as well?

"You could have made more rooms." Why was he hung up on that, of all things? Maybe because he desperately needed something to cling to that he understood.

"I could have. You were listening when I said we should enjoy ourselves?"

That was innuendo he couldn't argue with. He was

lost in this narrative of hers, but he'd catch up. "I was. Show me this room."

She led him up the stairs—solid wood with no creaking or give—to a hallway that ran in a direction that should be impossible in this building. Two doors were on each side. Her structure might be physically sound, but it didn't appear to be physically possible.

He should be appreciating the view, watching her ass in those trousers, as she showed him to the farthest doorway.

They pushed inside, and he blinked several times, to make sure he saw correctly. The bed was king sized and covered with a stark-black comforter that didn't have a speck of dirt on it, the furniture was stained as dark as possible without being black, and posters of dragons hung on the walls.

"I like your room," he said.

She tugged him in, kicked the door shut behind him, and draped her arms around his neck again. Her body molded to his, singing to his memory and fantasy. "How are we going to keep ourselves occupied until tomorrow morning?" she purred.

Fuck, she was tantalizing. He dipped his head and drew his nose up her neck, not making contact, but feeling the heat crackle between them. "I really should rest."

"That's a euphemism, isn't it?" She pressed into him.

Was it? She felt good. She smelled incredible. Desire floated from her, calling to something primal inside him.

"We need to make a plan." That was a lot harder to

say than he expected. "Figure out what we're doing on this quest."

"Do we?"

He kissed along her collarbone, down to the top of her breasts. This was ridiculous. He knew how to control himself. How was she undoing him like this? "We do." He pressed his lips to her skin.

"But that's not us." She shifted her weight, and her hip rubbed against his erection.

He summoned a sliver of restraint, unclasped her hands, and put some distance between him and her. "What is *us*?"

"We fight—each other or something else. We fuck. You save my ass. Rinse and repeat. We're not currently fighting, though we're closer than five minutes ago. I don't need to be rescued. What's left?"

He rested his hands on her hips, keeping her at arm's length, and guided her back to sit on the bed. He pulled up a chair, straddled it backward, and faced her. It wasn't much of a barrier, but it was the representation that mattered. "We talk, too."

"Eh. I vent. You listen. That's kind of the foreplay."

He wanted to argue that there was more to their relationship than that. He wasn't losing his mind, swearing he was in love, over something that could be deconstructed so easily.

Was he?

Fucking Icarus, putting thoughts in Actaeon's head. And being right. Actaeon groaned mentally. "There could be more. Most long-term relationships have more."

"That's what I hear. I'd hate to bore you, though."

Wow, he must come off as an asshole. Though, after the conversation they'd had before they fought Hades, he wasn't surprised there were still unresolved tensions between him and Lexi. "What about what you want?"

"I already have a guy who stimulates my mind, and one who loves me unconditionally. I can afford to be flexible with you."

This was a lot to unpack. "I don't want you to be flexible. I want *us* to be happy."

"Me too. I didn't mean otherwise," Lexi said.

Actaeon had no idea where to go next with this. He wanted to spend the next several hours talking through his relationship with Lexi, but they also needed to define what they were going up against.

Was he the only one struggling with this? She seemed content.

Was Charon wrong? She didn't look out of place here. It might take her some adjusting, but none of this was causing her visible stress.

"I don't want to stay here forever." The sudden change in her tone clenched around his chest like a fist.

Her expression wilted, and her posture drooped.

"You don't have to."

Was it true? He didn't know if he could promise that.

"You're lying," she said.

"I don't know if I am or not. I know I'd rather have you leave with me. I'll do what I can, to get you out of here."

"So I guess I need saving, after all."

Actaeon couldn't tackle all of this at once, and neither could Lexi. If he had his way, he'd charge full-speed ahead into any battle that awaited them and beat it to a bloody pulp.

It didn't seem like that was the answer this time. He moved to sit next to her on the bed. his tattered, bloody clothes needed to go, but addressing the sudden sadness in Lexi's voice was more important.

She leaned her head against his shoulder. "I don't know what I'm doing," she said softly. "I'm making it up as I go along."

"So far it's working for you." Their relationship would take untangling. More than they could do in a night. But it didn't have to be put on hold while they tackled everything else. "Tell me about this quest."

"I've told you everything. Mostly."

"Then how do you know there's a quest?"

"Because there's this insistence in my brain, this bit of... I don't know what to call it... insisting I need to find... something... and defeat... another thing... . And that I need your help—everyone's help—to do it."

Actaeon sighed and wrapped an arm around her waist. "That's appropriately vague. Welcome to immortality."

"Were you born cynical and grumpy?" Lexi's question was soft and without accusation.

He fell back onto the mattress, pulling her with him. "No. Once upon a time, many many years ago, even I liked hearing the stories my mother would tell me."

Lexi adjusted her weight, to settle next to him instead of half on top of him. "What kind of stories?"

"The same stuff everyone post-Enlightenment was raised on. Lightning and thunder and crashing waves and *Zeus is great* and *Poseidon will free you.*"

"But back then, the stories weren't part of the standard curriculum." She rolled onto her side, propped herself up on one elbow, and studied him. "I want to hear you tell one of them. Did you have a favorite?"

"I had one." He didn't have to reach for it. "They don't tell the story the same anymore, but *back then* it both terrified and fascinated me."

"Tell me."

He hooked his hands behind his head. "It's a kid's story."

"Tell me anyway."

He could ask her why it was so important, but he didn't mind, so there was no reason to argue. "Before the Olympians, the Titans ruled the world. Cronus was their king. He wasn't the first king. There was one before him, and others before that, as with all kingdoms. However, he wanted to be the last."

Lexi worked her jaw, and he paused. She shook her head. "I won't interrupt."

"There was an oracle—they even had them in those days," Actaeon said. "She told Cronus one of his children would overthrow him. So he ate them all."

"Just like that?"

Actaeon raised an eyebrow. "You said you wouldn't interrupt." He wasn't upset.

She shrugged one shoulder. "You said it was scary."

"I said when I was ten, it was scary. And Mother told

the story better. She had a trick that cast shadows on the walls and made the lights flicker."

"I've never heard you call her *Mother* before."

Because when he was a kid, Artemis *was* Mother. "Time changes things. Anyway, Cronus ate all his children, but his wife, Rhea, didn't like it. So instead of bringing him Zeus, she wrapped a rock in swaddling."

Lexi snickered. "There are so many possibilities in how she even got away with that." Her amusement was contagious.

"It was probably a metaphor. But perhaps not. Rhea took her son and hid him on an island. He trained for years, to be stronger and faster than his father, but he knew he couldn't confront Cronus alone. When the time came, he returned to his father's castle, and fed him a poison to make him expectorate."

"Eww," Lexi said. "Cronus puked the other kiddos back up?"

"Not as poetic as the version I grew up on, but yes. Hades and Poseidon helped Zeus overthrow their father, and then the three split the world among themselves."

"It isn't particularly scary. The story's been told better since then."

Actaeon agreed. "That's not the part that got to me." He sat and pulled Lexi upright too. He took her fingers, the way Artemis used to do with him, and pressed his thumbs gently into her knuckles. "She'd look me in the eye, and her voice would deepen." Actaeon held Lexi's gaze. "Zeus swore on that day that no one would be king after him. He would never be overthrown by his children or their creations. He swore that mountains would rise and crumble, and oceans would swell and shrink, and he would ensure that he always sat on the throne."

Lexi stared back in disbelief. "No real subtlety there."

"Did I mention I was ten?"

"A few times, yes." She smiled. "But I would have been terrified too. Dad told me a similar story about The Enlightenment. He said Mom taught it to him. But he left out the *eating babies and puking up siblings* bit. That's pretty gross."

Actaeon couldn't argue that.

A crack of thunder filled the room, and they both jumped.

Lexi laughed nervously. "I guess it got to me a little."

Actaeon was glad it was only a story.

FIVE

THE SCREECHING STOPPED AFTER A FEW SECONDS, AND Cerberus could think again. He had no idea where the sound came from. It was almost like someone set off an alarm, and it echoed across the world.

"What was that?" he asked.

"Irritating." Lexi sounded frustrated.

The clouds cleared, except for a handful of white wisps, and the sun beat down on them.

She sighed and sat up. "I don't want to stare at a blue sky. The world shouldn't keep spinning as if someone wonderful didn't just pass away."

Cerberus hated the sadness in her voice. "You can't stay trapped in grief forever."

"I know. But I should be allowed a little time to mourn."

"That's fair." He stood and offered her a hand. "I'm going to walk. Would you like to join me?"

If this was her memory, could he walk without her? How did any of that work here? Could he interact with anything besides her? The environment was real enough, but would he be able to talk to people?

"I was thinking of getting some lunch. I haven't eaten all day." She accepted his help up. Her palm was warm and familiar pressed against his, and longing spiked through him.

How did he miss her when she was right here?

Because this wasn't his Lexi.

"I'll buy." He patted his pockets. He didn't have his wallet or phone, which meant no access to his accounts. Even if he had anything on him, would digital currency work in here? "On second thought…"

"It's all right. Dad left me a few things. I can afford a sandwich for myself and the cute-but-clueless homeless guy." She took off toward the edge of the park.

Cerberus didn't care for the description, but it was as accurate as anything, given the circumstances. He walked with her. "Have you decided to trust me?"

"Yes. It might be a stupid decision, but you're the only honest person I've talked to in a while, so I'm going to take a risk."

"Thanks. I think." He jammed his hands in his pockets, to resist the desire to tangle his fingers with hers. It felt wrong, not sharing the little touches, but it wouldn't be right to do so, either.

"Are there immortals who can lie and hide it?" Lexi asked.

Cerberus scrolled through the list of those he'd encountered over the centuries. "I don't know. I don't suspect if I'd met one that they'd admit it to me."

"That's fair." She shrugged.

As they strolled down the sidewalk, they had to weave between people. Cerberus' nose was going nuts. He couldn't smell any of them. It was like having a bad cold.

The crowd was loud, but nothing distinct stood out in the conversations. Snippets of gibberish blended with traces of perfume and something that smelled really good. Roasting meat.

His stomach growled.

She pointed him toward a shop with *Stateman's Deli* panted in large red letters across the glass window. Curtains hung behind it, blocking the view of the interior from the street. "This is my favorite place."

He opened the door for her, and a symbol caught his attention. A triangle with an eye in the middle, tucked above the handle. This place accepted barter, instead of or in addition to digital currency.

The food smell was stronger in here. It made his mouth water. The chatter wasn't any easier to decipher, but it was quieter.

"What do you want?" She nodded at the menu board.

There were several rows of text, but only a few words were legible. The soda, chips, and cookies, as well as five different sandwiches. "What do you recommend?"

"I'm having the Reuben. Their dressing is drool worthy, and they make the bread here."

"I'll have the same." If he had to guess, he'd say turkey and avocado, grilled ham and cheese with tomato, and the pastrami sandwiches were her other favorites. Oh, and the peanut butter and jelly.

She ordered their food and paid with a cufflink. The gems on it sparkled under the lights when she handed it to an older balding man in an apron.

Cerberus expected her to pay in credits, but he shouldn't have. She'd lived the barter lifestyle for a while. He'd assumed there was a point in her life when that wasn't the case.

Did her stepfather ever even put her in the system?

Cerberus hadn't found any record of her when he was hunting for her, so maybe not.

They sat at a booth with a decent view of most of the room, and Lexi put her back to the wall.

There were a few seats behind here, and someone with a silvery aura occupied one. The man looked disheveled, and his face was hidden.

A young woman set their sandwiches in front of them almost immediately. Lexi's wasn't corned beef, though. It looked like the grilled cheese.

Her clothes were different, too. Jeans, a T-shirt, and a leather jacket. He wasn't sure if it would make her mood better or worse to comment on the change.

His food was he ordered, though.

He waited for her to eat, before digging in. The flavors washed over his tongue in a sharp burst. At least his taste buds still worked. "This is good."

"Told you." Lexi grinned.

The bell on the front door chimed, and Lexi's eyes grew wide. She sank lower in her seat and spoke through clenched teeth. "Can you stop glowing?"

"I don't have a way to turn that off." He doubted she'd believe him if he told her there was a slim chance anyone saw him. Even though it was the truth, it felt one step too far past the point of plausibility.

He glanced over his shoulder.

"Don't look." Lexi's voice was tiny. Tension spilled from her, heavy enough to coil in his neck and set him on edge.

He turned back to her. He tracked the movement of her eyes as someone approached, then came into view.

Artemis? She looked out of place in the modest deli. Her cream pantsuit and matching silk blouse were probably valued at more than the daily receipts of the place. She settled in across from the a man behind Lexi whose hair looked like it hadn't seen a comb in months.

The stranger looked up.

Actaeon? Cerberus should have smelled him the instant they walked in. Not only was his scent missing, but his aura was all wrong—brighter and colder.

Artemis didn't look right, either. Threads of moonlight wove around her and flashed over any exposed skin. And a severed red cord dangled from her ring finger. The edges were frayed, but the color was as vibrant as the vinyl bench she sat on.

Was this how Lexi saw her world?

"Have you ever been to Los Angeles?" Lexi's question drew him back to the conversation.

Cerberus nodded. "It's pretentious and crowded, but the smog is almost gone, especially compared to two decades ago." The Enlightenment had one nice side-effect—the gods didn't like their world being polluted, so they'd magically cleared out the debris. Relocated and recycled what they could, and incinerated the rest. They had strict laws in place, to keep things from getting out of hand again.

Lexi plucked a piece of ham from the edge of her sandwich and nibbled on it. "I want to be an actress."

"You seem as though you don't like people noticing you."

She frowned. "I'm not supposed to tell anyone who I am, but I don't have to use my real name, and auras don't travel on camera."

"But the people who cast you will know. They'll wonder why you don't have ID. Why you're not in the system." His counter points didn't matter. She'd already made this decision. Why didn't he just let her have the dream? He'd never known this about her. An actress?

"I could get myself put in the system. Maybe I shouldn't tell you this, but you have to suspect there are people who make fake identities."

Cerberus only had one real argument for her, outside of all of her considerations. "I don't think you'd like the people. Hollywood is all lies."

She twisted her face. The expression said she was considering his words. "But there, I'd expect it. They're honest about their deception."

"Good point."

Silence settled between them as they ate. Cerberus couldn't keep his attention from drifting to the booth behind her.

Actaeon looked so different from the man Cerberus knew. This hero's hair was longer. Dingier. Pulled into messy ponytail. His eyes were sunken, and his clothes tattered.

Was this why Lexi didn't remember she'd seen him in her past, or was this a memory Aphrodite took from her?

Cerberus still wasn't one-hundred percent sold on the *this is Lexi's past* theory, but he was sticking with it until something else made more sense.

"Did you have any luck?" Artemis asked. Her voice was kind, but something hostile lay underneath. It wasn't a sound so much as a sensation.

"No." That was Actaeon's voice.

They didn't move as they spoke. It was as if Cerberus watched cardboard cutouts having a conversation.

Lexi glanced over her shoulder, and Actaeon dropped his face into his hands.

She turned back to Cerberus, and Actaeon remained frozen in that pose.

It made sense. In her mind, Actaeon and Artemis only existed in this moment the way Lexi had seen them.

"What's so fascinating about them?" Lexi asked.

"I know them. So do you."

Lexi snorted. "The goddess Artemis? The purest of the pure? The embodiment of moonlight? The mistress of the hunt?" Disdain leaked from her words. "And some random hero? I don't know anyone like that. The gods are bad fucking news. Deadly, you might say."

"I just might."

"You need to give this up," Artemis said. "It's

destroying you."

"I have to find her. She said I'd come for her, but she's not there. Where else would she be?" Actaeon sounded tortured.

Was he talking about Cassandra?

"What happens if you do get her back?" That same hostility lingered in the air each time Artemis spoke.

"She's lying," Lexi said.

Was it deception he heard, not disdain? "She asked a question. How can that be a lie?"

Lexi shrugged. "She wants him to think she cares, but she's manipulating him. There's a twist to her words. She wants him to see the world through a different perspective."

"He's looking for his dead lover. Why would Artemis stop that?" Cerberus was asking himself as much as Lexi.

Lexi stiffened and glared. "You're making a lot of assumptions based on a snippet of conversation. Why would you say that?"

"It's a hunch."

"Fighting only ever brings you pain." Artemis sounded kind, but that sensation—the lying—lingered. "I hate to see you like this. Tortured. Lost."

"What am I supposed to do? Walk away?" Actaeon was forlorn.

Lexi stretched and rolled her neck, taking the opportunity to glance over her shoulder.

Cerberus wouldn't have been certain, but when she moved, Actaeon did as well, focusing on Artemis.

"He's in pain," Lexi said, "but she doesn't care. I'm

not sure what she wants, but it's not for him to heal. This is why I don't deal with the gods."

Artemis sighed. "I don't know how many more times or ways I can say this, your suffering hurts me too, so I'm going to try again. You can't save the world. You want to. It's admirable, but it will destroy you, and you won't be the only casualty."

"But—"

"Remember Las Vegas?" Artemis cut him off.

Lexi's expression soured, and she pushed aside the last few bites of her sandwich. "I'm done." She stood and walked out the door, without waiting for Cerberus.

He jogged to catch up with her, passing two-dimensional blurs until he was by her side again. "Are you all right?" he asked.

"Dad told me once that there was an old saying. A stupid marketing motto. *What happens in Vegas stays in Vegas.* They should have thought that one through a little better, because it's utter bullshit."

"The battle. I know. Did you lose someone?"

She glared at him. "You know I did. And I don't want to talk about it."

Great. What kind of minefields would they navigate while he was here, and how was he supposed to get out?

How did he get here in the first place? Were he and Lexi both stuck here? Did Hades send them here? Have one of his accomplices do it for him?

Was Cerberus capable of having any conversations with her that extended beyond what she knew at this point in her life?

There were too many questions.

Lexi stumbled, and Cerberus wrapped an arm around her waist out of instinct.

"I'm fine." She didn't pull away. "Tripped over an invisible crack in the sidewalk. Clumsy me."

He'd never seen Lexi as clumsy, but everyone had their moments.

A crack of thunder split the air, and they both jumped. She let out a nervous giggle.

Lightning lit up the sky.

That wasn't right. Thunder didn't come first.

Fear spread through Lexi. Heavy and tangible, it clung to Cerberus' skin and coated his tongue.

"It's Zeus." Her voice cracked.

Zeus didn't make entrances like this unless he wanted *everyone* to know he was in town. New Orleans was Poseidon's—or it had been—and the brothers didn't infringe on each other's territory.

Lexi pulled from Cerberus' grip and ran toward the nearest alley, and he followed without hesitation.

"He's not supposed to be here." She fidgeted with the cuffs of her jacket. She pressed her back to the brick, as if she wanted to fade into the dingy-blue and cracked yellow paint. "Why is he here? Is he looking for you?"

"No. I can guarantee that." Why *was* Zeus here? "We have to get you someplace safe."

"No shit, Shifter-Boy. Any bright ideas?" Despite the sarcasm, her voice wavered, and she cast her gaze around the alley every few seconds, not focusing on anything for long.

He knew, because he only saw things move if she paid attention to them. "No."

SIX

"Lexi. Come on."

Cerberus didn't recognize the voice. A girl about Lexi's age stood next to them, tugging on Lexi's arm.

Where did she come from?

She looked directly at Cerberus. "You too. Let's go." She led them further into the alley and through an over-sized metal door.

Was Cerberus playing the part of someone else in this memory? The girl was familiar, but he couldn't place her, and with Lexi's unique interpretation of auras and lack of a sense of smell, identifying her was more difficult.

"Where'd you come from?" Lexi asked in a stage whisper as they passed through an industrial-grade plastic curtain into a room filled with conveyer belts.

"I've been looking for you since Zeus showed up. I was worried about you," the girl said.

Cerberus took in the room while they walked. To his

right, hung a row of uniforms that swayed each time an invisible breeze blew through.

Lexi touched his arm, drawing his attention. "Cerberus, this is Clio. She's my best friend."

"Hey." Clio wiggled her fingers in a wave. "*The* Cerberus? Wow."

Was she being sarcastic?

Lexi slapped her arm. "Be nice. So far, he's not a bad guy. And he's not Zeus, so there's that."

"*Clio*, like the muse?" Cerberus asked. A lot of parents gave their hero children classic names, but this was a very specific name.

The girl shrugged. "My mom thought I was inspirational."

"Where are we?" Lexi hovered her hand above a conveyer belt.

Cerberus hadn't noticed before, but the room had a faint blue glow, as though ethereal dust had settled over everything.

"It's an early Enlightenment facility. They wanted to blend electronics with god magic, but they couldn't figure it out. The residual energy should keep us from standing out to Zeus while he's in town."

"Oh. Okay."

Lexi might be fine with the explanation, but Cerberus wasn't. "Why is that a concern today, but not most days?" He asked.

Clio narrowed her gaze. "Because *Zeus* is in town."

Zeus could be in any town at any given time. Then again, he rarely made it a point to announce his arrival.

Their settings changed. Instead of being in the

warehouse, they stood in the middle of a crowd, in an amphitheater. Several large screens surrounded the stage, displaying an empty podium.

"We should move to the edge of the crowd." Cerberus didn't like being confined this way.

Lexi grabbed his hand. "We'll be fine."

"No one would be king after him." The voice in his head was hers but not, and overlapped her spoken words.

He didn't agree with her assessment that they'd be okay. "Do it to make me feel better." He pulled her toward the entrance.

"Let's stay." Clio stepped into their path.

He moved around her and guided Lexi through the crowds. They walked for a couple of minutes but didn't get any closer to the edge of the field.

"I really feel we should stay," Clio said.

How did she keep up with them so easily? He growled. He was tempted to shift. The *alert* bells were screaming fifty shades of red in his skull. He reached for his hellhound form but couldn't grasp it.

Lexi squeezed his hand. "We're only sticking around to hear the highlights. The instant he's covered the high-level stuff, we'll be gone."

"Right." Cerberus looked at the people around them, while Lexi focused on the stage. A sea of faces, all talking and jostling each other. And the smells were so potent. Twenty kinds of beer and weed and mustard. Sweat mingled with sex mixed with vomit.

It was enough to make his stomach churn.

He expected to sit through an hour or two of live music and choreography. Poseidon liked his stage shows.

Poseidon's face filled the screens at the front of the stadium. "It's always great to have such a huge turnout." His voice boomed over the auditorium without the use of a microphone or speakers. "I think you're going to like what we have to say today. And without further fanfare, give a warm welcome to everyone's king —Zeus."

A great thing about living a memory, apparently— fast forwarding to the important bits.

Zeus took the stage to a chorus of cheers.

Also a little odd. These events drew mostly believers, but there was always a pocket of people who were there to heckle, regardless of the consequences. Sometimes they just had a death wish, other times they'd decided showing the world their disdain in a public forum was the most important stand they could take.

Cerberus expected those people to stand out more distinctly to Lexi, rather than vanishing completely.

"We're rolling out a new program around the world." Zeus was already diving into the meat of the speech. "And I'm pleased that we can make this wonderful city the home of our announcement. This is a program that's been in the making since the start of The Enlightenment. Another way we give back to you, as a *thank you*, for everything you've done for us."

Standard rhetoric. Cerberus wanted to fast-forward through this part, too.

"This new program will make sure everyone is taken care of."

Cerberus actually might be sick. He remembered this event now. He hadn't cared for watching it on TV the first time around. Living the in-person version wasn't any better.

"Everyone who's part of the system will be provided for. Food, work, education, entertainment—all of it covered, regardless of your status. But in order to do this, we need everyone registered," Zeus said. "We're at ninety-percent today, but we'd like to be at one-hundred."

According to people Cerberus knew on the inside, they were actually closer to about seventy-five percent. The thing about *registration* was it made it difficult to track those people who didn't register. Lexi, for instance.

Zeus continued. "If you have friends, neighbors, or colleagues who are heroes, especially those not as gifted as the heroes who help us keep you safe, please urge them to register."

Because a hero who wasn't on the records was one of the biggest dangers there were to the gods. Cerberus glanced at Lexi, who watched the news with a scowl.

"Great. All I have to do is tell them who I am, and I'll never go hungry again." She said sarcastically as she turned from the stage.

"You wouldn't be who you are if you'd been smothered by the system. Look at that kid Hermes and Eros had. He's a tool." Clio spoke up before Cerberus could. She looped her arm through Lexi's, and the girls wove their way through the crowds.

Cerberus followed them to the exit. He was glad to be leaving. He remembered the propaganda around this campaign. The *See Someone, Say Something* and *It's Only a Problem if You're Hiding.*

Lexi was hiding arguably the biggest secret of any of them—being Hades' daughter.

They were outside, back on the city streets again. Zeus, Poseidon, and Artemis strolled along the sidewalk. Gargoyles flew overhead.

"How strong are you?" Lexi asked.

Cerberus was unsure how much information to give her. In real life, he could take on two or three of those gargoyles without a problem. In here? There was no telling.

"He's pretty strong," Clio said. "There's a lot of power in a creature like that." Something lined her voice, but he couldn't identify it.

Cerberus realized what they were looking for. "I'm not strong enough to kill Poseidon."

"Even if I give you a gargoyle claw?" Lexi reached for her backpack.

"You still carry that with you?" he asked.

"It's a reminder." The *duh* was implied in Clio's tone.

Cerberus pushed Lexi's hand down, and her bag swung back on her shoulder. "It's not a weapon," he said. "It's a sacrificial blade, meant for an incapacitated target."

The pain that flashed over Lexi's face gnawed at him.

"Insensitive much?" Clio pulled Lexi closer. "We don't need him. Between the two of us, we can accomplish anything. Look. They're heading inside." She pointed to the restaurant the gods had entered. "Their beasts are on the roof. They can't fit in there. You can see through that stupid shield they put up. In, knife in the back, and out before anyone realizes what's going on."

Lexi nodded and grabbed the claw from her backpack. "All right."

"Whoa." Cerberus yanked her to his side. "You can't kill Poseidon. Are you going to take all three of them out?"

"The other two didn't kill her dad," Clio said.

Concern and confusion mingled inside Cerberus. Something about this wasn't right. Lexi—*his* Lexi—was smart about how she moved in this world. She missed her stepdad, but had her grief driven her this far?

He didn't know everything about her past, but this didn't make sense.

The three gods were shown to outdoor seating, in a table away from everyone else, but appropriately on display for the world.

He wrapped an arm more tightly around Lexi's waist and pulled her behind the corner. "Just listen to them for now." He didn't know what he was doing. If she'd tried to assassinate a god, he couldn't stop her, and she obviously hadn't succeeded.

But that wouldn't keep him from trying. He refused to be a passive observer when her life was on the line.

The gods were served. It was a habit of several of them to walk among the people like this. They claimed it was to let everyone see they weren't above humanity. It was exactly the opposite—they did it to prove they were untouchable, even surrounded by the masses.

At the beginning of The Enlightenment, people

threw bottles and rocks, and even shot at the gods on a regular basis. None had any effect.

"You read comics, right?" Clio was looking at Cerberus. "Registration is always bad."

Odd assumption to make, that he'd be familiar with something decades old that had been phased out when the gods returned. He wanted to argue this wasn't X-men, but there were enough parallels. And she was right. Altruism that required turning in one's neighbors and created second-class citizens wasn't actual altruism.

"Forget him," Clio tugged Lexi's arm. "No one is around them. The gargoyles are on the roof, and this is a narrow space. We can be in and vanish and leave before anyone sees us."

Except Lexi hadn't known how to make herself invisible back then. And he doubted she'd told many people, even if she could.

Lexi nodded.

He grabbed her wrist and held tight.

The hateful glare she fixed on him seared through his veins, but he refused to let go.

Clio rested a hand on Cerberus' cheek, and he growled at the jolt of pain. What the fuck?

He wasn't letting Lexi do this.

"It won't be a problem," Artemis' voice carried distinctly over the crowd. "I've taken care of things on my end."

This wasn't right. Artemis abhorred the events of The Enlightenment. Especially the selective death and discrimination. He only had a piece of dialog, though. He couldn't draw a conclusion from it. It also wouldn't distract Cerberus from his primary objective of detaining Lexi.

"I wish you'd get rid of him," Zeus said.

Artemis pursed her lips. "Unlike the rest of you, I don't have hordes of them. He's still mine. I'm telling you he won't get in the way, and that should be good enough for you."

"I've got things covered on my end, as well. The Death girl is grief stricken and terrified. She has no parents to pursue in the underworld. Of the others on my list, one is institutionalized, three work for me and have sworn loyalty, and seven are dead."

They were talking about Actaeon, Lexi, and other heroes. Cerberus knew conversations like this happened, but experiencing one was a different story.

"Now." Clio yanked, and Lexi broke free. The girls vanished before Cerberus could grab her again.

"Lexi, don't," he shouted.

Zeus looked directly at him, and Cerberus' blood turned to ice. "There you are." Zeus' smile was terrifying.

Poseidon vanished.

Lexi and Clio reappeared, within arm's reach of the gods. Lexi froze, gargoyle claw clutched in her hand and raised to head-height.

Cerberus ran toward them at full speed.

Artemis held a blade. Where did that come from? She glanced at Cerberus, then sliced Clio's throat.

Blood, dark red and thick, spilled over everyone. More than there should be.

Lexi's scream was of fear and grief, and shook the world.

Before Cerberus reached her, the gods and Clio disappeared.

Lexi went limp, and he caught her before she hit the ground.

"Lexi?" he asked. What did he just witness?

No one around them was moving. Then there was no one around them. The city blurred at the edges. The skyline grew closer, as their surroundings licked away into a void of blue sky.

"*Lexi*." Cerberus wasn't prepared to find out if this disappearing scenery would make his situation better or worse. "Wake up, please. I need you here." He might not survive if she didn't come back.

Worse, he didn't know if she would survive.

SEVEN

Icarus studied the device on his nightstand. It was a lot smaller than the ley line portal in the other room. He didn't need to stand on it, though. He would connect to the device, and with a little skill and a lot of luck, follow it back to Lexi's mind.

A *lot* of luck.

"We agree this isn't going to hurt her?" He didn't know why he was asking. The design was his. He didn't have the time he wanted, to think it through. If he had Lexi's help… He shouldn't be so reliant on her already, but she made things clearer. She helped him see answers that were previously hidden.

Conner leaned against the doorframe, doubt splashed across his face. "It's plugged directly into her lifeline. I'm not guaranteeing anything. Especially since there's no telling what condition she's in."

Icarus was hoping for more reassurance, but he didn't expect it. "We know she's breathing. Aphrodite and Hermes say she's not hurt."

"What term did they use? *Fractured?* That doesn't sound healthy. Psychological breaks are ugly things. Do you want me to define *fracture* for you?"

"No." Icarus wanted a guarantee this would work. He wouldn't get one from someone else, though. He glanced over the titanium box one more time. It glowed with traces of his power, mingled with Conner's. The infusion linked the device to an individual's lifeline and made it possible for Icarus to see what Conner did.

There was nothing else to check. "I'm going in," Icarus forced confidence through his veins. "Yank the cord if either one of us doesn't look good."

There was no cord, but Conner could take away his contribution and shut the contraption down.

Icarus closed his eyes and focused on calming his racing pulse. He needed to slip into a meditative state. He could see the ethereal outline of the device and the cord running through it, from Lexi to someplace unknown.

He mentally grasped the line. *"Please, let me in."* He probed the edges of Lexi's mind.

A new sliver of light appeared. He nudged harder, to toe his way in.

An unseen force slammed into his chest and shoved him back hard enough to steal his breath.

His eyes tore open, and he gasped. He was back in his room.

The device on the nightstand hissed and sizzled, then a shower of sparks erupted from it.

He snapped his fingers, and the glow vanished.

"That's not good." Conner's statement forced Icarus' attention to Lexi.

Her aura danced across her body, like flames licking at her skin. She arched her back and opened her mouth, but no sound came out.

Icarus grabbed her wrist, trying to force some control into her.

She landed flat on her back, and her breathing went shallow.

"Fuck." He couldn't risk doing that to her again. "What went wrong?"

"I don't know, but I'm not playing mad scientist with a goddess anymore. Doctor, maybe." Conner's laugh was tight. "This isn't the right time for that joke, is it?"

Icarus raised an eyebrow. "I don't think there's ever a good time for that joke. Call me possessive."

"That's your right." Conner raised his hands, palms out. "But unless you have any other ideas…"

"I was so close. She keeps kicking me out. Or something does."

"Did you try asking her permission? Consent, dude."

Icarus stared at him in disbelief. "She's unconscious."

"But you're poking around in her head anyway."

"Why did I call you?" Icarus let out a long groan and raked his fingers through his hair. "That's rhetorical, by the way."

"Figured. I need a drink."

"Fridge is stocked. Grab me one, too?"

"Sure." Conner walked away.

Icarus studied Lexi. It was a stupid idea, but he didn't have any others, and at least this was less likely to hurt her than what they'd just tried. He sat on the bed next to her and caressed her cheek. "You have to be around somewhere. I'm having a hard time figuring this without you, my muse." He spoke softly, searching for the right words. "Wherever you are, I'd like to be there with you. I'm not trying to trespass. If you don't want me there, that's okay, but I want to help. I hope you trust me enough to let me. Can I come in?"

The pink and purple smoothed out, curling around her like water instead of fire, and her lips moved.

"If you're talking to me, I can't hear you." This was beyond far-fetched. She wasn't a coma patient.

But in a way she was.

He closed his eyes and edged himself toward that line between consciousness and sleep. "If you're talking to someone else, I'd like to join you," he said aloud and in his head at the same time.

The darkness fell away, and he found himself surrounded by tombstones. A light patter of rain drizzled around him, but none of the drops struck him.

"They're so sad," Lexi said.

She stood a few feet away, wearing the same clothes she had to George's funeral. The black pantsuit fit her perfectly, as nymph clothing tended to. She was dry, despite the weather.

He wanted to wrap her in a hug. He settled for moving next to her and grasping her hand. "Who is?"

She nodded at the group of people gathered around a fresh grave. "Them. They want their son back. So many of them are thinking it. They want to know why Hades forsook them, when he gave others life. Why does Steve Jobs deserve a second chance, and their boy doesn't?"

"Hades is dead," Icarus said.

Her chuckle was dry. "Is that irony or just really unusual? I've never used that word right. I want to help them."

"Can you? Is it your place to bring their son back?"

"No. The dead need to stay dead. They inhabit a different world than the living."

It was a wise observation. He was unsure what else to say, so he watched with her. It was too intimate, peering into people's lives this way. Was this taking place in her head? Was it from her past?

The graveyard was replaced by a university commons building. Icarus recognized it immediately— this was where Conner taught, and where Esper was enrolled in post-grad studies.

In fact, she sat at a nearby table, talking to a young man who was about her age.

They were too far away for Icarus to hear. Esper's companion looked in Lexi and Icarus' direction—he might as well have looked through them—then turned back to Esper.

"She's so sad." Sadness flowed from Lexi's words, so heavy it was tangible.

This must be now. Esper lost one father a few years ago, but the other passed away recently.

Somehow Lexi was sliding through the lives of people close to death.

"I want to help." Lexi hugged herself. "It's screaming from them. They need comfort. Relief. What am I supposed to do?"

The prayers Aphrodite mentioned.

Icarus clenched his jaw, as her grief encompassed him. Was Lexi projecting, or was this empathy that came with the connection he had to her?

"You can't save the world," Icarus said.

She frowned and looked at him. "What?"

"You can only do so much, even as a goddess. You can reach out to, but you have to pick and choose."

"That's not fair. Why do some people deserve my presence more than others?"

"I'm not saying that's the case. You're not here for the living, though. They may call your name as their loved ones pass, but they're not yours." Why did he say that? "You can't stay trapped in their grief forever."

"I know. But they should be allowed a little time to mourn." Lexi frowned. "Déjà vu."

Esper turned toward them, and her eyes grew wide. Did she see them?

Her friend said something, and she shook her head.

Icarus read the words on her lips. "I thought—"

"We should go." He grabbed Lexi's hand again. Esper had never displayed any gifts from her Titan heritage, but now wasn't the time to push their luck.

Lexi shook her head. "I don't have a lot of control…"

Their environment changed.

"Or maybe I do?" Lexi turned in a slow circle.

They stood in an open field that stretched forever

with its tufts of dried grass. It looked like Icarus' setup outside the labyrinth he'd created, but there were no walls or maze.

There were also no grieving people.

A growl filled the air. Icarus and Lexi spun. A chimera stood behind them. Flaming nostrils flared, and a string of threatening grunts echoed from her throat. "You killed my sister." Her words were in Icarus' head.

"Technically, *we* didn't," he corrected her. Actaeon and Cerberus had killed the chimera who attacked at the apartments near Icarus' place.

"Your clan did. And you displaced us. I'm sorry to be cliché, but I'd like vengeance," the chimera said.

"Take a number." Lexi still sounded mournful.

The chimera snarled and charged.

Icarus' heart leaped into his throat. A wall appeared between them and the beast.

"I've got this." Lexi wore a tiny smirk.

The chimera crashed through the illusion, still running full-tilt, and barreled between them, knocking Icarus away from Lexi.

"Why didn't it work?" Lexi looked at him, panic written across her face.

He'd tell her, if he had any idea.

The chimera lunged for Lexi.

Icarus wasn't a skilled fighter, but he had the strength of a powerful immortal. He sprang forward, arms outstretched, and tackled the beast. The heat seared his flesh and ate away at his clothes.

Was it real, or a mental projection?

It didn't matter. It hurt like fuck. He gritted his teeth

and screamed through the pain, focused on pinning the chimera to the ground.

"Duck," Lexi said.

He did. She sliced the air above his head with a blade, driving for the monster's throat. The illusion passed through without slowing, and Lexi stumbled with her own momentum.

"I don't understand," she muttered. "It worked. I learned how to do it. I could make them real." Her panic was growing.

He didn't blame her. The chimera shook him aside. When he hit the ground, the impact jarred through him.

The chimera charged Lexi again. Lexi leaped to the side at the last minute, but the beast caught her ankle in its jaws and snapped.

Lexi's scream shattered Icarus' heart. He had to do something. He had to—

His eyes flew open, and he was in his room. Lexi's body lay on the bed, where it had been when he closed his eyes. His heart hammered in his ears.

Her aura was controlled, though. She wasn't thrashing or making any noise.

"That seemed like a good sign," Conner said. He set a beer on the nightstand. "Consent worked?"

Icarus didn't have time for this. His hands and body burned. His real clothes were intact, but when he examine his arms, he saw bright red flesh with emerging blisters. "I have to get back to her. She's trapped... somewhere, with a chimera."

"Fuck."

Good call. He could try to return to Lexi the same

way, but what would he do when he got there? He still wouldn't have the skills to fight. "I need a way to bring an ethereal shotgun with me."

Which summoned another question—why weren't Lexi's illusions tangible in there? Wherever *there* was.

And how much longer would she survive if he didn't figure it out?

EIGHT

Lexi bolted straight up in bed, startling Actaeon.

He lay next to her, but sleep hadn't come. There was too much on his mind.

Her chest heaved, and her eyes were wide.

"Lexi." He covered her hand.

She looked at where he touched her, but it seemed to take a moment before she registered what she saw. She broke the contact and rubbed her bare ankle.

"What's wrong?" he asked.

"I had a really fucked up dream." She was breathless. "That the chimera you and Cerberus killed had a sister who wanted revenge."

As far as dreams went, that sounded pretty tame. "You said you wanted a quest." He tried to joke.

She gave him a withering look. "Why does my ankle hurt?"

He pulled her hand away. Bite- and burn-marks scarred the flesh. That was bad. "Tell me *everything* about your dream."

"There's not much to tell. I was in this vast nothing-ness. Well, not quite. It wasn't a blank slate; it was more like an eternal stretch of barren land. A lot like what you saw outside the labyrinth, but there was no maze."

"But you saw it? Your environment, that is." When they'd been in the labyrinth, Lexi hadn't seen anything until she connected with Cerberus. It had been so much of an illusion, she'd looked straight past it.

He flopped back on the bed. There were so many pieces here, and he didn't know how to assemble them.

She nodded. "I was there with Icarus, and I was saying something about control. It was so real. He was as tangible as you are. Except my illusions weren't. I couldn't make them take shape. She attacked us—the chimera—and I didn't have any way to fight. I could make knives, but they went right through her. And then she bit me, and I woke up."

A teensy-tiny, itty-bitty part of Actaeon's ego demanded to know why he wasn't in her dream. He would have protected her. But then it wouldn't be the same nightmare.

It was more, though, if she came out of it with bite marks.

"What are you thinking?" Lexi asked.

"That in our world, dreams that come with real wounds aren't dreams."

"Morpheus?"

Actaeon considered this. "Perhaps. Snarling beasts aren't his MO, but I don't think we're in Kansas anymore."

"No. We're in New Orleans." Lexi knit her brows

together and shook her head. "Sorry. Weird memory."
She met his gaze. "Do you like corned beef?"

"Depends on my mood." He was more concerned about why hers was so mercurial. What was up with these tangents?

She rubbed her ankle one more time—the marks were fading, but they'd probably leave scars—and swung her legs over the edge of the bed. "You ever visit a place called *Stateman's Deli*?"

"Possibly. I don't keep a list, and a lot of those places blur together. Why?"

"I don't know. Curious, I suppose." She stood. Last night she shed the bustier, trousers, and boots, but kept the loose white top on. Now it hung off one shoulder and fell past her waist. It stopped just below her ass, leaving her long legs on display. She glanced back at him.

He didn't try to hide that he'd been staring.

One corner of her mouth tugged up. "Join me in the shower?"

"You have indoor plumbing?"

"Would you want to stay in a place that didn't?"

Good point. As far as he was concerned, it was one of the greatest inventions in history. "Are you going to magic me up some questing clothes after?"

"Are you going to make fun of me for not being period-specific?" Challenge and teasing lined her words.

"Nope. Not even close." He was curious to see what she came up with. As long as it was more comfortable than the tattered, blood-soaked clothing he'd discarded before bed, it was fine with him.

She knelt on the bed and crawled toward him. "You didn't answer the shower question."

They had to get clean anyway. Her top dipped low, giving him a full and stunning view of her unbound breasts. He pushed up to press his mouth to hers and locked a hand at the base of her neck, holding her captive.

Lexi moaned and leaned into the kiss.

This was good. Better than good. It was an assurance things weren't completely fucked up, only mostly. Need raced through him, and he nudged her back as he sat up the rest of the way.

"Is that a *yes?*" she murmured against his lips.

"Yes." It was easy to tumble into the energy that wrapped around them. He swore it was stronger today than in the past, flowing through and over him, binding them to each other. Every inch of him sprang to life.

He hopped to his feet and hooked his arms under her legs and behind her back in a single swoop.

Lexi squealed in delight. Her happiness joined the incredible swirl inside him.

Actaeon carried her into the bathroom, which was huge. Marble lay beneath their feet. A freestanding tub sat in one corner, and a large shower with glass doors was in another. "I like what you've done with the place," he said.

"No reason to skimp on the luxury."

He set her on her feet, then stripped her top off. She stood in front of him in nothing but her panties. Realization tickled his thoughts. It was the first time he'd seen her mostly naked.

He dragged his gaze along her smooth skin... The curve where her hips met her waist... Her full breasts. "You're fucking gorgeous."

The pink that spread over her skin added to the stunning sight. "You're biased."

"Maybe." Actaeon brushed his lips over hers and rested a palm on her stomach. "But I'm still right."

She dragged her nails up his back, drawing closer and molding her body to his. She jutted out her lower lip. "You know, I had to take care of myself the entire time I was down here alone."

"You poor thing." He nipped her exaggerated pout. "Unless you prefer it that way."

"Not so much."

He kissed along her jaw to her ear. "No? What if you had an audience?"

"Then I'm not technically alone, am I?" Lexi stepped out of his grasp and put a meter or so between them. "Is that what you prefer? Watching?" She hooked her thumbs in the elastic of her panties and slid them to the ground.

The playful teasing danced over his nerve endings, and her scent filled his thoughts. He reached her in a few quick strides. "I'm more of a hands-on kind of guy."

"I was hoping you'd say that." She pushed off his boxers, draped an arm around his neck, and fumbled behind her for the shower door handle.

Actaeon was so hard it hurt. Pressing into Lexi didn't sate his need. Hands on her hips, he guided her backward into the shower.

The desire to pin her to the wall and fuck her hard and fast was potent. Nearly overwhelming. He wanted Lexi to enjoy herself first.

He turned on the water, leaving it at almost-but-not-quite too hot, and let the scorching heat encompass them. He grabbed the bodywash and squeezed out a dollop. "Lilac. How appropriate."

"Cerberus says that's what I smell like."

Actaeon dragged his nose up the side of her neck. "You do. And you wear it well." The perfumed scent was a poor imitation, but combined with her natural scent, it was a perfect complement.

He glided soapy palms up her torso, to cup her breasts.

She gasped and pressed into his hands.

"We have a little time, don't we?" Actaeon asked as he pinched her nipples and let them slip and twist between his fingers.

Her reply was a sigh and a moan.

The sounds enticed and enthralled him. He explored her body, memorizing every inch, and the delicious noises that accompanied each touch.

"A girl can only take so much teasing." Lexi covered his hand and pushed it lower.

He didn't need to be told twice. He spun her away from him, drawing another squeal. That was rapidly becoming one of his favorite sounds.

Actaeon pressed his erection into her back and slipped his fingers down her stomach. When he brushed her clit, she gasped and bucked against his touch. He teased and stroked.

As she neared climax, he pressed her back, prompting her to bend at the waist, but didn't let up his attentions between her legs.

He fisted his cock and slid inside her. His groan mingled with hers. Fuck, she felt good, wrapped around him, tight and slick.

She fell into orgasm as he thrust, gripping his shaft and milking him.

He gripped her thigh with his free hand. He didn't have any restraint left. The need that had been building inside tightened in his balls, and he came hard, filling Lexi, pounding against her until they were both spent.

This was all perfect—the noises she made, the scent of sex, and the hint of perspiration that greeted him when he licked up her spine.

There were only a handful of moments in his life that lingered in his thoughts centuries after the fact. Those wonderful, incredible instances that filled him with joy that defied words. This was one of those.

It was both too bad and a good thing that they had to go back to the real world soon. He could see himself getting lost in a life like this.

***

LEXI LEANED into him with a sigh, and pulled his arms and the towel tighter around herself. "We should get dressed. Our quest awaits."

"Are you going to tell me what we're questing for?"

"The others," she said, as if it should be obvious. "Clothes, by the way." She gestured to one stack on the bed and grabbed the other. Those hadn't been there before. Neat trick.

He pulled on a long-sleeved T-shirt, that was some of the softest cotton he'd ever worn, boxers a lot like the ones he'd discarded, and a pair of stiff jeans.

"Why'd you skip the videogame getup?" he asked.

Her outfit was similar to his. It fit well, was simple and attractive, and could probably be purchased at any generic store in any country in the world. Their socks were nondescript, and a pair of ankle-high hiking boots waited for him on the floor.

She finished dressing. "The pirate bar-wench look is fun, but we might need something more practical."

He hoped not. His plan was to lead her back to Styx, and fill in the missing pieces for her along the way. In a couple of hours, Charon would take them back to the other side, and this would be over.

"What else do we need to bring?" she asked.

Actaeon looked them over. "We have comfortable clothes and walking shoes. We're set." She'd put more thought into the stroll than he tended to when he went out for a walk.

"We can't be. In the books, they always have hard cheese and bread. Flasks of water or wine. What kind of things do you bring with you?"

What sort of answer was she looking for?

"I can't draw a lot of parallels between my life and fantasy novels," he said.

"Have you read many?"

He stalled. His answer would contradict what he just said.

"Well?" She studied him expectantly. "I'm guessing *no*. Because they're too much like real life for you."

Sort of. "Except that in real life, the hero doesn't always win."

"That's the fun of the books. At least in those, you're guaranteed to slay the beast." She slung a backpack over her shoulder.

He had no idea where it came from. It was battered and dark green, with dozens of pockets, like an old Army backpack.

"Honestly? I don't prep for much of anything. You saw me when we were looking for a way to get to Hades. I took whatever I had on me. If it fits in my pockets, it comes with me. The rest either presents itself along the way, or it doesn't. Then again, I've never taken a months-long trek through the mountains, to drop a ring in a volcano." *Ha*, he did know one of those references.

"So you have read some fantasy."

"I watched the movies."

Lexi swatted his arm playfully. "Blasphemy."

This was fun. He was pretty sure quests—trials, whatever—weren't supposed to be fun. "This is your show. What do you think we need?"

"Food. Water. Weapons." She ticked off the list items on her fingers.

He held out his hand, and a dagger appeared in it. "We have weapons. We summon them out of midair. And you said you have a… blade of plus-ten cool stuff?"

She blew a puff of air at her hair. "Plus one dagger of strength. I'll have Bob put something together for us. Supplies that will travel."

They headed downstairs. Actaeon needed to give her the full story about what was going on. He wasn't sure how she'd handle it, so he was hesitating.

But besides the way she treated parts of this like a game or a book, she was coping just fine. She was more carefree than usual. She acted younger. A decade or two shouldn't make a difference, but there was a bigger gap between thirty and forty than there was between three-thousand and three-thousand ten.

The downstairs was mostly empty, but Bob was behind the counter, pouring himself a cup of coffee. From a Mr. Coffee machine.

"Where does the electricity come from?" Actaeon asked.

"The power socket in the wall." Lexi stood on a metal rail that ran along the bottom of the counter, bent at the waist, and reached behind the bar.

Good view.

She straightened and held two travel coffee-mugs. Stainless steel. She handed the mugs to Bob. "Pretty please?"

"Sure." He turned away to fill them.

Lexi looked at Actaeon. "Yes, I know electricity doesn't come from a magical place that lights things up because I plug them in. The entire building is wired. I'm not sure about the source… But I like my coffee strong-but-not-burnt, and the bread is a lot easier to bake in an electric oven. We only had wood burning for the first couple of weeks, and I couldn't figure out how to cook the food evenly."

Actaeon was only out for a few minutes after they

killed Hades. Or so his fresh wounds had implied when he woke up. "How long have you been here?" he asked.

"Don't know. A couple of months? The sun didn't really rise or set when I first showed up. That made it hard to keep track."

Time passed differently on different planes of existence, so there was no telling how long they'd been here, relative to an earth clock. And he was someplace else before this.

Bob handed them each a travel mug full of coffee, and nodded to a carafe of milk with a sugar bowl next to it. "Prep it the way you'd like."

"Can you do something else for me?" Lexi asked sweetly.

Bob gave her a huge grin. "Of course, love."

"We need questing food."

Bob furrowed his brow. "You're going to have to be more specific."

Actaeon was glad he wasn't the only one confused by all of this.

"You know—like cheese, bread, fruit, and nuts. Stuff that's good for traveling. Dried fruit, probably. I don't want to squish it."

Why don't you just summon it out of mid-air? The question died in Actaeon's throat. If she enjoyed doing things this way, he didn't see the harm in it.

Bob seemed to consider her request. "I can throw together something like trail mix. Fill some canteens with water. Or booze. Give you a tin with ground coffee in it…"

"That'll work perfectly." Lexi dropped on a stool and poured milk in her coffee.

While Bob fetched their *questing food*, she sipped her drink.

Actaeon sorted through his thoughts for the best place to start the reality part of this conversation.

Bob returned a few minutes later and set Lexi's backpack in front of her.

"Bob, tell me something," Actaeon said.

The bartender looked at him. "Sure."

"What did you do before you came here?" If these people had wandered into the town, they were displaced dead. Actaeon was curious about how out of place they were.

"I was a bartender at Kings of Hustler."

"The male strip-club in Las Vegas?" Actaeon hadn't expected that.

Lexi looked at him, mouth twisted. "You know that, but you can't remember if you've ever been to the best fucking sandwich shop in New Orleans?"

It did sound a little suspicious. Actaeon shrugged. "Some beef is more memorable. Besides, I haven't visited as many strip clubs as I have delis." He preferred a hands-on experience, and typically didn't have an issue finding a willing partner.

There was one he'd surrendered the opportunity with, and he was a little jealous Lexi had that with Icarus, when Actaeon no longer did.

"This place is epic, compared to that Hustler." Bob's comment rooted Actaeon back in the now. "Do you know how many women expected Tom Cruise Cocktail moves from me?"

"Who what now?" Lexi looked confused.

Tom Cruise? "When did you work there?" Actaeon asked.

"As in, the year? Late eighties."

"Nineteen Eighties?" Lexi might as well be asking if he was from the middle ages, for the disbelief in her voice.

Actaeon bit back a comment about post-enlightenment immortals. "How long were you wandering after you died and before you wound up here?"

"I wasn't," Bob said. "I died. I woke up. There was this bar. Thirty seconds? A year? Beats me."

Lexi covered his hand. "I'm glad you found it. You're awesome. And I'm sorry to cut the reminiscing short, but we need to get going. I don't know how far we have to travel, and we want to cover as much distance as we can while it's still light."

Odd statement, for someone who controlled the sun rising and setting on this plane.

"Sure." Bob pulled a book from under the bar and flipped to a bookmarked page. "I'm to the good part, anyway. Good luck." He looked at Actaeon. "Bring her back safe."

"Always." The assurance came easily.

Was it a promise he could keep this time?

They were walking a few miles to the shore of the river. How hard could it be?

NINE

Cerberus rocked Lexi in his arms, muttering, "Please wake up," over and over, as the edges of the reality disintegrated.

Her eyelids fluttered, and she groaned softly. The world swam back into view, but they weren't in the same place anymore. This was a suburban street, lined with rundown houses that had overgrown yards.

She looked up at him. "Are you all right?" Her question was sweet and concerned.

"I was worried about you."

Her clothing had changed again, too. Her jeans were worn in several spots, she didn't have socks, and her shoes looked as though her force of will was the only thing holding them together. Her T-shirt was dingy white, with scraps of red silkscreen print that had faded beyond recognition. "Why would you worry about me? You don't know me. You say you do, but there's no way you could."

"I *do* know you. I love you intently and dearly and

completely. I've given my life for you, and I would again." He shouldn't have said so much, but he hated picking and choosing his words.

The corners of her mouth pulled up. "I should be really creeped out by that."

"You're not?"

"Can we go someplace less public?" She extracted herself from his arms and stood.

He joined her. "You name it, and we'll go."

She took a step, wobbled, and let out a faint, *Ow*. She bent at the waist and rubbed her ankle, before straightening again. "This way."

She led him down a few blocks, to a two-story house that had probably been pink at one point.

"What happened with Poseidon, Zeus, and Artemis?" Cerberus asked.

Lexi furrowed her brow and confusion drifted around her. "Is that a general question? It's a shitty conversation starter."

The scream she'd let out when Clio died echoed in Cerberus' ears. Even a few years later, it would still affect Lexi. "The day Zeus announced mandatory registration. When... Clio died." He winced on the last words.

Lexi stared at him blankly. "Who?"

"Your best friend, Clio?"

She gave a dry chuckle. "I think you've confused me with someone else. I don't really trust enough people to make friends." They picked their way through weeds, along a broken concrete path, and up a crumbling porch. She paused at the door, hand on the knob. "If we don't fuck with anyone else in here, they won't fuck with us."

He nodded and followed her in. Was Clio an erased memory? But Zeus saw him. How was that possible?

Lexi didn't have the same lilt to her walk that she had before the amphitheater—if that had even been real—but now she walked with her shoulders hunched, and her gaze darting around her every few seconds.

This must be a later-in-life memory, but how much later? And what was the significance of this one?

They made their way up a staircase. She stepped cautiously in certain spots, and he followed her example. It was unlikely he'd make any noise. He didn't want to risk it, though.

They stopped in front of the last door at the end of the hallway. The entire building reeked, but he couldn't identify the smells beyond rotting things and bodily fluids.

The room they entered was clean. A black sheet was draped over the window, and a charcoal gray comforter covered a mattress on the floor. She gestured to a box in the corner that held food. "Do you want a granola bar or anything?"

"Thanks, but I'm fine. There's no lock on the door. Aren't you worried about people stealing your stuff?"

"If they need it, they can have it. As long as they don't piss on my mattress. Guy downstairs did that. He's not here anymore."

Cerberus had so many questions. One of the bigger ones, he hesitated to ask. He needed to know, though. "Why don't you live in your stepfather's place?"

Sadness whispered across her face before vanishing. "The gods found him. The house was a sacrifice spot. It was only a matter of time before they would have realized I was there. I haven't been back in three years."

That gave him some idea of where they were in time.

Lexi sat on the mattress. She rubbed her ankle, her forehead creasing, then patted the spot next to her. "I'm sorry I don't have better seating."

"This is fine." The one thing that was wrong with it wasn't her fault. He hated that she'd lived through this. That it didn't faze her. If he'd found her a couple of decades earlier...

He might not have been strong enough to turn Hades down, when he was ordered to kill Lexi. He might not have had the ability to help her out of this. If that was Actaeon in the deli, the hero had been in no shape to help—

"Who's Icarus?" Lexi asked. "Rather, I know who he is on paper. Guy with the wings from legends, who died when he flew too close to the sun."

"He faked his death. Daddy issues, I think."

Her laugh was dry, but there was no bitterness in it. "I should be surprised he's alive. I'm not. The history books say Hades is dead too, but dead men don't have daughters, do they?"

"Not last time I checked." Cerberus wouldn't ask if she was referring to herself. He knew the answer and didn't want to spook her. "Why did you ask about Icarus?"

"You obviously know me. A version of me? I don't understand that bit. Do you have a TARDIS?"

"No, but Icarus has something a lot like one, minus the time travel."

Lexi massaged her leg again. "You're yanking my chain, but I like it. So do I know Icarus the way I know you?"

It was a far more loaded question than she probably realized. What was that pre-enlightenment phrase? She knew them both *biblically*? He doubted her stepfather taught her that reference. "You do. Why?"

"I dreamed about him. We were fighting a chimera."

Was she talking about what happened in the apartments near Icarus' shop? Were her memories bleeding together? And if so, was there an answer in that to why Cerberus was here?

Her hand went to her ankle again, and Cerberus grasped her wrist. The contact jolted through him, and she gasped. She looked at him, eyes wide.

"It's a quest." Her voice was in his head. *"We have to find the others."*

"What?" he asked.

"I didn't say anything."

Of course she didn't, because he wasn't bonded to this Lexi.

"I didn't mean to startle you." He let go. "Why do you keep reaching for your ankle?"

"It hurts. In my dream, we were standing in this barren field—me and Icarus. We knew each other. He was trying to protect me, but the chimera bit me."

That wasn't the fight Cerberus was part of. He lifted

the hem of her jeans. An ugly red mark ringed with teeth glared back. It was healing, but not well. "What happened next?" he asked.

"I woke up in your arms."

Cerberus had pieces to this puzzle, but he didn't know how they fit. He was missing far too many to make a whole picture. There were gaps in his observations, and what little information he had was based on assumption.

"Do you want to see a magic trick?" she asked.

"Sure."

She took his hand and held it out, palm down. He braced himself for another rush. Heat flowed between them, carrying desire, but it was faded. A memory, like this Lexi.

She traced her fingers in the air above his arm, and an intricate design began to appear on his skin. It was a dragon. The jaws were open along the patch of skin between his thumb and finger, and the tail wrapped around his forearm, ending just below the elbow.

"Wow." He studied the detail and bright colors.

"Do you like it?"

"It's stunning." He wiggled his fingers, and the illusion faded. "Incredible." Was this something she'd done to someone else, at this point in her past? Had she been experimenting on herself?

Laughter, loud and jarring, drifted in from the hallway.

"Ignore them," Lexi said. "They're not here for me. Do you want to see something else?"

He'd seen her illusions before. They were so much

stronger in his present. Tangible when she wanted them to be. But he needed to see where this memory went. Why she was stuck at this point.

It had to be significant. Seeing Actaeon in the deli was. Her father's death certainly had been.

He nodded. "I'd love to."

She held her hand up, and a knife appeared a few feet above it, floating in midair. This wasn't like the weapons of Actaeon's that she liked to imitate. He leaned closer. It was… "Klingon?"

"Yes." Her smile was bright. Captivating. Innocent, but having seen too much. "You can't touch it, though. You can try, but it won't work."

"I don't need to touch it. It's incredible." He adjusted on the mattress, so he could examine it from different angles.

"What the fuck?" A woman's voice startled him from behind.

The blade vanished.

Cerberus looked to see a young man and woman, about Lexi's age, in the doorway.

"What was that, and where did it go?" the guy asked.

"Nothing. I don't know what you're talking about. You're drunk. High. It was a hallucination. You didn't see anything." The words tumbled from Lexi's mouth at high speed.

The other girl was glowing. Why didn't Cerberus see that before? Her aura was faint, which meant Lexi might not have noticed until now either.

The girl took a step closer. "You're one of us. Daughter of war, with a knife like that? Duplicity?"

Lexi shook her head. "I'm no one's daughter. I'm homeless and destitute."

"You're a hero." The girl sounded certain. "Holy shit. Your dad... The gargoyle claw..."

Lexi crawled closer and knelt in front of her. "Please don't tell. You can have all my food. My room. Please?"

The guy stepped between them. "We're not going to tell anyone. We don't need one of those assholes coming down hard on us."

"You're supposed to get her stuff, first." The girl pushed him aside. "Before you make the promise."

He shook his head. "She's a good roommate. I'm not risking someone else coming in and taking her place." He looked at Lexi. "No worries. Your secret is safe with us."

"Thank you." Lexi stood and backed up.

The instant they were gone, she grabbed her backpack. "He was telling the truth," she muttered. "She was lying. I have to go."

She shoved a handful of things into her backpack but didn't touch the food or bedding. "I promised him he could have it. He's not the one who will sell me out."

Cerberus walked out the back door with her, cringing at the feeling of her panic as it crackled in the air around them. The instant they reached the street, she ran.

This was like being trapped in a bad dream. Where were they supposed to go? She sprinted for a few blocks, then ducked into a crowded Chinese restaurant.

She looked different. Her clothing was the same, but an image of something cleaner and tear free hovered above it. Another face floated in front of hers too.

This must be what it was like for her to look through an illusion.

The host showed her to a table and asked if anyone was joining her. He never looked at Cerberus.

Lexi said *no*, as Cerberus sat across from her.

She ordered one dish, but as hers was delivered, his appeared as well. He was eating the same thing as her.

He was almost getting the hang of the rules down here.

The chair next to them creaked across the floor, and Aphrodite sat down.

"Aphrodite?" Lexi sounded scared. "What are you doing here?"

Lexi recognized her as a goddess here, but years later, she didn't know this was Aphrodite. That didn't make sense.

Aphrodite took her hand. "It's all right." She looked at Lexi's wrist, then where Cerberus sat. The goddess looked through him, but he swore she was trying to see him. She shook her head, then turned back to Lexi. "You can't be here. *Gaia*, I hate screwing around in your head, but I don't have a choice."

"Sure, you do," Cerberus said. "You could just not do it."

Lexi raised an eyebrow in his direction.

Aphrodite didn't flinch. "The girl in the house is a child of the ocean."

"Poseidon?" Lexi's terror was back, amplified by a thousand.

"Yes."

Why hadn't Cerberus smelled the salt water?

Because Lexi hadn't.

"She's not strong, but she can walk between realms on her own," Aphrodite said. "I was with him when she found him."

"That was only ten minutes ago," Cerberus said at the same time Lexi said, "It's only been a couple of hours."

He glanced outside. The sun was much closer to the horizon than it should be. Fucked up memory clocks.

Aphrodite stroked the back of Lexi's hand with her thumb, tracing the same path back and forth along her wrist. "I'm guessing she sought him out immediately. We were having breakfast in New Zealand. She appeared and told him she'd found that Hades-girl."

Several missing pieces collided in Cerberus' skull. Poseidon had known about Lexi? He stared at the side of Aphrodite's head. "How many memories have you taken from her?"

"I need you someplace safe. Cheyenne is landlocked. You set up there about a week ago." Aphrodite cupped Lexi's cheek. When she drew her hand away, something appeared in it. A delicately crafted rose with a pearl nestled in the middle. She pressed it into Lexi's palm. "This will pay for your room for the next few months. You need to forget today ever happened. For your own safety."

Lexi nodded. "I didn't care for most of it, anyway. How did you find me here?"

Aphrodite stroked Lexi's wrist one more time, then kissed her on the forehead. "I'll tell you someday. And this is the last time I can dig in your head this way. If something happens again, if I need to make you forget one more time…"

"What?" Lexi asked.

"Nothing, child. Enjoy Wyoming."

The Chinese restaurant was gone, and Cerberus stood with Lexi in a new apartment that put the old one to shame.

Polished hardwood stretched in all directions. He knew without looking that the fridge was stocked. The neighbors were quiet. The front door locked, and Lexi had the key.

"The next time I see Aphrodite, she's got a lot to account for," Cerberus said.

Lexi crossed her arms. "I can't argue that."

TEN

Icarus got in once. He could do it again. He
needed to curb the panic that Lexi might be fighting for
her life alone, and calm himself long enough to get back
into her head.

"What are you going to do about the chimera?"
Conner had dragged a stool in from the other room and
sat in the corner, watching and nursing his beer.

Icarus didn't know. "If Lexi's illusions didn't work,
I'm tapped. I'm only taking my brain, and it can do
amazing things, but summoning objects from thin air
isn't among them."

"Did you look around last time you were in there?"

A sarcastic answer flew to Icarus' lips. That wasn't
what Conner was asking, though. He wanted to know if
Icarus had seen any electricity. Auras. The kind of thing
Icarus worked with. "I didn't notice. I'll take better note
next time, but even if there's something there, I'll need a
physical object to bind it to."

"You talked to Zee while you were in there, though.

Right? She's your muse. She might spark something if you bump your heads together."

She was a hell of a lot better as a sounding board than Conner. "I could try that."

Conner took a long drag off his drink, then set it on the dresser with a *thunk*. "She ever tell you her favorite class as a kid?"

"We don't have time for this."

"You need an answer before you go back in."

"Fine. English lit?" Icarus was grasping, but she loved to read, so that made sense.

"Character class, genius."

That made even more sense. "I haven't known her long enough to get that intimate. It's not the kind of thing a guy asks on a first date if he's not descended from gods of love and sex." Not that Icarus had a chance to take Lexi out. He owed her a date. Or as many as she wanted.

"Touché." Conner smirked. "She liked to play an illusionist. Go figure, right? Talk about hiding in plain sight. So the year I went to school with her, she invited me to play with her and her friends one night."

"You rolled dice and crawled dungeons?" Icarus couldn't picture it. Conner might be fighting with his grandmother, but he had the same traits as the rest of his family. Oozed sex appeal and knew it. Role playing games, at least the D20 kind, didn't really sing *sexy*.

"Zee was the only other immortal in town. She was also a fine piece of ass. I did a lot for her."

Icarus didn't care that the two had a history. He didn't like the objectification, though. "She was sixteen."

"So was I. Anyway, we're out questing, and we reach this room in the basement of the castle. It's kind of half-castle, half-carved out of the cave, and there are spikes hanging from the ceiling. Our thief steps into the room—after checking for traps, of course—"

"Of course." Icarus bit back his impatience, along with the urge to ask if this had a point.

Conner raised his eyebrows. "He steps into the room, and one of the spikes falls. It barely misses him. High dexterity. Turns out the spikes are alive."

"Are you serious? Sentient stalactites?"

"I didn't write the adventure; I was just a quester. Everyone in the party panics and starts discussing what to do. We have to go through the room. The thief wants to risk running across. He rolls against his dexterity again and gets… I don't remember—whatever *not quite good enough* is. He sprints, a few of the spikes fall, and he breaks a leg."

"The spike didn't tear it off?" How did that work?

Conner tilted his stool back on two legs and knocked his head against the wall. "You're being too literal. This is role playing. Keep up. The entire party is discussing strategy. See, arguing at the top of our lungs. Zee says, *I cast an illusion on the floor, about… How tall do we need to be, to crawl? Three feet above the existing floor.* She has to roll her intelligence versus the spikes'. They're a three, she's a seventeen, it doesn't take much to beat them. She casts the floor illusion, we all crawl underneath to the other side of the room, and bing-bang-boom—no one else gets hurt."

"There are so many flaws in the creature construction—"

"Zee liked First Edition rules. *Focus*. Chimeras aren't the brightest creatures in the world. You run into another one, or the same one, and it doesn't have to know Zee's illusions aren't solid, as long as she casts them right."

"You're scary. I love it." Icarus couldn't believe he didn't see the answer himself, but it was good to have one.

Conner winked and blew him a kiss. "I get that from a lot of guys."

And now the conversation was deteriorating. "You're not my type."

"I know. You're keen on the brunette passed out on the bed. Or would you prefer my hair was lighter, and I looked more like a marble statue carved in the moonlight?"

An entire immortal bloodline of irritation. Icarus turned to Lexi. "I'm going back in."

There was no give-and-take this time. Icarus nudged, and the door opened. He found Lexi at another funeral. She looked up when he appeared. Sadness marred her face.

It was a lot better than chimera burns. He wrapped an arm around her waist, and she leaned into him while they watched the mourners.

"What happened?" he asked.

"I don't know. She bit me, you vanished, I felt like I was being torn to shreds, and then I was here. Can you hear them?"

"Delivering the eulogy, yes. Asking for comfort? No. I think that's only you."

She rested her head on his shoulder. "Why do you say that?"

"Aphrodite told me the voices you were hearing were prayers. The whole goddess thing, and all that." Was it disrespectful to have this conversation while they watched someone else's funeral? Or just eerie?

"Did she tell you how many times she wiped my memory when I was a child?"

That was a random question. "I take it that means it was more than twice?" He knew about the erasure the night Lexi and Conner slept together, and the one Aphrodite had a siren help with.

"I think…" Lexi pulled away and looked at him with a frown. "I can't remember. Go figure. What's going on?"

He wished he had some long, drawn-out story to tell. It would mean they had information to dig through. "What's the last thing you remember?"

"You told me I was a goddess, and that you'd teach me how to make the ceiling disappear so I could watch the stars from inside. Did you find Cerberus and Actaeon?"

She was halfway to caught-up.

"I didn't. Hermes found Actaeon."

"Cerberus?" Sadness spilled from her.

It sank into his pores and infected his thoughts. This was potent shit. Icarus wished he had better news. "I don't know. I'm sorry. What I do know so far is you're becoming the underworld. You're taking Hades' place."

"How does that work?"

"I suspect if we had that answer, this wouldn't be an issue. You don't know how to deal with it, so you've fractured. Actaeon is supposed to be helping from the underworld—"

"But I'm the underworld? Does that mean he's in me? That should be sexier." Her smile looked forced.

Icarus wished he could laugh. "Now you know what I know. I need you to come back with me."

"I can't. Not *I won't.* I don't know how. I feel these pulls, these pleas, and I'm drawn to them without my permission. I don't know how to help, but that doesn't stop me from being anchored here. It's like I'm required to watch their mourning through their collective thoughts."

Grief weighed on his chest and soul, suffocating him. Was that from her or the mourners? It was a good thing *magic* was a valid answer for *why*, or Icarus would go insane, figuring out how this made sense. "You need to be more selective and learn to block them out."

"I don't suppose you have any advice on how to do that? And I swear to me, if you say *meditate…*"

"Clever." He managed a smile at the underlying joke. "I've never lived through it, so I can only guess." He settled his hands on her hips and stepped behind her. Intellectually he knew this wasn't physical contact—it was literally all in their heads—but it felt good to be close.

It felt better when she leaned more of her weight against him. "I don't suppose you have a god on speed-dial who you're on speaking terms with, who isn't currently fucking with our lives, who wouldn't balk at helping Hades' brat…"

"Conner is with me."

"No shit." Relief trickled into her laugh. "Tell him I said *hi*, and that he owes me a trip to Germany."

"Tell him yourself."

"Don't do that. Don't be clever and hyper-positive, and say, *you'll tell him when you pull through*."

This felt good. Incredible. Stimulating. Swapping thoughts with Lexi was already on the top of his list of favorite things. "That's not what I'm doing. You get to deal with him pretending to take the offer the wrong way."

This time her laugh vibrated through her back. It didn't lift the sadness that saturated the air, but it made it easier to breathe through.

A loud blaring cut through the sky, drilling into his thoughts and making his brain shut down. Concern shoved aside everything else. That wasn't good.

"What the fuck is that?" Lexi covered her ears.

"Proximity alarm. I need to go. I'll be back if you don't find me first." He kissed her on the cheek, then forced himself back to his room.

No one else was in here with them. Where was Conner?

A wince-worthy noise came from the other room, like several objects scraping across stainless steel, then clattering to the ground.

Icarus sprinted toward the sound.

Conner stood several meters away from Icarus, and between them was a… dragon? Not one of the originals.

This was more like Smaug, but with green and blue scales.

"What the fuck?" Icarus' question drew its attention.

As the dragon spun, its tail whipped out in Conner's direction. Instead of knocking him back, it passed through him.

The beast was transparent, like a weak hologram. "I don't see any aura. Or anything," Icarus said.

Conner backed out of its way. It didn't seem focused on them. It was thrashing and roaring, but only occasionally made contact. "I don't, either. But I don't think it's attacking us."

"It's more scared of us than we are of it doesn't make me feel better." Icarus had never seen anything like this outside of a movie screen. He'd worry about it being a hydra, but heads growing back didn't matter if he and Conner couldn't connect with it long enough to cut one off.

And he needed to shut off that fucking alarm. He snapped, but it didn't go silent.

The dragon flapped its wings, and Icarus jumped away. Scattered puffs chased stray papers, and then his laptop flew across the room.

"Could you make that stop?" Conner shouted.

"I'd like to." If the alert wasn't stopping, it knew he felt like he was still in danger.

The dragon reared back and opened its jaw, and a rush of flame shot out. It passed through everything.

Icarus would have to turn the alarm off completely, rather than resetting it. And it would take days to get it back online again.

Was it worth it, to shut off a little irritating sound?

Considering his eardrums might liquefy and leak out his ears if he didn't… though, probably only figuratively.

But it wouldn't get rid of the dragon.

The beast shot another breath of flame at a shelf, and about half the contents burst into flame.

Icarus grabbed the nearest thing to him—a coil of insulated copper cable. He maneuvered to the side of the dragon and tossed one end of the wire to Conner, holding tight to the other.

Maybe they could clothesline the beast.

"On *three*, charge it and pull it tight," Icarus yelled.

Conner nodded. They'd done smaller scale versions of this and knew how to insulate themselves against each other.

"Three." Icarus gathered all the ambient electricity and forced it through the cable. The power that crackled along his skin, raising the tiny hairs on end, said Conner had done the same.

They hit the dragon in the throat, and lightning crackled along its scales everywhere the line rested. It screamed, louder than the alarm, and reared.

It was working.

The beast shimmered, and the line went slack, cutting in half when the beast's neck faded, then reappeared.

Well, fuck.

ELEVEN

THE SCENERY HADN'T CHANGED SINCE ACTAEON WAS here yesterday. Once they cleared the heavy cloud of dust that separated whatever Lexi had created from the rest of the underworld, the ground was cracked and the air was still.

He had the backpack slung over his shoulder, and she walked next to him as they headed toward the river.

"How do you know this is the right way?" she asked.

"It's the way I came in."

"Did you pass Cerberus along the way?"

"No. If he were down here, Hermes would have found him, the way he did me." Actaeon didn't know if that was true. Technically, Hermes found people who were waiting to get in, not who were already here. But walking around, sniffing the air for a single hellhound's scent, wouldn't get them anywhere.

She kicked a loose pebble, and it skittered to a stop ahead of them. "You don't believe that."

"Can you sense him?"

"No." Her pout was evident in her voice. "That doesn't mean he's not here. It could mean he's really badly hurt."

"And he'd heal, if that were the case. This is his element. You're his goddess. He's going to be strongest here."

"Wait. What?" Lexi grabbed his arm as she stopped, spinning him to face her. "I'm his what?"

Actaeon wanted to have this conversation anyway. Why would he rather face another chimera than explain this to Lexi?

Simple—if she didn't take it well, her reaction would destroy his attempts to convince himself this would be easy. "You're his goddess."

He repeated what Charon said, about Hades and the underworld, and Lexi's becoming more.

"Oh. Okay." She shrugged and started walking again.

Easy was good. This was ridiculous. Nothing came without a trial. Perhaps the challenge here was accepting the ease of the situation?

He stared at her back, then quickened his pace to catch up. "Just like that? Did you hear what I said—"

"Goddess. One with death. Blah, blah, blah." She waved a hand dismissively. "I made an entire town because I wanted to, and people who've been lost for seventy years or more are occupying it. Your explanation makes more sense than *just because*."

"All right." Actaeon wasn't going to argue.

In the distance, thunder rumbled. Had she installed some kind of weather pattern outside of her pocket town, or was that instability in their environment?

"Tell me the truth about Cerberus," she said.

When Actaeon dated Cassandra, watching her suffer through visions of the future was painful. He hated to see her suffer.

He was still undecided on how it felt to be with a human lie-detector.

He wasn't going to make a joke about her being like a dog with a bone. Puppy jokes pissed her off on good days. "I don't know where he is. I'm not here to help you find him. I'm here to make sure this transition doesn't drive you insane. Charon understands it better than I do. He saw Hades go through it. We're going to talk to him. Then, you can look for Cerberus."

"I see." Her voice was tight. "You decided this. You neglected to tell me. You didn't think I'd have an opinion on the matter?"

Fuck. "We're questing, right? Think of me as your guide."

"Are you the guide who actually knows where we're going, or the one who speaks in cryptic riddles and then vanishes and reappears when it's convenient to the plot?"

Lightening split the sky, lighting up the clouds. It was far enough off they wouldn't run into it. The show was as pretty as it was worrisome, since Lexi may be responsible for it and not realize what she was doing. "I'm the guide who knows where I came from and would like to make sure that's where everyone ends up."

"Hmm… Anti-trope. I like it." There was an undercurrent in her tone that implied this wasn't the end of the conversation.

She tugged her canteen strap higher on her shoulder, never breaking stride.

He wasn't going to fall into the trap of over-explaining himself because she was silent.

They passed a patch of withering trees he recognized as about the halfway mark. They were making good time. He swore this took longer before. Being unfamiliar with the terrain could have that effect, though.

"What's Icarus to you?" Lexi asked.

Random. "We're old friends. I've told you that. He's told you that." A memory nudged his thoughts. Lexi waking him up, smelling of sex. Icarus' scent mingling with hers. It seemed like ages ago. It was probably only a day. "What's he to you?" he asked.

"Promise you won't get mad?"

"No. It matters to me, but I trust that you're following your heart. You don't owe me an answer right now, but if you're not comfortable telling me yet, I hope we reach a point where you are." There was more to the gnawing in his chest, but he couldn't name it.

"I've convinced myself it's my choice." Lexi sighed. "That came out weird. You know this whole *fated mates* thing that Cerberus is so enamored with?"

"That I didn't hear you complaining about, after you moved past the initial shock." His mind stalled, and he backed it up. There were a few reasons she might bring that up, but one key one he could think of. "Icarus made the list?" That pang was jealousy. Why? He and Lexi had something good.

"You don't have anything. You might, someday, but right now? It's lust." Icarus' argument was loud and clear in Actaeon's thoughts.

Lexi fiddled with the strap of her canteen. "I don't like the sound of a *list*. It's not as though I sat down and wrote out *these are the guys I'm crushing on*. Though, if I had… you'd all be on there."

That was reassuring. "Which is why it doesn't matter that it's fate." He could be the bigger man about this. He genuinely liked seeing her happy. She sparked when she was with Icarus. It wasn't *her* reaction he was hung up on. Slivers from an older past wormed their way in. "I'm not mad," he said.

"I hoped you'd get it. I couldn't have made it this far without you and your perspective." She grasped his hand.

"I could say the same about you." Was he getting giddy because they were walking and holding hands? Love was passion and heat and clawing, and sometimes tears. It wasn't a flutter because she chose to tangle her fingers with his.

A raindrop struck him on the nose, and another on the cheek, then a trickle fell around them. The air stayed warm and comfortable. He didn't remember this plane having a lot of weather, though.

Lexi turned her face toward the sky, slowing but not stopping. "I love the rain." She glanced at him. "And you didn't answer my question."

"I did, and you already had the answer."

"Is that all he's ever been?"

Actaeon stuck on the way she phrased her question.

It wasn't subtle, and her tone implied she had assumptions about the answer. "No," he said.

"So… fuck buddies? Sweethearts who decided you made better friends than lovers? The guy you jerked off with in the hot tub, but you never talk about it, because what would the neighbors think?"

"All of the above?" Actaeon wasn't in the mood to unpack that part of his past. The rain had dripped into the top of his boots and made his socks wet. His feet wouldn't blister from this, but it was uncomfortable.

Or he was looking for excuses.

"Why does it matter?" he asked.

Lexi stepped off the path, toward a large rock under a tree. The light drizzle tapped out a steady rhythm against the leaves, but it no longer reached them. She leaned against the trunk, one foot propped up behind her, and studied him. "Why do you think it matters? I'm grateful that you're open about who I may or may not fall in love with, but if the two of you have baggage… I'd like to think what I share with you is going to last beyond my father fucking with my life. Which apparently he can even do from beyond the grave. Probably a good thing death only had the one child."

"Now, who's getting distracted?" Actaeon tried to sound playful, but he had to force the words through a jumble of thoughts focused on Icarus. The last argument they had. The one they had last time they broke up. Funny how so many of those memories tied back to disagreements.

Her smile was flat. "I'm getting to my point. If our relationship—yours and mine—is more than an adrenaline-rush-fueled fuck fest, I'd like to know where you stand with him."

The skies opened up and unleashed what they'd held back. Rain slammed into the earth around them, hammering a deafening one-note song. It didn't reach them under the tree, though.

He didn't like her doubt. That it echoed portions of Icarus' accusations. That it chimed in with notions Actaeon tried to ignore. "Do you think we'll last that long? You're not considering this whole fate thing in your equation. That's not who you are."

"I don't know." Lexi didn't meet his gaze.

"Do you think you will, with him?" Actaeon didn't want her answer. It whispered in his ears before she moved her lips.

"Yes."

That hurt. It shouldn't. Hadn't Actaeon proven himself? "You've only known him for a few days."

"I haven't known you much longer."

"He and I dated a few times." He could tell her the truth. She'd learn it anyway, and none of it was a secret. "One of those off-again, on-again things over the centuries. We fight, we fall apart, we come together as friends, sometimes it grows back into more, and others we drift apart again before that happens."

"That's why you didn't know if he'd see you at the funeral."

Actaeon shook his head. "No. We haven't been together for more than a century. We finally admitted it was a bad idea." Any residual desire was lust-driven.

There was no love or romance there. Talking about it reminded him of that simple truth.

If he said it aloud, would Lexi call him a liar?

And why did it scrape his insides raw that Lexi and Icarus had this connection?

Because you can't form that with either of them.

But he would. He and Lexi would get there.

"Hmm... Wouldn't have guessed that. Obviously." She kicked away from the tree, and an umbrella appeared in her hand. She flicked her thumb over a black button. The handle telescoped, and the umbrella sprang into shape. "Thank you for telling me."

What was he supposed to say to that? *Sure? No problem? Anytime?* "Yeah. You ready to get going?"

She nodded and headed away from the path, at a ninety degree angle to the direction they'd been traveling.

Actaeon grabbed her arm and yanked her to a stop. "We need to follow the path."

"Why?"

"Because that's the way to Charon and Styx. We talked about this." There was more of an edge to his voice than he wanted, but digging up the past dragged like sandpaper over his emotions.

She looked at him, expression dark. "*You* decided it. You didn't ask my opinion."

"It's the way out." He wasn't in the mood to repeat himself.

We fight. We fuck. You save my ass. Her earlier words came back to haunt him. He shook them aside.

"You want us on the path? Fine." A stone walkway

appeared beneath their feet, replacing the dirt and dried grass. "We're not leaving without Cerberus."

"And I told you he's not down here. We can't keep playing this stupid fucking game." He tried to rein in his irritation, but she was pushing the wrong buttons. "This isn't a *quest*. We're not stuck in one of your step-father's stupid fantasies. This isn't a book or a fairy tale. We don't go looking for trouble. In those rare instances when life gives you a direct route out, you take it."

Thunder cracked loudly enough to rattle him, and lightning lit up and split the sky in half.

Lexi stared at him, the storm reflecting in her eyes. "That's not the right direction." She spoke through clenched teeth.

"You're being a child, Alexandra." He winced the instant her full name passed his lips.

Her mouth twisted into a dark, wicked smile. "And you're being an indifferent, apathetic asshole. I'm tired of being the maiden stuck in a tower, waiting to be rescued. If that's what you're looking for, go fall in love with someone else. I get an equal say in things, and I want to find Cerberus."

"How is this not you throwing a tantrum?"

Another clap of thunder boomed. The scent of sulfur mingled with rain. And then another roar.

This wasn't thunder. It was a beast. The crack of wings rent the air.

A dragon landed behind Lexi, wings stretched wide enough to block large portions of the sky, and jaw snapping in the storm. The rain glittered off the green and blue scales along its back, and its tail wrapped around its clawed feet when it settled.

Lexi turned and stumbled back into Actaeon. "Fuck me. Dragons are real?" she asked.

As real as stair trolls. As in, not the last time Actaeon checked.

The beast roared, and flame erupted from its mouth, turning a nearby tree to ash.

That was *very* real. *Creation*, this was bad.

TWELVE

"Hide. *Now.*" Actaeon summoned his bow as he barked the order at Lexi.

"Did you hear a word I said?" She really wanted to continue this argument, with a house-sized, fire-breathing dragon a short distance away?

"I heard every single one of them." Actaeon spoke through clenched teeth. "Now's not the time."

He notched an arrow and drew back the string. He wouldn't have many shots. Where was most likely to be vulnerable, and could he hit that spot?

"*Whoa.*" The dragon vanished, and glittering sparks showered to the ground around Morpheus. "I don't think I'll survive one of those arrows."

Actaeon wasn't in the mood for this. The last time he saw the god of sleep was in his dreams, and Morpheus was masquerading as Lexi. "Let's find out, shall we?" He didn't lower his weapon.

"I know where your gatekeeper is." A tremor ran

through Morpheus' voice. He looked at Lexi, but every few seconds, he flicked his gaze at Actaeon.

She gasped. "Cerberus?"

"Yes. And we've never been introduced. I'm Morpheus. It's a pleasure to meet you. Though it's always a little awkward, meeting someone whose skin I've worn."

Lexi gave a half-smile, half-grimace. "Someone dreams about me?"

"Multiple people dream about you." Morpheus gave Actaeon a knowing glance.

Tension quivered in Actaeon's arms. "Speaking of— you can't take other shapes unless we're dreaming. Where are we sleeping?"

"*You're* not." Morpheus spared him a glare. "Please, don't shoot me."

"Stand down, boy," Lexi said.

No wonder she didn't like the puppy jokes with Cerberus. That was fucking irritating. Actaeon growled and let his bow vanish. "Talk."

"You're both awake, but not all of the new goddess is. Part of her is asleep someplace else. It gets a little convoluted from here, but this place is taking the shape of her mind. I can manifest as her deepest dreams, and the dragon was one of them. She's broadcasting dreams, thoughts, and a variety of mystical signals, on every frequency I'm familiar with."

"You *want* to be attacked by a dragon?" Actaeon stared at her in disbelief.

She cast her gaze at her shoes. "No."

"She wants you put in your place," Morpheus said.

"I don't blame her, so I thought I'd have a little fun greeting the mistress of the realm."

"And Cerberus is here?" Lexi approached Morpheus. "I'm sleeping? Where?"

"He's deep inside Tartarus. I can't get to him, or I would have brought him to you. I don't know where you are, but he's trapped in the dream with you, and I can hear it. It's like someone left the TV on too loud and lost the remote, and I'd like you to stop. The sooner the better."

"You wanted to sic a dragon on me?" Actaeon didn't care for being ignored.

Lexi turned to face him. "I wanted something that would make you listen to me. I was also disappointed that out of all the things I've been able to create here, a dragon wasn't on the list. I didn't ever think, *I need a dragon to attack Actaeon.*"

Behind her, Morpheus shrugged. "Your subconscious did."

"You're not helping." Lexi shot him a glare.

"I don't have to. Unlike the gatekeeper, I'm not your servant. I'm a god as well—one who happens to inhabit your realm. I'm only here to get the dreams toned down and so you don't rip apart my home with your tantrums."

A hint of Actaeon's smugness slipped out.

Lexi clenched her fists, and her chest rose and fell. She looked between Actaeon and Morpheus. "Hi. New to being a goddess. I found out by having my soul ripped into pieces and part of me being shaped as a holding spot for *all of the dead*. You would have dealt with it

better? You"—she fixed her attention on Actaeon—
"destroyed half of Las Vegas because someone killed a
woman you don't even love anymore. And you knew
what you were capable of before you started. On a relative scale, I think I'm coping pretty well."

He refused to concede her point, regardless of how
true it was. "How do we get to Cerberus?"

"I can take you to the edge of Tartarus," Morpheus
said. "I can't bring you further, or I'd plant him at your
feet right now. That realm keeps me out."

"But we can get in?" Lexi sounded doubtful.

Actaeon knew the answer. He'd looked *everywhere* for
Cassandra after she died. "I can. And you're a force of
will, so I assume no place is going to keep you away
from Cerberus."

She smiled. "It's true."

Would she go to the same lengths for Actaeon?

Would he bitch about her putting herself in danger
if she did?

Probably.

That didn't make him a martyr, as Icarus had
accused; it meant Lexi's safety was important to him.

"Are you ready?" Morpheus asked.

Not really, but they might never be. "Yes."

Lexi nodded. "Me too."

Morpheus took their hands. The scenery shimmered, then reappeared, unchanged.

"Oh." Lexi gasped.

Actaeon followed her gaze. A door was behind them,
carved from marble and engraved with ancient Greek
characters.

Seeing the gate again sent goosebumps racing over him. He'd spent several long, torturous months in that place, fighting past damned Titans and others who had the nerve to piss off Zeus.

"Good luck," Morpheus said. "And, Alexandra—"

"It's Lexi," Actaeon corrected him without thought.

The corner of her mouth tugged up. "Hmm?"

"A moment?" Morpheus pulled her aside. He and Lexi moved far enough away to speak without Actaeon hearing.

Lexi did a lot of nodding and shaking her head, and in the end, she gave Morpheus a tight-lipped smile. "Thank you."

"Come out of this all right," Morpheus said. "You have the potential to be a good mistress, and I don't know if there's another spare."

Spare. Actaeon's chest tightened at the phrasing. As Morpheus vanished, the door swung open.

It didn't look like as though it led anywhere, but Actaeon knew better. He held out his hand. "Shall we?"

Lexi hesitated, then accepted the offer. Her skin was cool. The fit of her palm against his was perfect.

They stepped through the gate, and the door vanished, taking their previous location with it.

Tartarus was a gray landscape of rocks that stretched for an eternity. With fires and the scent of brimstone dotting the land, and screams punctuating the air, it resembled Dante's Hell.

"Which way?" Lexi asked.

There was no telling, but so far, picking a random

direction had worked in their favor. "That way." He pointed.

The cries of tortured voices didn't get any easier to hear, the longer he and Lexi walked.

Out of the corner of his eye, a movement caught his attention. Before he could locate the source of the shadow, another flickered in his periphery.

"This isn't good, is it?" Lexi's voice was tiny.

He spun around, keeping her at his back. Several figures—dozens—circled them, closing in quickly.

Women in tattered lace and torn gowns studied them. They were disheveled but whole. No torn skin or broken bones. Their faces were intact but marred with scowls.

Actaeon remembered this legend. It stood out in his mind from all the others, because of the magnitude of the death involved. He should have told Lexi this story last night. The Daughters of Danaus—fifty sisters, all promised to be wed on the same day. All but one of them killed their new husbands on their wedding nights.

"Hey. Howdy. Hi." Lexi waved. "We're not here to fuck with anyone. We'd just like to get in and out, and be on our way.

The woman in front of them replied in a dialect Actaeon hadn't heard since he was young. He repeated a more polite and formal version of Lexi's greeting, in Ancient Greek.

The woman in front introduced herself as Hypermnestra, the oldest sister, and smiled sweetly at Actaeon. *"I know you, child of the moon. Do you serve the new mistress of the neighboring realm?"*

"*Yes.*" It was best not to get into the details like *no, not really.* This was politics. The tiny voice in his head insisted he'd give anyone the same answer.

"What are they saying?" Lexi asked under her breath.

"I'll translate as soon as we're done," he said to her. He turned back to Hypermnestra *"We're looking for someone."*

"Kerveros. The gatekeeper. We know."

Lexi tensed at the name. *Cerberus* rolled off the tongue differently, but it was obvious who they were talking about.

Actaeon grabbed a polite reply. *"If you would direct us to him, we'll let you get back to——"*

"An eternity of suffering? Quite generous of you." Hypermnestra's reply was sarcastic.

Actaeon kept his muscles loose and his body prepared for the looming fight. It would be nice if, this once, he and Lexi could have a polite conversation and then leave.

Hypermnestra gazed at her sisters, then back at Actaeon and Lexi. *"No. You can't have the gatekeeper."*

Actaeon was disappointed by the answer, but not surprised. Could he take all of them without too much effort? Unlikely. *"Any particular reason?"*

"We've suffered for eons, deprived of love. Hades had no interest in alleviating that, despite his loathing for the brother that put us here. Because we cannot leave, we demand the new mistress of the neighboring realm to share in our futility. We'll kill her mate and force her to join in our suffering."

"Why does it feel like someone walked over my grave?" Lexi hissed.

Actaeon didn't want to be the one to tell her it wasn't her grave they were concerned with. He couldn't go hand-to-hand with this many combatants. And he didn't like being surrounded. The only chance for escape was to keep the sisters at range. He summoned his bow.

"I'm afraid that's not going to work for us." He spoke in English, for Lexi's benefit. The weapon should convey his meaning regardless of language.

Hypermnestra snarled, and charged.

He buried an arrow in her shoulder. The wound made her pause but didn't stop her. "Stay out of their range and behind me as much as possible," he said to Lexi.

She stepped by his side instead, two swords appearing in her hands. "I can handle anyone who gets close."

"Since when?" This was a bad time for this conversation. He let his attention fall in as many places as he could at the same time, turning and firing at each target before moving to the next.

Two of the sisters reached them and grabbed. He moved between them and Lexi. Their fingers dug into his skin, leaving welts that blistered and tore.

"Let me help." Lexi swung and sliced a nearby sister's shoulder. The sister howled in agony but recovered in a blink.

Actaeon wasn't doing so well. There were too many limbs, and he only had one set of eyes. He stumbled over Lexi's feet and lost precious seconds recovering. "I've got this." He spoke through a clenched jaw. "You need to be as small a target as possible.

It was partly because he needed to protect her, but as much that he didn't have a rhythm with her. Fighting with Cerberus was bad enough. He couldn't anticipate Lexi's next moves.

She put several feet between them, moving in an intricate sword dance that severed a sister's limb, disemboweled another, and decapitated a third. They all healed before she stopped moving.

Holy fuck. "Where did you learn that?" He fired off several more arrows, but two more sisters grabbed at him, leaving more smoldering wounds behind. Where they healed instantly, he wasn't recovering. The energy drain of using the bow, combined with his injuries, wore on him.

"The barber is a Japanese sword master. He trained me," Lexi sliced through another target.

He spun and shot at someone getting too close to Lexi, and fingers gouged his spine.

"You're the guy with the ranged weapon. You need to back up," Lexi said.

"You need to learn to read my moves better. I've been doing this a lot longer than you have."

Claws dug into his calf, and he stumbled. Another sister bit his other ankle, and he clenched his bow until his knuckles ached. He had to get back up. They needed to finish this fight.

Lexi dropped to one knee next to him, but her focus

was on the sisters. She crouched, pressing one fist into the ground.

Pain licked at his senses, spiking over every inch of his body. He needed to get up.

"I'm not a delicate flower," she muttered. "Are you really the guy who can't handle a woman as strong as him? *You?*"

"No." Why weren't the sisters attacking? It was as if something held them at bay.

"Then what's your problem?" Lexi asked.

He didn't have the strength to vocalize that *and* finish this fight.

"Great answer." Sarcasm dripped from Lexi's voice. The wind kicked up around them, sending debris flying and tearing at the sisters' hair. None of it reached him or Lexi.

The sisters vanished.

Lexi jumped to her feet. "I did it."

"Did what? Where did they go?" Even talking hurt.

"I sent them to the other side of Tartarus. It will be a while before they make their way back here."

"Awesome." He wasn't sure if he said the word or just thought it. Darkness licked at the edges of his vision. And then his world went black.

THIRTEEN

Icarus could put out the dragon's fires all night, but that didn't help them get rid of the creature.

Conner was backed against the far wall, doing a combination of avoiding the tail and trying to grab anything in order to do damage. He wasn't successful with either.

Should they call someone? Did he know anyone who could fight semi-tangible beasts who weren't supposed to exist?

The dragon vanished in a shower of translucent glitter. The alarm stopped.

"What the fuck?" Conner stared at the empty space between them.

Icarus didn't have any words. His workshop was a wreck. It would take weeks to put things right again. And none of that mattered until he could pull Lexi from whatever had her trapped.

Conner looked as disheveled as Icarus felt. He raked his fingers through his hair. "What now?"

"You tell me how you ignore prayers, and you let me stay in her head until she comes out with me."

"I wasn't the one who pulled you out last time. What if that fucking alarm goes off again?"

The only things in the house that couldn't be replaced were in this room. So many ties to his past. He let his gaze trip along the shelves. It would hurt to lose it all, but he'd still have the memories.

A glint caught his attention. He studied the silver chain with a cross that hung from a hook on his wall. A pang echoed in his chest. A past he thought he'd left behind, returned to engulf him. He looped the chain around his wrist three times, letting the cross dangle loose.

Icarus glanced at Lexi's prone form. Was he willing to give up all of this for her? This woman he'd just met? This fascinating creature whom he might or might not fall in love with?

These were things. She was more valuable than all of them put together. Maybe Lexi and he wouldn't work out, but he suspected they would. If they didn't, it would be another memory to add to those he cherished. He'd stow it with those of Actaeon.

"Well?" Conner asked.

Icarus steeled himself. "If the alarm goes off again, and you can't get rid of whatever caused it, get us out of here, please. Take us someplace safe, and don't risk yourself in the process."

"You're sure."

Icarus nodded.

"All right. This is what you need to tell Zee about

listening to—not ignoring—prayers." Conner blew out a puff of breath. "It's something most of us are born into. I don't really put a lot of thought into it."

"Try?"

The seconds that ticked away while Conner thought seemed to take an eternity. "Okay. Best I can come up with."

Icarus listened intently through the explanation, adding his own mental footnotes as needed. "Anything else I should know?" he asked when Conner was done.

"Distract her from the voices. Give her anything to focus on besides them, and that will help her slide over them. I don't understand how the two of you are sharing thoughts or dreams or whatever, but draw her into a story she doesn't want to escape. Take her on an adventure, if you can talk her into it. Something that forces the prayers to be background noise."

"I'll keep that in mind." Icarus lay down next to Lexi, arm pressed against hers, and took her hand. "Thank you. For everything." He closed his eyes and dove back in.

He found Lexi at a pub. She sat at a corner table, watching a large group sing loud songs and knock back shots and beers. A casket rested at the far end of the room.

He took the spot next to her on the bench, facing the off-duty police officers—the photos on the casket gave it away.

"I've never understood wakes." She slid her hand under his. "I guess they make more sense now than in the past, with Hades' bringing a couple of people back to life. But the dead are gone and moved on. They're in a different place. Why drag them back here?"

It was in interesting way to say *hello*. "You walked into the labyrinth, knowing it could kill you, to meet your dead mother."

"That's different."

"How?" He wasn't accusing; he was genuinely interested.

"First of all, she asked me to come, and second, I wasn't trying to resurrect her. I wanted the opportunity to say *hello*." Sadness spilled into her voice. "To tell her once what a difference she made in my life." She drew in a shaky breath. "Maybe I do understand it. Wanting that one last chance to say those things they never got to say."

"Is that what these people are asking for?"

Lexi shook her head. "Some of them, but not most. Several are happy it wasn't them, but others wish it had been. They're all mulling over what it would be like to be in his place, whether they know it or not. It's so loud. It's more deafening than their singing."

The grief pressed in, as it had before, gripping like a fist around Icarus' lungs. He knew this sensation—the sadness that accompanied the end of a life, the snuffing out of all of that potential—but he'd learned to ignore it centuries ago.

"That's a person." Lexi's statement caught him off-guard. "Not a collection of what they could have been if they'd lived longer. They already were something. To every single officer here, the man in that casket was already defined."

Icarus shifted in the bench to face her. "I didn't say anything."

"You didn't have to. But you do have to stop defining people as what they could be, and start accepting they've also got some glorious features as they are."

He didn't quite understand the words, but she believed them, so he tucked away the thought, to let his mind gnaw on it. "You can't stay here."

"I won't. Someone else will mourn or beg or plead louder, and I'll be whisked away."

He cupped her cheek and forced her gaze to his. "You have to stop letting these voices lead you. You're losing yourself in the individual."

"I have to do something. I'm a goddess now. I'm not going to be like the others. I have to help."

"You will." He traced a thumb along her cheek. "I don't want you to stop. But you'll do more good if you learn how to control this."

She furrowed her brow. "I don't suppose you came back with any brilliant advice on how to do that."

"I did."

Some of the lines in her forehead faded but didn't vanish. "Fill me in. But if you tell me to ignore them, I'm not going to listen."

Was that irony or just appropriate? "According to Conner, you have to stop focusing on the single voices." He wished he had a good analogy for this. "It's like... when you're standing in a rainstorm. If there are a couple of drops, you can feel each one. When it starts to pour, if you try to pick out the individual spatters, it'll drive you nuts. You have to focus on the entire storm."

Their world changed, and they were sitting on hard pews in the back of a chapel. A man in a suit stood behind the podium at the front of the room, reading verse and praising Hades for seeing his wife to the next world.

"That sounds like ignoring," Lexi said.

"It's not. You still feel the water, and part of you knows... Okay, this was a shitty analogy. Conner says if you can let it wash over you, your subconscious will learn to pick out those voices you can actually help. All of these people you've seen so far... Have you done anything for them?"

"Acknowledged their grief."

"Do they know that?"

Lexi wrapped her arms around herself. "I'd like to think they feel the comfort."

"Do you need to be here to offer comfort?"

"I don't know." Frustration leaked into her voice. "I have to do something."

So she'd said. "I understand. I'm not telling you otherwise." He tried to structure his thoughts. For the most part, he didn't explain how things worked, he did what needed to be done. This was something he couldn't even do for himself, and he had to put it to words. "As I understand it, if you're letting all the prayers rush around you, instead of stumbling over the one-offs, there's a part of you that will know how to help. To comfort. To soothe. To do those things you know are appropriate, without interfering or granting unreasonable requests."

"Just like that, huh?" She looked at him skeptically.

"I don't know." Three of his least favorite words, regardless of the language. "You'd have to give it a try and find out for yourself."

She squeezed his hand. "Help me?"

He didn't have any idea what he could do, but since she was going into this almost as blindly as he was… "Of course. Always."

She squeezed his hand. "Don't focus on the individual drops, right?"

"Exactly."

She closed her eyes. Seconds ticked away, turning into minutes, as the man at the pulpit recited from the New Book of Ares.

Non-denominational. Wonderful. Not.

Lexi looked at Icarus again. Frustration radiated from her, mingling with the sadness that filled the room. "This is all I can feel. It's the loudest."

"No, it's not. Before this happened, you heard all of them at once."

"I don't anymore."

"What about the place we were in before this?" He was grasping and had no idea if that would make things worse. "You know what that felt like. Can you find it again?"

"No."

Icarus wanted to be frustrated with her stubbornness. He stopped himself. If he was exhausted from being an observer through a few eulogies, what did she feel like, living all of them and more?

Distract her. Conner's advice echoed in his head.

That was all well and good, but Icarus needed her to

cope, in addition to that. He took both her hands. "Look at me."

When she did, the sorrow in her gaze devoured him to the core.

"You're probably exhausted and confused, and undoubtedly frustrated." He kept his voice kind. "I understand. I want to help."

"None of this is helping." Despite the words, some of the tension drained from her body.

He leaned in and brushed his lips over hers, then pressed their foreheads together. "Close your eyes again."

"Fine." She huffed out the word.

"And start by focusing on me."

"This feels an awful lot like meditating." There was a shift in the air, though. Sadness was muted with comfort.

Icarus hoped that was a good sign. "I can't say for sure, but I'd guess this is a lot like following different auras. You have to stop thinking about one, so you can see them all. If you step back from this group of prayers, can you feel those we came from?"

"No… Yes."

The fire and brimstone recitation of *The Tomes of Zeus* mingled with the drunken singing of the wake.

In his peripheral vision, Icarus saw their setting flicker between a bar and a chapel. "How about the university, where Esper was?"

The third setting blended into the mix, splatters of silence cutting off the noise, like a speaker with faulty wiring.

"You're doing it." He wanted to pull away and look

around, but keeping the physical connection was important— for him or her, he wasn't sure, but it needed to
stay.

The scent of damp grass mingled with that of
booze, and cool air brushed his skin before fading into
more scripture reading.

Lexi whimpered. "It's all so loud. I don't know
which one to listen to."

If Actaeon were here… Icarus was unsure why that
would make this better, but it wasn't an option. "You
don't need to pay attention to any of them. Listen to my
voice instead. Let them jabber in the background."

"I can't ignore them. I'm here to serve them."

"You will"—Conner had better be right about that
—"but only if you can learn to let them all run together.
They need to become white noise. Subliminal."

"I can't."

Icarus dropped her hands and cradled her cheeks.
He pressed his mouth to hers. It was gentle but unyield-
ing. *"Listen to me. No one else."*

When she didn't kiss back, he was ready to let go.
Then she relaxed against him, her lips molding to his.

A familiar jolt raced through his veins. This
shouldn't feel so good. He and she were mental projec-
tions, nothing more. But desire and comfort spilled
through his body.

When they broke apart, he gasped at the loss of
sensation.

They were nowhere. Vast nothingness stretched in
every direction.

"You did it." He grinned. "How do you feel?"

Her smile was tiny but stunning. "I can still hear all of it."

"I think it will take a while to turn it into background noise." He didn't expect it to happen in an instant. Despite his insistence, he was surprised she picked up on step one so quickly.

"There's a pull. Thousands of them. They tug at my thoughts and make me want to follow," Lexi said. "But I feel like I can tell them *no*."

That sounded like a good thing. "Do you want to come back home?"

"Yes. Please, yes. It feels like an eternity since I had a say in where I was."

This wasn't the time to point out what a real eternity felt like. He was grateful to have Lexi less compelled and more *her*. "Let's go." He took her hand and stood.

"How?"

"Uh…" He'd assumed once she fought the pull, she'd return to her own body. They'd wake up in his room. Conner would be happy he could go back home.

Lexi turned as much as she could without breaking contact with him. "Is there a door?"

"I don't know." He had to force the words out.

Grief and frustration pressed in again, but this time it was all hers. "I don't want to be here anymore."

FOURTEEN

If Icarus wanted to wake up, he could. He was unsure how he knew that, but there was no doubt. He wasn't going until Lexi did, though. He'd promised.

"Tell yourself to wake up?" he said.

"I'm trying."

Try harder. He bit off the words. No need to add to her frustration.

"*Hey. Me. Wake up!*" she shouted into the nothing.

Her volume left his ears ringing, but she didn't budge.

Distract her.

Perhaps Icarus wasn't done yet. If she was still struggling with the voices, she might need to be taken further from them.

"Since Conner isn't here, how about I take you to Germany?" Icarus clamped his jaw shut the instant the offer was out. Why couldn't he have picked anyplace else?

"It's not home, but it's better than staring at white space."

He didn't have to show her a memory. At least not one from centuries ago. They could go to pre-Enlightenment, post-Cold-War Germany.

The forest that appeared around them and the two-story villa in front of them said not all of his mind was on the same page.

Lexi's delighted gasp kept him from forcing a change in scenery. "This is amazing. It's straight out of a book. Did you make it up?"

"I lived here." Effective distraction for her. Great way for him to paint new moments over the past.

The flowering plants, the subtle blend of yellow and green in the leaves, and the faint chill in the air said it was spring. Icarus didn't have to wonder which spring. He needed to make a few changes to the house before they stepped inside. This was at least partly his mind, so he could erase any traces of Actaeon.

Lexi was busy taking in their surroundings as they strolled up the path. Her awe was contagious. It had been a long time since he saw the wonder in this place.

He pictured the interior. The weapons mounted above the fireplace needed to go. Easy enough to replace with a tapestry. Icarus changed the image in his mind.

A choir singing a modern hymn bled in with the chirp of birds, and Lexi faltered. "It's coming back." She spoke through clenched teeth.

That wasn't him, was it? She had no idea what he

was thinking. Best not to risk it. He left everything the way his mind pictured it.

She didn't need to know where the extra items in the house came from.

The stepped into the foyer.

"Wow." Lexi's awe was tangible. "It's so huge. Did you live here alone?"

"Not at first, but by this point everyone else was gone." There was a smaller house behind this one—living quarters for the people who had tended the home and grounds—but he'd dismissed them after Actaeon left. Icarus had stopped caring. He'd let the dust settle in, moved into a single room in the back of the house, and lost himself in creating.

But this version was frozen in time before he gave up. None of the wear or disrepair showed. On the main floor were the sitting room, dining room, and kitchen. The bedrooms were at the top of the grand staircase.

Before Actaeon left, they had lived a high-society life. Most eligible bachelors in the village. People were willing to gossip, but ignored the rumors about their sexuality as long as both men were flirting with all the ladies in town.

The only thing the house didn't have was indoor plumbing—nothing did back then. But since this was a memory, he didn't suspect that mattered.

"May I look around?" Lexi's question dragged him from his thoughts.

He gave a deep bow and gestured toward the sitting room. "Be my guest. My home is your home."

She walked with a light step, as if concerned she

might disturb the past. In the sitting room, she wandered among the sofas and other furniture, looking but not touching. She paused when she reached the fireplace. Above the mantle, a steel dagger was mounted under a bow, the faint silvery glow still radiating from both.

Of course he had to remember a detail like the weapons carrying hints of Actaeon.

"What is this?" she asked.

"Actaeon hunted with them. It wasn't practical to find food with his summoned weapons, so he kept real ones on hand. He used them so much, they absorbed some of his aura."

"Does he visit often?"

It was a simple question, but it gouged a hole, deep in Icarus' chest. "No. He'll never return to this place." He thought he'd gotten rid of that knot in his heart ages ago.

Lexi turned and strode back to him. She placed her palm on his ribcage, covering the pain. "There's something between the two of you."

"Not anymore." He shook his head. "There was. An on-again, off-again thing over the centuries. This time, in this house, was the last time."

"Is that why we're here?"

"I think we're here because it's Germany and I lived here for so long. Actaeon was sex, nothing more. There was never any conversation or exchange of ideas." Not enough, anyway.

Lexi dropped her hand to grip his fingers. "He's a good listener," she said.

Icarus couldn't argue that. "But he's a horrible talker." He didn't want to dig so deep into his past. "He and I fought, before we confronted Hades. I told Actaeon he didn't deserve you. That he needed to earn your love."

He expected her to get angry. To tell him he didn't have the right.

"Did you ever tell him that about yourself?" Lexi asked.

He shook his head. "It was never an option for him and me."

Lexi raised his hand and kissed his palm. "I was worried the first time I saw this." She drew her lips along the inside of his wrist. The sensation was sensual and soothing at the same time. "It's so faint. Invisible, compared to what you and I have. I didn't even notice it until after we killed Hades. Maybe it had faded into obscurity before then, or there were so many other threads it didn't stand out."

She was talking about a red cord.

"I don't… He and I don't…" Fate hadn't bound him to Actaeon. Icarus refused to accept it.

She shrugged. "It doesn't mean you and him falling in love will happen."

"Exactly." Fate didn't matter. They made up their own minds. "Besides, I'd rather focus on you and me right now."

Her smile was shy. "I'm not going anywhere."

Under other circumstances, that would be reassuring. Today, it wasn't quite what he wanted to hear. "I'd like it if we *both* left this place."

"I'm trying." With her frustration, the mood was lost.

"Me too."

"How long can we stay here?"

"I don't know." Time moved differently from one place to the next. "If this is all in our heads… It may be that only a few minutes have passed in the real world, but I can't guarantee it. Not that it matters. If you're stuck here, I'm not leaving you."

Lexi sank onto a nearby fainting couch. "I can't ask you to do that."

"You're not asking. You *can* ask me to leave, but I'd rather not. Conner will do something if we're gone for too long, if he can. There may not be anything for him to do, besides make sure our bodies are safe."

She rested her elbows on her knees and stared at her hands. "What do we do in the meantime, besides stare at our feet and talk about things that make you sad?"

"Actaeon doesn't make me sad." Did she hear the lie? "Would you like to see the city? Berlin, in the fifteen hundreds?"

The hint of excitement that pushed away her frustration made the offer worth it. "Yes. Absolutely yes."

He pictured them in period-clothing. Or a reasonable facsimile. The genuine articles were a pain in the ass to get in and out of.

"Oh." Lexi gasped and approached him. She touched something at the base of his throat, and he looked down.

He wore the silver chain with the cross. It shouldn't be there, but it was too late to take it back.

"What is it?" She traced her thumb along the intricate design.

"A cross."

"Thanks for that." Amusement tinged her sarcasm. "What's special about this one?"

He couldn't help a smile at the memory. "Martin Luther and the protestant reform. It began just a few years ago, and this was a trinket someone was selling, to profit on the movement. We thought it was funny, given our birthright and all..." He didn't want to say more and tumble back into that sadness.

Lexi followed the carvings on silver one more time before dropping the medallion. "It's from Actaeon. How long did you wear it after he left?"

"A couple hundred years."

"You're not going to correct me?"

He didn't expect her to be more fascinated with a necklace than with the stunning gown he'd dressed her in. "About what?"

"I don't know. I expected some sputtering protest about how he didn't leave, you threw him out."

Icarus didn't have the kind of ego that demanded that sort of lie. "He left. I suppose, in a way, it was mutual. Neither of us had what the other desired. He needed someone to die for, and I desperately wanted someone to live for." He couldn't offer more details. Not right now. "Shall we see the town? I can imagine us up a carriage."

"I'd love that."

With the past left in the house, Lexi was drawn more into the rest of the world—her dress, the view as the horse-drawn carriage took them into town, the lights and sounds of the city.

Their surroundings were a jumble of different time periods. There was no need to sort them, though. They weren't here for a history lesson. With Lexi trying to take everything in, Icarus wanted to appreciate her awe.

They went to the opera—Mozart, who should have been two-hundred years in the future, but was incredible tonight. Lexi sat captivated through the entire thing.

On the carriage ride home, she didn't stop talking. It was wonderful. "Dad raised me on well-orchestrated movie scores. I've always loved that kind of music, but I've never had a chance to see anything like a live symphony or a real, honest-to-Aphrodite opera. That was incredible."

They reached the house. Icarus was as enamored with Lexi's enthusiasm as she was with the evening. He adored the way her eyes lit up and her aura flared when she talked about her favorite parts of the opera.

She paused, and pink spread across her face. "What?"

"I like watching you." He caressed her cheek. "Then again, I also like touching you. Listening to you. Everything about you captivates me."

Icarus grasped her fingers and tugged her into the living room, toward a fainting couch. He kissed her knuckles, then tipped her hand up, to press his lips to each fingertip.

"There's so much to see here. We must have only scratched the surface." She nudged his shoulders, prompting him to sit, and straddled his legs. "And I don't think my skirts should bunch up this easily."

He glided his palm up her inner thigh, then hooked a finger under the crotch of her panties. "And you shouldn't be wearing these. But the clothing of the era was a pain in the ass to put on and remove, so I've taken a few liberties."

"Hmm… Have I ever mentioned I love the way you think?"

"The feeling is mutual."

She shifted her body, prompting him to adjust his fingers. *Creation*, she felt good. Her damp heat teased his skin.

She rocked against his touch and unlaced his trousers.

Something about this was muted. The sensations were incredible, but there was a hint of that extra *oomph* missing.

Because this wasn't real.

But if Icarus pushed aside that whisper, he could lose himself in this moment.

When Lexi gripped his shaft, he sucked in a sharp breath through his teeth. Her touch was electric.

He shoved her panties aside. "I desperately want to fuck you."

"So poetic of you." Lexi giggled.

"I'm not a word-guy." He lifted her enough to slide inside her.

She lowered herself, and a long moan tore from his throat.

They built quickly to a frantic pace, as he slammed against her.

"You're so incredible." He glided his hands up her sides, to tease her nipples through her dress.

She clenched around him. With each thrust, he inched closer to the edge of climax. His senses were alight with sensation.

Lexi's gasps became throaty cries. She was close to orgasm as well. He felt it flowing through and around him.

She dug her fingers into his arms when she came, grinding into him.

He couldn't hold back. He spilled inside her, grunting and hammering, until they were both spent.

Lexi's clothing faded to a thin cotton shift. Icarus discarded his altogether. She curled up next to him and rested her head on his chest. "I don't want to replace your memories of Actaeon. I don't want that to be what we're doing. I know this is a sad way to end the night, and I'm sorry for that, but your past is yours."

He wanted to tell her she was welcome to overwrite as much of his time with Actaeon as she wanted. The words stuck in his throat. "I don't want that either."

"If this is all imaginary, what's to stop you from bringing him back right now and having him join us?" She propped herself up and looked Icarus in the eye. "Not that this isn't lovely. I'm loving the time with you. But I'm curious."

"It wouldn't be him." That was one answer Icarus didn't hesitate on. "I'm not wishing some two-dimensional version of him into my life. If he comes back…"

What? Where was that thought supposed to end? "Then and now don't compare. I don't want him back." He tasted the lie, and it left a sour coating on his tongue.

Lexi settled against him again. "Curiosity sated."

Waking up next to Lexi was nice. The need to get out of this place still tugged at Icarus' thoughts, but without a solution, it was easy to shove the urgency aside.

A day became a week of nights filled with operas and plays, and mornings occupied by lazy breakfasts and discovering the best places in the house to have sex.

Time didn't move in complete days in here, so it was difficult to keep track of how much had passed.

They sat on a blanket on the back lawn, watching the stars. This was comfortable and right.

"Were we supposed to be somewhere?" Icarus asked.

"I'm not in the mood to go out tonight. This is pleasant."

That wasn't what he meant. There was a thought out of reach. A different time and place. He couldn't grasp it and didn't want to try too hard. "I didn't mean... Never mind. I don't know what I was thinking."

"I like it when it's just you and me. The way it's always been," Lexi said. "Or... is that right?"

He kissed her nose. "It sounds good." He was forgetting something, but whatever it was, it wasn't important. Being here with her was. Why would they need to be anyplace else?

FIFTEEN

Lexi knelt next to Actaeon, terror and sorrow choking her. This wasn't like when she thought she'd lost Cerberus. It hurt just as much, but in different places. Her body ached. Her tears were all dried up. She couldn't do this without him. She was death. Hades had brought people back. Could she? His soul hadn't left his body. But they were already in the underworld.

She'd built a village out of nothing. She'd pulled lost souls from the void and gave them a home.

She manifested her dreams into reality.

Why couldn't she wake up Actaeon?

His body lay on the ground, clothing torn, wounds closing, but not fast enough. She rested a palm on his chest. His heartbeat was so weak.

"Please don't leave me." She pressed her lips to his forehead. "I know you wanted to die for a cause." Where did that come from? It felt true, but how had she picked up on it? "No cause, no person or immortal, is worth that. I'm not worth surrendering your life for, and neither is anyone else."

She'd been a brat since he arrived. Insisting they do things her way despite his experience. Getting underfoot in the fight. Trying to help when she had no idea what she was doing. "Please, wake up. I don't want to be alone."

That was a shitty reason to want him around.

The thought jarred her, adding an acrid edge to her mounting panic. Would she pull someone back from the brink of death for a selfish reason like that?

Was that why she bonded with Cerberus? No. She loved Cerberus. That was real.

What was this?

Actaeon groaned and coughed.

Relief spilled inside Lexi, pushing out the questions, and sending fresh tears down her cheeks.

He pushed himself up on his elbows and looked at her. "Hey. What's wrong?" Concern mingled with the exhaustion in her voice. "Are you hurt?"

She laughed through the sobs. "I'm so much better now." She helped him sit, then threw her arms around his neck. "I'm sorry."

"For what?" Actaeon hugged her.

There was no hesitation in his embrace, there never had been. That was good, right?

Stupid fucking doubt. She squashed it. "For being a brat. For not letting you do what you excel at. For nearly getting you killed."

"Don't be, and you didn't." He nudged her back

enough to kiss her cheeks. His movements were slow and deliberate, and she felt each one echo in her bones.

"I'm sorry. You're in pain. I need to be more careful." She dropped her arms.

He grabbed them again, pulled her back, and hugged her tight. "You're fine. I'm bulletproof."

"But apparently not Daughters-of-Danaus-proof."

He crushed his mouth to hers, swallowing her fear and nipping at her lips. The energy that flowed between them was soothing, almost salve-like. It erased her aches.

"I can't lose you," he murmured against her kisses. "I'd do this all again in a heartbeat. I'd sacrifice everything for you."

That wasn't right. It was a sweet sentiment, but it crawled under her skin and chewed on her soul. She pulled away and stood, barely registering that his wounds were gone. "Don't." An edge slipped into her voice.

"What did I do?" Actaeon climbed to his feet with minimal effort.

She knew he could heal quickly, but how…? It didn't matter, because irritation had replaced concern. "I don't want you to give your life for me. Ever. I don't want you on a cross of your making, so I can live."

He rolled his eyes. "Glad to see you've caught it too."

"What's that supposed to mean?"

He shook his head. "It doesn't matter." He nodded at something behind her. "That's what they were guarding. What's inside?"

She'd been so worried about his stupid, self-sacrificing ass, she hadn't looked. She turned on her toe and stalked toward the cave.

As she stepped further in, darkness closed in around her. Their auras made things worse. The bright glows that circled them kept her pupils from widening but didn't cast an ambient light on their surroundings.

"Can't you magic up a torch or something?" Actaeon's tone was flat.

Why was she pissed off? Because she didn't want him dying for her? Stupid, arrogant fucking caveman. She held out her hand, and a flashlight appeared. She shone the beam forward, and it bounced off a tangle of vines, inches from her face.

"Oh." She jumped back, her heart hammering in her ears.

"Are you okay?"

And he was worried because she was in trouble. How cliché. "I'm fine." She bit off the words and progressed forward.

She had to sweep the beam around, to ensure she saw both ceiling and floor, as they walked. This was ridiculous. They needed real lighting.

In her mind, she pictured bulbs lining the walls, from here to the end of wherever this place led.

A few sparks flickered into view in front of them, and then vanished.

"What the fuck?" She didn't like these rules. Like with the fight, it seemed she couldn't make anything tangible that was outside of her grasp.

"I think the best we can get is making the flashlight brighter," Actaeon said.

Yeah, thanks. She'd figured that much out. How did she know which direction to head, anyway? Because she was being pulled.

She grew the beam of the light in her hand, making it cover everything in front of them—floor and ceiling— and they continued.

The light fell on a body, and she swore her heart stopped. The three dog heads overlapped by a human one were unique. "Cerberus." She sprinted forward. It was tempting to drop the flashlight, but she needed to see him.

She fell to her knees next to his body and pressed two fingers to his human neck. His pulse was strong, and his chest rose and fell easily. There were no visible wounds on his body.

"Cerberus, come back to me." She didn't feel the panic she had with Actaeon. The tug in her heart insisted her hellhound was fine. He just wasn't here.

She leaned forward and pressed her lips to his fore-head. *"Wake up. I need you by my side."*

There was no response to her mental words. No emotion or murmuring or stirring.

Then— *"Lexi? My Lexi?"* Cerberus' voice was loud and clear in her thoughts.

"Yes. Is it you? Of course it's you." She knew his heart anywhere. It was part of hers.

His eyes opened, and he met her gaze. "Hey, gorgeous." He smiled.

She felt more right than she had since she arrived in this fucking place. "Hey, yourself."

A freight train of thought slammed into her skull,

assaulting her with words and images and thoughts she couldn't process. Her brain screamed in protest, and the pain ripped from her throat in a shout of her own.

***

CERBERUS DIDN'T FEEL RIGHT in this strange place Aphrodite had set Lexi up in. It was comfortable and secure and a bribe of a whole new sort, since Lexi didn't remember how she'd gotten here. As far as she was concerned, she had the right barter at the right time.

She watched TV, and Cerberus tried not to pace. He needed to get out of here.

"Wake up. I need you by my side."

That was her voice, but it was in his head. There was no question. *"Lexi?"* He risked broadcasting the question. *"My Lexi?"*

"Yes. Is it you? Of course it's you." Her voice sounded glorious. It should be identical to the one he'd been hearing for days, but it wasn't. This one knew him. Loved him.

A caress that wasn't there brushed his face, and longing burst through him. He winced at the onslaught of sensation. Scents that didn't meld with this world. Dirt. Death. *Actual* Lexi.

He squeezed his eyes shut tight, until stars danced behind the lids. Cool, heavy air pressed in on him, clogging his nostrils. His back was pressed against something hard. Was he lying down?

Cerberus dared look, and found Lexi kneeling next

to him, darkness behind her. She grinned, brighter than the sun when she met his gaze.

"Hey, gorgeous," he said. She was, too. The most incredible sight he'd ever seen. The smudges on her cheeks. The mark on her neck that said *Truth*.

"Hey, yourself."

She leaned in, and he expected a kiss. Instead, she wobbled and grimaced. Then she threw her head back and let out the most horrifying scream he'd ever heard. She grabbed her head, and the room went black.

"Lexi?" His concern overlapped with another voice. Actaeon. At least she hadn't been alone. Cerberus sat up and reached for her. *"Lexi?"*

Images assaulted him when he sent the thought. Betrayal, longing, fury—it all rode on snippets of the events he'd watched her live. Those moments he'd traipsed through in her mind.

It wasn't sequential, the way he'd seen, though. The jumbled Picasso of the past sliced at her in shards, cutting his mind in the process.

And then it stopped, and so did her screaming.

"Shit. That's not good," Actaeon said.

"What happened to the light?" Cerberus scooped Lexi into his arms. Her body was light and warm against his.

"She was making it. I assume it vanished when she passed out."

Great. "Do you know the way out of here?"

"Yes," Actaeon said. A moment later, he grasped Cerberus' shoulder. "I have more sure footing. I can carry her."

Cerberus growled. "No. Where are we?"

"Tartarus. The daughters of Danaus were planning to kill you. She sent them away. I don't know how long until they find their way back."

Cerberus gave a grim smile in the darkness. "Don't let go." Magic flowed differently down here than it did on earth, and he'd been created for this. He pictured an intricate gate, scribed in iron and gold and waiting for them.

They wouldn't be able to see it in here, but he knew where it was. "Walk behind me. Don't let go," he said to Actaeon.

"All right?"

Cerberus reached out and shoved the gate open. He stepped through.

Tartarus vanished, leaving the underworld in its place.

"Neat trick," Actaeon said.

"They call me *Gatekeeper* for a reason." And his being able to open the gate meant he once again served the ruler of this plane. His goddess. He wasn't surprised. Cerberus set Lexi on the grass. *"We can't keep missing each other like this."* He tried to keep his teasing light in the mental words, but concern flowed through him.

Actaeon knelt on the other side of her.

Were they wearing matching outfits? And why was Actaeon's more rips and blood than fabric?

Hardly important right now.

"I'm here." Lexi's reply echoed in Cerberus' head. *"Holy fuck. What's going on in my thoughts?"*

"Wake up, and I'll tell you what I know."

She groaned and pushed into a sitting position. "Three for three?"

Actaeon's chuckle was strained.

"What?" Apparently Cerberus needed to be brought up to speed.

"Third one of us to climb out of unconsciousness in the last couple of hours." Lexi massaged her temples. "Don't suppose you can pull Icarus through one of those gates? I could go for four."

"He's not with you?" Cerberus should have noticed sooner.

Actaeon shot him a glare. "Does it look like he is?"

They had a *lot* of catching up to do. "What's going on?"

"I can only tell you what we know, and it's not the entire picture. But there are so many thoughts in my head that weren't there before. My past, with you in it?" Lexi pulled his arms around her.

It felt good to hold her again. He was reluctant to ever let her go. He had a better idea of who Lexi was and where she came from. "We need to talk about what Aphrodite's done to you," Cerberus said. "That's probably the best place to start, because it explains what you're seeing."

He'd never had access to the images in her mind before—only feelings and words. Was this a good thing? The bond between them was stronger than it had been with Hades. Or was this because she trusted him more as time went on?

He didn't dare linger on the fear that it meant something in her mind was breaking.

SIXTEEN

Actaeon was grateful to have Cerberus back. The thought caught him off-guard. It wasn't only because Lexi had relaxed after the initial shock of whatever happened, but also because Actaeon had missed the hellhound.

The middle of an empty field wasn't the best place to catch up, though. "Can you give us another of those gates?" Actaeon asked. "We can step through it into this little place Lexi set up down the road."

"The gates only allow us to move between underworld planes, not individual places. So if it's in the underworld, no." Cerberus shook his head.

Lexi looked pale. "I can take us back, now that I know where we're going." A tremor ran through her voice. She looked as shaky as Actaeon felt.

He was trying to shrug off the exhaustion, but like when he'd woken up, it wasn't leaving him.

She grasped Cerberus' hand, and then his. Some of

his weariness faded. He wasn't instantly healed, but the fog lifted from his joints and his mind.

The tension faded from Lexi as well, and she sat up a little straighter. Then they were on her bed, in her room back at the saloon.

Cerberus didn't look surprised. "You made this?"

"Yes. Did you know Persephone was a goddess before she hooked up with Hades?" Lexi didn't let go of Actaeon's hand.

"I would have told you if I did." Cerberus stood and wandered around the room. He examined everything without touching any of it. "You used to have a room like this."

"Not exactly like it. But the one you saw, in my memories? I wanted it to look this way."

Actaeon was missing a few pieces in their conversation, but he could make assumptions to fill in the blanks. He expected a tug of envy—the same persistent feeling he got whenever Cerberus and Lexi went off on a tangent meant only for them—but it wasn't there.

It might partly be because Lexi still clung to Actaeon. He didn't feel smugness about that, though. It was more gratitude and… rightness.

Cerberus returned to sit next to them. "How are you feeling?"

"My head doesn't hurt, but my brain is killing me." Lexi pressed her free palm to her forehead. "Like a billion memories were crammed into it at the same time." She laid her head on Cerberus' leg and moved Actaeon's hand to her thigh. "I shouldn't be surprised Aphrodite locked so much away from me."

"She did it for love." Cerberus made it sound rational. "That's kind of her thing."

Lexi's laugh was bitter. "Not a great reason. Does this mean, if I'm the new goddess of death, I'll go out of my way to ensure people die if fate wills it?"

Actaeon knew the answer to that one, without question. "That's not you. It will hurt you to see them suffer, but you understand everyone has to be allowed their individual lives."

She rolled her head, to look at him. "That's some pretty wise insight."

"I'm more than a muscle-bound bruiser." This was the missing element before. The easy flow of a conversation everyone was a part of. "What kind of things did Aphrodite hide from you?" He swallowed a joke about more fated loves. It felt like poor taste.

"The ritual that killed her stepdad," Cerberus said.

A shadow passed over Lexi's face. "It was meant to destroy his soul. Intentionally done to keep me from finding him in the underworld, later in life."

That implied— "Poseidon knew who you were?"

"He knew I existed. I don't know why Aphrodite hid that from me. But his goal with me was the same as Artemis' with you."

The words sliced through Actaeon like a blade of ice. He didn't have the best relationship with his mother, but she hadn't sacrificed anyone he knew. "I don't see a correlation."

"Deli in New Orleans, after you returned from your search for Cassandra..." If Cerberus thought letting that hang would provide answers, he was mistaken.

That wasn't completely true. Actaeon understood now where Lexi's earlier question came from. "I don't remember much about that bit of my life. I was a wreck after the Cassandra thing."

Lexi jumped from the bed, jarring the mattress and catching Actaeon off-guard. "Is anyone else hungry? I'm hungry. I'm going to have Bob make us something."

"Who's Bob?" Cerberus asked.

"Bartender. Nice guy. Doesn't he go home at night?" Actaeon was curious about where the sudden change in demeanor came from.

Lexi walked toward the door. "Then I'll go grab something from the kitchen. Any requests?"

She could make it appear here, but some habits must be hard to break. That, and if she was like the other gods, she wasn't actually plucking things from midair; she had to take them from someplace else. Were the rules different here, since she was the realm? What did that make the food, then?

Actaeon didn't want to tumble down that rabbit hole, and it hardly seemed relevant to the conversation. "We'll go with you. Give Cerberus a tour along the way."

"Sounds good to me. So does real food. What have you got?" Cerberus fell into step with them.

Lexi didn't skip down the stairs like she had when they left on their quest. That was more normal as well, but it was also a little sad to see. "Cold cuts. Chips—chocolate and potato—"

"No bread or cheese, apparently," Actaeon teased.

She shot him a withering look.

Okay, so they hadn't moved past her irritation over the *quest*. Or he was getting hung up on it and needed to move on.

"You were a fighter before Cassandra died." There was an edge to Lexi's voice. "You stood up to Zeus, even though she begged you not to."

"How do you know that?" He'd talked about Cassandra's visions but never shared details about their relationship.

The kitchen was a stark contrast to the bar, but Actaeon expected that. Industrial stainless-steel counters and appliances. A restaurant-grade dishwasher. Two huge refrigerators.

Lexi opened one and started pulling out storage containers. "Lucky guess. It's who you are. You wear this pathetic mask of indifference, but you've never turned your back on the mess we're in. Or anything you've come up against since I met you."

"You make for a good view." Why was he brushing her off? She was paying him a compliment.

"You can't help yourself." Cerberus grabbed three plates from a stack on the counter. He opened one of the containers and started dishing out sliced ham. "Despite what Artemis said to you, it's who you are. How many months did she pick away at your core, while you were miserable and lost, to get you to back off for even a couple of decades?"

Actaeon was losing the thread again. "Artemis didn't... She wouldn't... I still don't understand what you're talking about."

"Like mother, like son." That was what Lexi said the first time she met the goddess.

Cerberus handed him a plate stacked with sliced meat, cheese, and olives. The hellhound leaned against a nearby counter and ate. "The gods forced all of the heroes to pick a side or be destroyed. That's part of Enlightenment history. They've never hidden that."

"They didn't destroy me, because they couldn't." That was the point of drawing Actaeon to Las Vegas. "Heracles tried."

Lexi sat on the counter, kicking her legs back and forth, only picking at the dinner she insisted they have. "So they took you out of the picture another way. Artemis convinced you fighting the establishment was futile."

Actaeon couldn't believe he was listening to this. "Why would she do that?" Motivation was the glaring hole in their theory.

"I don't know," Lexi said.

He tossed his plate aside, and it skidded across stainless steel before stopping. Olives rolled onto the floor. "This is ludicrous. I don't know what kind of shared hallucinations—"

"Stop." Lexi's command rumbled through the floor. "I'm sorry you don't want to hear or accept this, but don't push it back on us. I know what I saw and heard down there."

He was sick of this. The games. The denial. The way she'd had them chasing their tails. "You were correct about one thing, when it comes to you and me."

He looked at Lexi. "We fight. We fuck. I save your ass. Right now, I'm not doing any of the above, so you don't need me here."

"Now who's throwing a tantrum?" she asked.

Actaeon wasn't sulking or angry, but he was annoyed and tired.

Because she's right?

Because she was drawing conclusions from a limited forty years of experience. Cerberus wasn't much better. He'd been involved in post-Enlightenment politics from the fringes, observing as an outsider, because he served Hades at the time.

"Believe what you'd like." Actaeon wasn't going to argue in circles. "Artemis didn't participate in some sort of farfetched conspiracy with Zeus and Poseidon years ago, to ensure you and I wouldn't interfere now."

"You and dozens of other heroes. Some Poseidon's children. Anyone they thought they couldn't get rid of otherwise." Cerberus looked calm. He was almost done with his food.

"Give me a motive." That was the one thing Actaeon didn't see in this weird and wacky tale of theirs.

There was no response.

"Because they wanted to rule the world?" Now he was getting angry. "They have that. They're not comic-book villains. This isn't a stupid movie or a fucking game. Zeus is all ego, but he's got what he wants. There's no reason for him to squash the little bugs because they annoy him."

Lexi hopped to her feet and stepped in front of him.

"Then help us figure out what their motive was," she said.

Actaeon turned away. "I'm sick of this. Icarus is waiting for us on earth. Hermes confirmed that. We found Cerberus. I'm going back to Styx, to go home. You can stay here and keep *questing*, or you can come with me."

"Why are you convinced what she saw in the past isn't real?" Cerberus asked.

"I'm not saying it was fake, but the interpretation doesn't make sense. You're going along with it because you're a loyal fucking lapdog." He winced at the insult. He shouldn't have fallen back on that.

"Again with this? Really?" Lexi's tone implied she agreed. "Fine. You want to go home? Let's go home." She grabbed his hand. The spark that flowed between them was almost uncomfortable. "Join hands, boys and boys." She tugged him so she could reach Cerberus as well. "Let's get the fuck out of here."

Nothing happened. Seconds ticked away, and Actaeon waited for the familiar shift in environment.

"This isn't funny. If you don't want to go, don't pretend otherwise." He tried to pull away.

She held tight. "It's not meant to be funny." The room vanished, and they stood in the middle of the field again, a nearby scorched tree taunting them. "This isn't where I wanted to be."

"Ignore him and concentrate." Cerberus was kind.

Actaeon wanted to deck him. "Don't you think she might already be doing that?"

"Trying again." Lexi spoke through clenched teeth.

Their environment wobbled, like the vertical hold was broken on an old TV, then solidified as Styx. Charon waited for them at the shore.

Finally.

"You found her." Charon spoke in his normal tones.

Lex stepped forward. "Yup. Here I am. Happy and healthy and really fucking irritated. We'd like to go home. Drop us wherever, like last time. I'll give you…" She patted her pockets, then frowned. "Can I owe you?"

Charon covered her hand with long, bony fingers. "You never have to pay again, but you also don't need my services. You can come and go at will, Mistress."

"I'm trying."

Charon pulled back his hood and studied her, then turned to Actaeon. "You were supposed to help her become complete."

"She looks complete to me. Feels it, too."

No, she didn't. She was missing that piece that he clicked with. She wasn't whole, and neither was he. He clenched his fist. Why wasn't there something around, for him to punch? It wouldn't solve anything, but it would make him feel better.

"But… they don't want to be here." Lexi's frustration bled into hurt.

"Then I'll take them home," Charon said. "You give me the word, and they'll go. Once you find your balance, you'll be able to travel back and forth, as part of you will always be in both places."

How did that make sense?

"I don't know what else to do." Lexi's shoulders drooped. "Any great and grand advice?"

Charon looked sympathetic. "Don't let it drive you insane, the way it did your father. I didn't experience it, so I can only tell you what I saw. I can tell you the story of how Hades was bound to the underworld."

"Did Cronus really eat a rock dressed like baby Zeus?" Lexi asked.

"No." Charon stepped onto the docks, and four chairs appeared. He settled into one. "Cronus did want to kill his children, to keep his throne. Rhea wouldn't let him. The compromise was to lock them away. They stayed in their cells for centuries, growing up with only their minds and each other's voices to keep them company. After a time, Rhea couldn't stand to have her children locked away. She went to visit them.

"She started with Hades. He was the youngest, but he was also the most powerful. I know, the stories say Zeus was, but he wrote those stories. Rhea saw the madness in her boy's eyes, and realized she hadn't done him any favors by imprisoning him. She said she was sorry and promised that soon he and his brothers would be together for eternity. She tried to sacrifice him."

This was far more gripping than the tale Actaeon heard as a child. Probably make a better movie, too.

"Zeus and Poseidon heard the noise in their cells," Charon said. "They broke free to save their brother, and destroyed Rhea in the process. But she'd already plunged the dagger into Hades' heart. His brothers didn't know if they could save him. Their next act was one of desperation. They bound him to the underworld, trapping him between life and death, to keep him from passing on. He was already on the brink of madness, and becoming this place didn't do him any favors. But Persephone was good for him. She absorbed the madness. Healed his mind... for a few centuries, anyway.

"When Zeus and Poseidon started The Enlightenment, Hades refused to join them, and they bound him in the labyrinth to keep him from stopping them. But that's a different tale for a different day."

Actaeon understood why the other version was more popular. This one gave actual insight into the three brothers. He glanced at Lexi, who looked transfixed.

"As Rhea lay dying, she begged for her sons' forgiveness. She made Zeus promise that he would never let the misguided dominate the world, the way his father had. She knew Zeus was good and kind, and made him swear he would keep everyone—Titans, humans, and his siblings—from destroying each other. That he wouldn't walk in his father's footsteps, even if it meant lives like hers had to be sacrificed for the greater good. And Zeus swore to his mother he would do as she asked."

"Wow. Much better than the myth." Cerberus summed it up perfectly.

Charon shrugged. "Much darker, as well. It won't help you get out of here, though. The realm has bound itself to Lexi, and until she becomes whole, she's stuck here."

Actaeon could leave. Charon already said as much. Cerberus could go with him, not that the hellhound would willingly leave her side. Not in a situation like this.

Actaeon wouldn't either. Despite his irritation, he wasn't interested in walking away. He needed to protect Lexi. To love her.

And to be honest with yourself about her.

That wasn't helpful.

SEVENTEEN

THE RIVER AND CHARON VANISHED, REPLACED WITH Lexi's new room. Cerberus was impressed she'd adjusted to this so quickly. What was incomplete about her? Charon had to be wrong.

She let out a groan that mingled with the frustration spilling from her, and fixed her gaze on Cerberus. "I don't know what to do."

"We'll figure it out," Actaeon said.

She pursed her lips. "I so desperately want to say, *I told you so*. We did things your way. How'd that work out?"

"It was a plan. I gave us a direction. I'd do it again in a heartbeat, because it's better than *let's go on a quest*." Actaeon paced like a caged animal.

Apparently Cerberus had missed a lot, being trapped in Lexi's past. He wrapped an arm around her waist and pulled her to sit next to him on the bed. "Freaking out doesn't help. Fill in the blanks for me, about what happened while I was gone. Maybe if we have more of a complete picture, we can make some new decisions."

"*Ugh.*" She raked her fingers down her face. "I have the complete picture. I remember you traipsing around in my head. I lived what happened here. Why do you have to be rational?" Some of her anger evaporated as she spoke.

"It's a thing I do—being rational. Maybe part of the problem is that it's all still in your head. Not as in you imagined it, but talking it through may help you sort it out." Cerberus didn't like being stuck down here, but as long as they were, it was a chance to slow down and catch up. He'd missed Lexi. Spending time with her back then, it was clear how she'd grown into the woman he loved.

"And who knows? Maybe one of us has information you don't. Centuries of it," Actaeon said.

Cerberus didn't know what to make of the tension between Actaeon and Lexi, but it wasn't helping. Lexi's reaction to it clawed his skin like a million needles on a roller. "Not to side with the hero, but I feel like I'm missing a big part of the picture here. Do you hate each other now? Is this a new kind of mating ritual the kids are trying?"

"He's treating me like I don't know anything." Lexi's reply was calm.

Actaeon stopped his pacing, to glare at her. "Because you're acting like an impulsive child."

"Because I'm new to being a goddess and trying to figure things out."

"But you won't listen to anyone who has experience."

"Whoa." Cerberus felt like he was watching a tennis match. "How long have you two been alone together down here?" Months? Years? What kind of isolation bred this level of hostility?

Lexi sighed. "Two days, give or take? And we weren't really alone. There's Bob. We talked to Morpheus for a while."

"Is this like a sexual-tension thing?" Cerberus was grasping at straws. "An instance of *oh just fuck already*?"

"We tried that." Actaeon's stony expression threatened to crack.

"It was good," Lexi said.

Actaeon shook his head. "It was amazing. It gets better every time."

Relationship Counselor wasn't among Cerberus' skills. When things started to fall apart between Persephone and Hades, he'd listened to both of them bitch, but he hadn't had any brilliant insight for either of them. Especially since telling Persephone *just leave* was against Hades' orders.

"Maybe that's the only way we know to communicate." Lexi slid from Cerberus' grasp and pulled her knees to her chest. "Maybe we don't have anything else in common."

She wasn't completely herself yet. Charon was right, after all. It was as though she was stuck between stages in her life and growth. And he suspected the issue between her and Actaeon had more to do with them being too alike, rather than too different.

"I'm a fantastic listener." Actaeon crossed his arms and leaned against the wall.

"Unless you don't like what's being said. And you're a shitty talker." Lexi frowned and worked her jaw. *"Where did that come from?"* The mental question was soft, as if meant only for herself.

"If you're going to get *insight* about my past from Icarus, you might want to hear my side of the story, too. Even Fate gets some things wrong." The fire was fading from Actaeon's tone.

Lexi's was evaporating as well. "Are you talking about you and me, or you and him?"

"What?"

Cerberus was more concerned about the conversation she was having with herself than about the dwindling argument.

"Is that really what you think of us?" Actaeon asked her. "That all we ever do is fuck and fight—each other and monsters?"

Lexi shrugged.

"To be fair, you haven't had a lot of time for much else. Life has been a series of complications since you met." Cerberus should stay out of this, but he was already square in the middle, and it ached to see Lexi so frustrated.

She didn't want to be in this rut. He didn't have to guess; it flowed from her in waves. But she didn't know how to change things.

Couples counseling for the woman he loved and another man looked like the best option. He was okay with that, as long as it got them somewhere.

"I don't want to be stuck down here." Weariness filled Lexi's admittance. "Bob is nice, and learning to swordfight is fun, but I miss the freedom of coming and going. I miss that in general. I'm not staying here because I think this is some kind of super-awesome-keen adventure. Believe it or not, I know how harshly parts of this reality suck, and I'm trying to make the best of it."

Actaeon leaned his head against the wall behind him. "You could have said so a lot sooner."

"I shouldn't have had to. I'm under no obligation to justify my optimism to you. I haven't had control over much of anything since those lost and confused moments before you picked me up in your cab. Down here, I do. Wouldn't you embrace that, even for a little while, if you could? I turned it into the best thing I could think of, while still working toward a solution."

"That sounds fair." Cerberus wasn't only siding with Lexi because it was her. He hoped he could be as reasonable in a similar situation.

"Besides," she added, "you wouldn't leave me behind, and I'd never abandon any of you. There's no way you can blame me for wanting to find Cerberus. You didn't agree with me when I wanted to check on Persephone. You argued when I wanted Cassandra gone. You don't trust my opinion."

Actaeon stared at ceiling. He kicked away from the wall and approached them. "You're right. If it was you, and Cerberus insisted you were here, I would have searched everywhere. I'm sorry I didn't afford you the same luxury. It's not an easy thing for me to do— trusting someone else's instinct over my own. I can't take it back, but I can try harder, going forward." He settled on her other side on the mattress. "In that vein, what do you think we should do next?"

"Because you're tapped for ideas?" she asked dryly.

"No. My idea is still the same. We go back to Styx and hang out until Charon takes all three of us across. That's obviously not the right answer, so I want to hear your thoughts."

Mischievousness mingled with the emotions flowing from Lexi and blanketed them. "We got the fighting out of the way, and asses have been saved today…"

"No." Actaeon rested a hand on her cheek.

The spark of desire and rush of attraction raced from his touch through the bond Cerberus shared with Lexi. That was new. And if it was even a hint of what flowed between Actaeon and Lexi, no wonder sex was the one thing they didn't argue about.

Lexi's pout was exaggerated. "Why not?"

"Because I'd like to be more than that to you. I want to get to know both of you," Actaeon said.

"Do we get the same in return?" Lexi wanted to accept his proposal. She heard his sincerity. She didn't trust her response.

Cerberus wished he could make this easier on her.

"You already are, by being here," she said mentally.

LEXI DIDN'T REALIZE she suggested sex with Actaeon out of habit, until he told her *no*. What he asked for instead…

If she had to be honest—and the fact that she was a shitty liar, plus she hated deception meant she did—letting Actaeon in terrified her. She wasn't sure why. The whole *fate* thing made her take a step back when it came to Cerberus and Icarus, but things were easier with them. Everything clicked.

But Actaeon… He didn't know his own heart well enough for her to get an idea of what was there.

"Falling in love isn't always easy." Cerberus' words echoed in her head. *"You have to open yourself up, without knowing for sure it will work."*

She liked the wisdom in his words, but the idea scared her as much as anything. She pulled away from Actaeon's touch, but held his gaze. "What do you want to know?"

"What happened after Cerberus woke up? What happened before? The whole story, rather than fragments."

It seemed like a simple question on the surface, but there was so much turmoil attached to the memories. "Cerberus was stuck in my memories."

Cerberus was hesitating. He didn't want to say too much, in case it betrayed her trust.

"It's okay. You can tell him whatever you believe will help," Lexi said mentally. *"I have to make that leap at some point, and now seems like as good a time as any."*

"This is the equivalent of three people having a conversation, and two of them whispering so the third can't hear." Actaeon interrupted.

He had a good point. "I'm sorry," Lexi said. "Half the time, I'm not even aware I'm doing it until we're several sentences into the discussion." Something occurred to her. "How did you know we were talking?"

"You both go quiet and stare at each other. There's also a feeling, I can't describe it. I just know."

Lexi had lived her entire life without talking to anyone telepathically. She could survive the occasional pass now. "I think it's a fair request. I'm still learning to set the mental boundaries, but I'll try to keep it under control."

"That's all I ask." Actaeon relaxed.

She swore she felt it, and the sensation was unsettling. Tension she didn't realize was there, and his, uncoiled in her neck when he spoke.

"I lived parts of Lexi's past with her," Cerberus said. "Memories of points in her life that were traumatic. That's where I was when I was unconscious."

"Literally stuck in her head?" Actaeon covered Lexi's hand with his. Icy concern and comfort wrapped around her—the familiar sensation his touch always brought, but there was more behind it. A tenderness she'd never noticed before.

She nodded. "It's as though, while he was there, I relived all those parts of my life. Some of them I'd forgotten, and others I just wished I could." A knot rose in her throat at the nudge of images she'd tried to bury long ago.

"And Aphrodite was responsible for hiding several of them," Cerberus added. He wrapped an arm around Lexi's waist and pulled her back into him.

Actaeon's frown was one of worry. It was so odd,

knowing that instinctually, but she'd adapt. "Do I dare ask for details?"

A simple question, but one that broke the dam holding back the potent pieces of her past. "I found him, memory-time-wise I guess, after Dad's funeral."

"I'm sorry." Actaeon stroked his thumb along her skin in tiny circles. "I've never asked, and I don't know if you want to tell me, but how did he die?"

She could do this. She'd relived the grief already. Now all that was required was a short answer. "Sacrificed to Poseidon. No one said so, but it was for sheltering me." Her voice cracked, and she swallowed a sob. "Because apparently the gods have known about me for years, and taking away Dad was one way of keeping me from standing up to them." The bitter words tumbled out and spilled tears down her face.

Actaeon drew a finger across her cheek, leaving a damp streak. "I know how much that hurts. I wish I could take that ache away from you."

"How do you know?" She wasn't trying to be cruel, but he still had his mother.

"I wasn't always a grumpy old man. I told you I was a kid once. Had a mortal father." Actaeon sounded kind, and the comfort he brought was tinged with sadness. "He died when I was little. Maybe five or six? I cried for a week."

"I didn't realize." Lexi's frown deepened. She hated to admit it, but she forgot sometimes there was more to the figures from history books than what it said on the pages.

Cerberus squeezed her. She was grateful for the silent support.

Actaeon moved closer, half-pulling her into his lap, without taking her from Cerberus. It was a neat trick.

"A couple decades passed—that's a literal thing; I was probably in my late twenties—and I thought I had gotten over it," Actaeon said. "And then I found out it wasn't a hunting accident, as I'd been told. Zeus was responsible."

Lexi might have laughed at the cruel parallels, if his story plus hers didn't leave her raw inside. "Is that the first time you went after Zeus?"

"No." Actaeon gave a dry chuckle. "Artemis talked me out of it… Did you really see her and me?"

Lexi would rather hone in on the scene from the deli than most of the other memories. She was grateful for the change in subject. "She was convincing you to give up, after you talked to Cassandra."

Something caught in her thoughts and snagged. "Cerberus tried to talk me out of it too." That wasn't right. Cerberus was part of the memory, not real life.

"You tried to go after Poseidon?" Actaeon's question was a combination of concern and awe.

"It wasn't her idea," Cerberus said.

When Dad died, Lexi didn't see herself as powerful. She could make intangible knives. She wouldn't have pursued Poseidon. "I never did that. Did I?" A stabbing pain pulsed behind her eye, as she tried to grasp the thought.

"Clio talked you into it." Cerberus' concern spiked.

"Who?" Lexi's head pounded.

"Clio. Your best friend?"

Actaeon squeezed her leg. "Clio, the muse? I didn't realize you knew her."

"I don't." Snippets of a memory that wasn't Lexi's invaded her thoughts. "Do I? She's there, but she's not. I didn't know her, but… She's not part of my past, outside of that day." The harder Lexi grabbed, the more difficult it was to find answers.

EIGHTEEN

Lexi and Icarus strolled along a street in Berlin. This wasn't the same place it had been just a few years earlier. The plague killed thousands, and now the streets felt vacant.

Immortality kept them safe from the disease, but required them to maintain a low profile, not to draw suspicion. It felt like ages, since they'd been able to stroll through the city.

Laughter reached Icarus' ears. It was a welcome but out-of-place sound. He steered Lexi toward the noise.

A large crowd had gathered in an alcove at the edge of the city, and at the front of it all, someone had set up a stage.

"Traveling actors," he said. It had been ages since troupes stopped here.

Lexi hugged his arm. "Can we watch? We have time, don't we?"

"We do." They had all the time in history.

The man on stage was dressed in oversized robes,

with excessive padding underneath. The effect was comical as he stumbled and sat on his throne.

Another man strode in front of him. He wore a fitted toga and a long, dark wig, and he carried a wooden piece of lightning. *"Father. I have returned."* His overacted lines were in German.

"Do you want a translation?" Icarus whispered in Lexi's ear.

She shook her head. "I get the gist of things."

It was a little odd. They'd lived here for as long as he could remember, and she didn't know the language. But it was what it was.

"Zeus. I thought you were dead," the king said.

Icarus knew this story—how Zeus overthrew Cronus, freed his brothers, and became king of the gods. A child's tale, but every few centuries, it made a resurgence in theater. From the way the characters were presented here, Zeus was very much meant to be the hero.

Two more actors joined Zeus on stage. It was odd that the woman playing Hades had a faint glow.

She turned and looked at the crowd, and Icarus swore her gaze met his.

"Does she look familiar?" Lexi asked.

He dug through his thoughts but ran into several walls of nothingness. "Clio?" The muse of history? What was she doing with a traveling acting troupe?

"Clio. I know her..." Lexi pressed a palm to her forehead, and her face twisted in pain. "Don't I?"

"They don't really do meet and greets." Why couldn't Icarus access those bits of his mind?

Lexi's frown deepened, and she stumbled back, away from the stage. "I need to get some air."

A strange thing to say, given they were outside, but he followed, concern pulsing through him. He didn't remember this from… From what?

"She died. I saw," Lexi muttered. "On the street. A café."

The walls in Icarus' head pulsed, then shattered, and a lifetime of memories rushed back. Hundreds of years surged in, in a blink, reminding him there was more outside of this world.

The stone buildings and streets splintered. Not the way breaking rock should, but more like it was all painted on glass that someone threw a rock through.

"When I was younger, I met her. She was my best friend." Lexi was still talking. "But she wasn't. There's a memory there, but it's not mine…"

"It's mine." Clio appeared in front of them on a blank white landscape. "Hello." She waved and smiled.

This wasn't good—understatement of the century they'd just not-lived.

"Where are we?" Icarus asked.

The muse shrugged. "Same place you were before you noticed me. Your head. Her head. It's all kind of a deliciously messy and fucked up blur."

Lexi massaged her temples. Icarus knew the feeling. This was a lot to be shoved into a brain at once. "In case you missed the news," Lexi said, "a siren already tried trapping me in my thoughts. Lorelei didn't fare well."

"Trapped? I haven't trapped you." Clio tilted her head to one side and then the other, studying Lexi.

"Then why can't I leave?"

Icarus remembered more now. He was supposed to pull her out. Instead, they'd gotten sucked into a life that was half-mishmashed memories, half-fantasy.

"That's on the two of you. I'm only here as an observer, and maybe to poke and prod a little, to see how the two of you react." Clio's tone was light and playful. She bounced from one foot to the other.

"Why? On whose behalf?" Icarus wanted to know. Their settings hadn't re-solidified. If he or Lexi focused, would they go back to Germany? Would they lose themselves again?

"Why did you pretend to be my best friend? If you're only here to watch, why did you interfere in my other memory?" Lexi added to the stack of questions.

"I'm not supposed to tell." Clio sang the words.

Icarus didn't care what she was or wasn't supposed to do. On earth, he might not be a fighter. When it came to the mind, he was a master. He pinned her to a non-existent wall with invisible force. "Explain, or stay in here with us."

"You can't keep me here." Clio's playfulness faded as she squirmed. "I'm here because you're creating new worlds within your own history. I'm just inspiration. I can leave anytime." She twisted her body but didn't otherwise move.

"Then, go." Icarus poured the menace into his words. "If I can't stop you, why are you still here?"

Panic tinged her laugh. "I like it here. The two of you are fun. Plays and operas and sex every day. Why would I leave?" She clawed at the air but remained pinned in place.

He advanced on her. The gods' fucking with his life was status quo, but that didn't mean he had to like it. "I want to know why Zeus sent you. Simple question that requires a simple answer. Talk, and you can go."

She stared at him, eyes wide and chin quivering. "I told you already. He wants to know how the new goddess of the underworld reacts. He needs to know what he's up against."

"Is that all?" The answer was stupidly straightforward. He pushed a little more pressure into the force that held her. It wouldn't do physical damage, but the mind was a dangerous playground if someone let themselves get lost in it.

As he and Lexi had discovered.

"Nothing more. I promise." Clio's glee had vanished. "I was there with the hellhound, and I'm here now, to see how she responds and report back to Zeus."

"Wonderful." Lexi spat the word. "Another god poking in my thoughts for his personal gratification. When do I get to do the same to them?"

Icarus relaxed his hold, and Clio vanished. "If I could tell you how, I'd let you play around in any one of their dreams," he said.

"On second thought, it's probably nasty in Zeus' head. Like all… superiority complex and shit. I'll stay out, thank you very much."

He was glad she saw the humor in the whole thing. "I can't believe we got stuck here."

She leaned into him and pulled his arms around her. "I don't know how much I mind. We had fun, right?"

"True."

"As long as we get to keep the memories…"

He wasn't getting rid of those, ever. Not if he had any say in the matter. "Yes." He wrapped her in an embrace and kissed her the top of her head. "I'd still like you to join me in the real world, though."

"Me too." Lexi sighed. "And then go kick Zeus' ass for thinking he had the right to jab me in the feels. How much of this was real?"

"None of it, except for the impressions it left behind." And the most important thing. He'd never said it. How had they gone decades without the words passing his lips?

"You're so smart. Dad would be proud of me, finding a smart guy who's as irritated with the gods as I am."

He laughed and pulled her closer. Trepidation coursed inside, over answers they didn't have and Zeus' involvement, but Icarus could set that aside to appreciate this moment. "He'd be proud of you anyway. And you need to know something."

"What? Are you all right?"

"I'm worried about you being stuck in here." He was stalling. "Which is why I need to tell you, and I should have said this sooner."

Worry whispered across her face. "Tell me what?"

"I love you." He brushed his lips over hers. "That's the one thing down here that's real. I love you wholly and completely. I'm so glad I found you, and wherever we are in history, or in planes of existence, or trapped in a dream, I'll always find you."

Her smile was worth more than all the money in the universe. "I love you too."

That sounded incredible. Better than he thought possible. He kissed her hard, drinking her gasps and falling into the scrape of her nails up his back. He pulled away with a gasp, not wanting the moment to end. There was a critical issue at hand. "I need you to come out of this. Please?"

"I still don't know how."

"Meditate?" He tried to laugh as he said it, but he was tapped for other answers.

Lexi whirled to face him and grasped his hands. "Or hold me tight and take me with you."

"I don't like the idea of leaving you in here."

"But you've come back every time. It's not like it's difficult for you to climb into my head at this point. If it doesn't work, we try something else. *Not meditating*. Not only because I'm stubborn, but also 'cause I'd rather not get sucked even deeper into my head."

He didn't have an argument for that, and they were out of ideas. He tugged her close again. "See you soon, one way or the other," he murmured against her lips.

He felt her smile. "See you soon," she said.

Icarus closed his eyes and pictured himself in his body, in his room. He looked again, and his ceiling stared back. This was promising. He sat up.

"That didn't take long." Conner was sitting on the stool again. "Oh, fuck." He looked to Icarus' side.

Icarus followed his gaze to the empty space on his

bed, where Lexi should be. Everything was still in his head—the last few years of fantasy, the talking, the falling in love—but she wasn't here anymore.

Fuck was putting it mildly. Fear and anger filled him. "Where is she?"

NINETEEN

LEXI DIDN'T CARE FOR HAVING A THIRD SET OF
memories jammed back into her skull. Especially not in
the middle of this made-up town in the underworld,
while she tried to figure out why she couldn't get out of
this place. Was anyplace she'd been in the last few days
—years?—real?

Her heart swelled and broke in seconds, as another
lifetime flooded inside. Falling in love with Icarus. Seeing
his world. Watching him try to ignore how much losing
Actaeon had hurt him.

This was going to take a lot longer to explain than
sharing a few memories with Cerberus. Did she want to
go into any of it?

"Lexi?" Cerberus watched her with concern.

She might let him in once she'd had a chance to
process.

"Are you all right?" Actaeon rested a hand on
her arm.

And him. It wasn't her place to share how Icarus

felt, but she needed to find a balance with Actaeon. "Four for four."

"What?" Actaeon asked at the same time Cerberus said, "Where?"

"Why and how?" Lexi was so sick of not having answers. "Mysteries of the universe." She knew one thing though. She was whole.

She took their hands and transported them to Icarus's shop.

A siren blared, beating against her eardrums.

Actaeon covered his ears. "What the…?"

"I hate that sound," Cerberus said.

"Proximity alarm," Lexi said at the same time Icarus did.

She spun to find him standing a few feet away, and the gnawing pain in her chest lessened.

He snapped his fingers, and the noise stopped.

Lexi threw her arms around Icarus' neck and wrapped her legs around his waist, kissing him hard. This was real. She wasn't stuck in anyone's head. She was no longer a series of fragments. This was right.

He held her up even after they broke the kiss, and pressed his forehead to hers.

"We missed you," she murmured.

He sighed. "It feels like it's been centuries."

"Am I the only guy here no longer fucking you?" Conner's dry question shoved its way into the moment.

Lexi smirked and dropped to her feet. She looked at Conner. "You saved my sanity. These three have no idea what godhood is like."

"Sounds like a *yes*. Welcome back, Zee." Conner was

seated on a stool. One of the few items in the room that wasn't charred, upended, or in pieces.

She'd find out what happened in a moment. So many parts of her heart and mind ached, but it was all back where it belonged. She wanted to laugh and cry and scream and cheer and fight and fuck and everything, all at once. "Do you know everyone?"

"By reputation," Conner said. "Not many of us have met servants of Death."

Icarus gestured. "Conner, Cerberus. Cerberus, meet the God of Internet Dating."

"That doesn't roll off the tongue the way *Death* does. I'll leave the heavy sexual tension in the room to use that innuendo however it would like." Conner traced the mark on her neck. "Or are we calling you *Truth?*"

"We're calling me *Lexi*. *Zee*, only because you're cute." She'd let Icarus get away with it from here to eternity. She glanced around the room. "Did a tornado touch down while we were gone?"

"Semi-tangible dragon," Icarus said.

Actaeon cleared his throat.

Lexi wouldn't look at him. She wasn't in the mood for one of his accusing glares. "Oops."

"Are you sorry now that it impacted more than me?" Actaeon asked.

"I said I was sorry before." She was a lot sorrier that she'd destroyed Icarus' workshop than she was about Morpheus' showing up in the underworld as a dragon.

"We have a lot of catching up to do still, don't we?" Cerberus' voice was in her head.

She'd missed that, too.

Conner clapped Icarus on the shoulder. "Call me if you need anything else. Thanks for the biggest brain bender I've had in ages." He hugged Lexi. "I'm glad you're safe, Zee. And one of us."

"I'm not sold on the second bit, but otherwise, me too. Thank you again."

As Conner left, Lexi took in more of their surroundings. She shouldn't know what was intact and what had been destroyed, but each item she checked out, she could put in one category or the other. "I'm so sorry." She'd done this because she was upset with Actaeon. She didn't know how the dragon appeared to her, but it made sense, given the rest of the overlap in her experiences, and that Morpheus said she was broadcasting.

She really had been a child. "We'll clean up. Tell us where to start."

"It's not a priority." Icarus covered her hand. "We'll get to it. My money says I'm not the only one who's exhausted. We need to…"

She could guess where the thought was heading. There wasn't space here for the four of them. Not to be comfortable and stay in the same room.

"You're always welcome in my home." Actaeon almost sounded hesitant.

Icarus frowned. "I haven't been for a long time."

Lexi felt his hurt. It ached with a past she and he lived outside of this one.

"You were, you are, and you always will be." Actaeon was sincere this time. "We're all exhausted, and there's a lot to talk about."

And Actaeon's house was as neutral as it got.

"I love you boys," Lexi said, "but can we decide sooner, rather than later? I've lived three lifetimes in the past twenty-four hours, and saying *I'm drained* is an understatement."

"Actaeon's place is fine," Icarus conceded.

Lexi took their hands and blinked them to the foyer. It wasn't the destination she preferred, but she didn't dare assume yet, with Actaeon. She fixed her gaze on him. "Biggest bed in the house? Puppy pile?"

"You get to make dog jokes?" His face was sunken. She'd never seen this kind of exhausted before.

"I'm the mistress of the underworld. Of course I do." She didn't feel it, though.

He nodded up the stairs. "My room, it is."

The four collapsed in a tangle of limbs on his mattress. She was surprised anyone had the strength to take off their shoes. She wanted to sleep for a decade, but her mind refused to be silent. Too many thoughts. Too many lives. Too many memories.

"Give it time. Try not to focus." That was Cerberus.

"What he said." Icarus chimed in.

Apparently they could hear each other now.

Lexi couldn't do this. She needed silence. It had been centuries since she had her own thoughts. She wanted the men all close, but she couldn't... "I need a little time."

She was grateful no one stopped her as she climbed from the bed. She wandered onto the beach. Warm sand squeezed between her toes. The ocean air caressed her cheek. It was all real. If she could ground herself here and never leave, it might be heaven.

She sat near the water, close enough for the waves to lap at her feet. The soft crash of the surf mingled with the night, providing the only sound. Walls in her head kept the voices out.

In a few hours, she could face it all. Cerberus and Icarus—even Actaeon—were close enough she felt secure, but far enough she could think.

She stayed there until the sun crested the horizon. It was a beautiful sight.

Actaeon's icy aura caressed her skin before she heard his footsteps.

Thank her, he didn't speak. He sat next to her, pressing his arm to hers. The simple contact quieted her thoughts further.

"Cerberus is your heart, child. But Icarus is your mind." Aphrodite's words taunted Lexi.

It made sense now. Actaeon was her strength.

"I don't need you." Lexi's quiet words mingled with the morning.

"I'm hurt."

She rested her chin on her knees and stared at the vast stretch of blue. "No you're not. You're waiting for me to finish my thought."

"Am I?"

"You don't need me, either."

"I'm going to let you keep talking, because I'm tired of sticking my foot in my mouth."

She smiled. "Life has taught us both that we can only rely on ourselves. That we don't need anyone else." The words didn't taste quite right, but they were close. "There's a bit of you—I know, because I hear a similar voice—insisting that, if we fall apart, you can still stand on your own. I'm my own backup. I can't afford to rely on anyone else."

"That does sound familiar."

"Then you can guess what I'm going to say next."

"Is this what it's like with them?" Actaeon asked. "Finishing each other's thoughts?"

"No. I hear them in my head." She couldn't explain why Actaeon wasn't there. She didn't want him to be. Didn't know if she ever would. "This, right now—it's instinct."

Actaeon chuckled. "You're right. I don't need you. Who I am won't let me. But I sure as fuck want you here, and I'm going to be lost if you leave."

That was exactly what she'd being going to say. She leaned her head against his shoulder. Silence settled between them as yellow and orange cascaded over the ocean.

She was done trying to figure out time and clocks. The sun was a few inches above the water when Actaeon spoke again. "You're going to have to sort through what happened."

"It's all a jumbled mess." Her heart was, anyway.

"Talking about it may help unjumble things. We could have breakfast. Icarus makes a brilliant berry cobbler."

"I know he does, and I'm not telling you how I do. You haven't earned that detail." She wanted Actaeon around. Felt his strength whenever he was near. They still had issues, though.

"That's fair." Actaeon stood and tugged her to her feet. "May I ask you something?"

"You can ask…"

"That doesn't mean you'll answer. Thanks." His smile was soft. "I still want to take you on a date. Or more than one. After you're back in a better spot and feel like your head is on a little straighter, may I buy you dinner?"

"That's what you wanted to ask?" She hadn't seen that coming. It seemed like so long ago that he'd promised to take her out.

Actaeon rested a hand on her back and pointed her toward the house. "Yes. You. Me. Night on the town—this one or another, you pick."

"I'd like that." A date. With a hero. One of the big ones in history. The idea made her heart skip in a giddy hop. Dad would be so disappointed. But he might like Actaeon. Lexi almost laughed at the ridiculous ramble of thoughts. It felt so normal.

They stepped inside, and the sugary scent of cobbler greeted them.

"It cooks more evenly in the modern oven," Icarus said when they found him in the kitchen.

Lexi grinned. "I know how that goes."

She and Actaeon took seats at the breakfast bar.

Cerberus passed out mugs with coffee, while Icarus dished out food.

Shadows fell across the marble, and she spun toward the glass doors at the back of the house. The sky was black. Lightning shattered the darkness, leaving an after-image when it vanished. Thunder shook the building.

"Zeus." She wasn't certain which of them spoke, or if it was everyone.

Energy crackled in the air, and their phones all screamed high-pitched whines at full volume.

Icarus furrowed his brow and clenched his fist, and the noise stopped. His nostrils flared, and his breathing was heavy. "He's doing this to every device in the world that can broadcast. We need a TV."

"I don't have one," Actaeon said.

"Of course you don't." Icarus turned to Cerberus. "You have something."

"Yes." Cerberus reached into the air, and a laptop appeared in his hand. He set it on the table. The instant he opened the lid, it blared to life, and Zeus appeared on the screen.

"He shouldn't be able to do this." Icarus sounded concerned.

"We'll figure out the *how* after we hear what's so important that he did." Listening to Zeus was at the top of Lexi's list of *things that suck worse than getting shot*, but if he'd gone out of his way for a stunt like this, it needed to be heard.

"I come to you today, regardless of the time where you are in the world, to share some tragic news. But out of the saddest moments come some of life's greatest triumphs." Zeus was seated on a plus recliner, in a simple living room.

How domestic of him. Lexi's muscles tensed. She rolled and stretched her neck, but it didn't help.

"Discovering my brother Hades wasn't dead was simultaneously horrifying and heart-wrenching." Zeus' tone was somber. "And to hear otherwise as he returned to destroy so many lives, because he could… I blamed myself. I still do."

"Bullshit." Actaeon voiced everyone's sentiments.

"As you all know by now, this happened because his daughter was misguided," Zeus said. "Lied to her entire life, and led to believe freeing her father was a wise decision. She's learned from her mistakes and taken steps to vanquish the former god of the underworld. She's stepped up to fill her father's shoes and take his place. So, this evening, as we mourn and celebrate the passing of a great and terrible god, I'd also like to welcome a new one to the pantheon."

An image of Lexi appeared on screen. It was altered—she'd never worn a blue evening gown in her life. They made her look good. She'd be grateful for it, if her gut wasn't twisting in on itself at seeing her face on a global broadcast.

"In two weeks, we'll introduce her properly to all of you. A live event and a global series of accompanying banquets, for everyone registered, to usher in this new age."

This was so very bad.

TWENTY

"You're not attending this bullshit event."
Actaeon shouldn't be surprised by Zeus' gall, but he
never would have guessed the god would pull something
of this magnitude.

Cerberus flipped shut the lid of his laptop and
stashed it in his pocket reality. "She has to. He's told the
world to expect her. If she doesn't show up, that's instant
antipathy."

Actaeon couldn't believe that Cerberus—her fucking
guard dog, of all people—was even considering this.
"Who gives a fuck what the general population thinks?
The dead are her followers. The living, as a collective
anyway, will always been indecisive assholes. And doing
anything because Zeus suggested it, especially if you're
not getting something in return, is a stupid idea."

"Or," Icarus said, "you could both keep in mind that
Lexi's not only a god, she's also an adult, and she can
make her own decision."

Actaeon looked at her.

Lexi gave him a thin smile. "Door. Heracles."

"What?" That wasn't an answer.

Someone knocked.

"How—?" Actaeon wasn't sure he wanted to know.

She jammed her hands in her pockets. "He's really bright. Like you, but in a sunshiny, painful-to-look-at kind of way. Can't you two smell him or something? And do you want me to get that?"

"No. I've got it." Actaeon stood and went to let his cousin in. When he was paying attention, he could smell the change in the air, and Heracles' presence was obvious, but it wasn't something he usually gave thought to. In Actaeon's experience, he was happier when he ignored the other hero's presence unless it was a threat. "The gang's all here." Actaeon nodded to the kitchen. "I'd offer you breakfast, but we already ate."

"Thanks. I'm not here to socialize." Heracles followed him further into the house.

Cerberus had his fists clenched, his body coiled in his seat. Icarus didn't look any friendlier.

Lexi gave Heracles a tight-lipped smile. "Your dad is a dick."

"Lovely to see you again." Heracles' formal greeting was as stiff as the tension in the room. "And to be fair, so was yours."

Lexi shrugged. "Sperm donor. And we killed mine."

"So I've heard. I'd love details sometime, about how you managed that," Heracles said.

Icarus gestured to a free stool. "I bet you would. Are you staying? Have a seat."

Presumptuous ass. Actaeon wanted to be upset at the

gesture, but that tiny bit of him that he'd tried to ignore for so long was happy to have Icarus back in the same house again. Almost like he belonged here.

"I'm only here to talk to the newest member of the pantheon." Heracles was focused on Lexi. "To extend an invitation on Zeus' behalf, to join him and the others for dinner."

"He sent you for that? He didn't have someone who could drop off a message?" Actaeon wanted the retort to sound belittling, but he knew why Heracles was here. Actaeon should be pleased this group posed a threat, but if Zeus was worried enough to send his toughest champion, he'd take other extreme steps as well.

"Do you think the invitation might be more sincere if you showed up *before* he told the world I was attending?" Lexi asked.

Heracles rubbed the back of his neck. "I would have preferred to do things that way. This was his decision, though. You can still say *no*."

"These three have some very specific ideas of what happens if I turn Zeus down. What's your insight into the situation?" Lexi hopped from her stool and approached Herc

"I don't speculate like that." Heracles wouldn't meet her gaze.

The only person in the world who was a worse liar than Lexi. She was going to call him on it, without question. Under other circumstances, Actaeon would have laughed at the two meter, one-hundred-ten kilo wall of muscle being intimidated by a woman almost a foot shorter and half his weight.

Lexi studied him through her eyelashes—a deceptively demure posture, with her hands clasped behind her back. "Go on. Speculate. Consider it a good deed for a god who's new to this entire thing? Please?"

Was she batting her eyelashes? Actaeon was almost entertained.

"I'd suggest you attend," Heracles said. "You can refuse the invitation, and I don't expect Zeus will come after you. Right now, the world knows you as Hades daughter—the post-Enlightenment immortal who loosed his wrath on hundreds of thousands of people. And I know you can hide your appearance, but an eternity is a long time to live with that kind of animosity, and you strike me as a person who's tired of hiding. It's dinner. Come meet the gods. Enjoy the spectacle. Go home at the end of the night and let your friends tell you whatever stories they want, about who everyone actually is."

"Told you so," Cerberus muttered.

Actaeon rolled his eyes. The mutt had to choose that one thing to say aloud.

"Do I get a *plus three*?" Lexi was still sweetness and sunshine.

Which was probably adding to how uncomfortable Heracles looked. "A what?"

"A party invitation, as books would have me understand it, frequently comes with the option to bring a guest. But you're trying awfully hard to ensure I say *yes*, so I'm being presumptuous and asking if I might bring three other people with me."

Heracles looked around the room. "Heroes tend to

make the guest list anyway, but servants aren't typically welcome. But I'm only delivering the message; I can't say for certain."

A chill passed through the room, and Lexi's spine stiffened. "Try. Give me your best guess. If I tell you I'll attend, may I bring my guests?" Her sugary tone was developing crystals.

"I'd like you there, regardless," Heracles met her gaze head-on. "I don't know who you are or what bizarre twists of fate put you in this position, but I think you're a good thing. Bring whom you'd like. I'll tell Zeus this is your answer."

Lexi mimed curtsying. "Then, we'd love to attend."

"No. Hang on." Actaeon might be enjoying the show, but experience didn't like the situation. "We want your word that Lexi will be safe. That this isn't an excuse for anything."

Heracles gave him a withering glare. "It's dinner. Like the hundreds we've been to in our life. It's not an ambush."

"Your word," Actaeon said.

Heracles turned back to Lexi. "You have my word. These soirees tend to be glitz and glam and fluff, but you don't invite guests into your home—or temporary dwelling, in this case—to ambush them."

Heracles' word was worth a lot, but Actaeon still didn't like this. Every warning bell in his head was screaming this situation was wrong.

"All right." Lexi nodded. "Tell Zeus *yes*, and that you deserve better than to be a messenger."

ICARUS WANDERED through the main floor of Actaeon's house. *Make yourself at home.* It felt awkward to hear. The kind of thing one told people to be polite, and coming from Actaeon, it slid over Icarus uncomfortably.

It was fascinating to see what Actaeon kept on display from things he'd collected over the centuries. On the surface it was all decorative, but Icarus recognized several of the pieces and knew which vases, paintings, and sculptures were gifts. There weren't many items worth more than sentimental value.

That was one thing he'd always loved about Actaeon.

Icarus stalled in the doorway of a room at the back of the house. It was like a museum, but more personal. Curio cabinets along the walls. Paintings of and from lovers over the millennia.

And in the center of the trinkets on the mantle at the far end of the room, the mid-morning light reflected off a vibrant piece of crystal.

Seeing it again clenched like a fist around Icarus' heart.

He crossed the room and hovered his fingers over the puzzle box, before gingerly grasping it. Time hadn't touched the carved crystal and pewter. Icarus had vivid memories of creating the spring-loaded toy. Actaeon loved pieces like this, and he was a master at figuring them out.

Over time, Icarus had lived so many lives, but right now was different from anything he'd experienced. He was used to floating on the fringes of the gods' affairs. Having his finger on the pulse, and not being an insider, but always able to reach into their world and participate when needed.

Actaeon had floated in and out, pissing off members of the pantheon, and then finding their favor.

And overlapped on all of that was the life Icarus had lived with Lexi. She'd thrown his world into disarray, and he adored it. He didn't take issue with her love for Cerberus. It was genuine, and separate from but complimentary to what Icarus shared with her.

He still had his doubts about Actaeon, though. He didn't want to see him tear Lexi apart, the way he had Morpheus. Cassandra was a different story, since she'd died—twice—before she and Actaeon split. And that was its own set of unresolved issues.

"I like your bracelet." Actaeon's quiet comment startled him.

Icarus glanced at his wrist and the silver chain with the cross that hung from it. He'd forgotten he put that on, but there was no reason to hide it. He'd rather talk through things than fight again. It wasn't his right to tell Lexi whom to love, but he needed Actaeon to understand where he was coming from. Why he was so stubborn when it came to that bond.

"I like your puzzle box." Icarus held up the toy and let it catch the sunlight. "I'm surprised you still have it."

"I am, too."

Not the response Icarus expected. He didn't know what to do with it. "So, this is us. Forced proximity, because we love the same woman."

"You're going to give me that, now? You admit I love her?"

"That's between you and Lexi. I'm going to trust it if she does."

Silence lapsed in the room, creeping and growing until it was suffocating.

"What happened?" Actaeon's question shattered the stillness but not the awkwardness.

Icarus wasn't ready to share the intimate details of what he'd lived with Lexi. "That's a vague question. Narrow it down for me."

Actaeon puffed out his cheeks, then exhaled. "Where to start? Let's see… After the fight with Hades, Hermes found me in the middle of nowhere. Literally. And brought me to Charon." He laid out a tale about Lexi being torn apart by becoming the new goddess of the underworld. It was similar to what Aphrodite explained—how Actaeon was supposed to find her. The details about what happened when he did were vague. "When we found Cerberus, we thought she was whole again. Apparently not. She was stuck in her past with him. Since you showed up about the time she deemed herself *complete*, and based on that kiss she gave you, I assume you were the missing piece."

The explanation filled in a few blanks for Icarus but didn't inspire him to open up. "We were in my head. We got to know each other and fell in love."

"I see." Actaeon's tone was flat. "Lucky you. I guess I got to be the other side of that coin. We were doing the opposite of falling in love." His voice cracked. "I was focused on getting out."

That hint of accusation didn't sit well with Icarus. He didn't know which of them it was directed at. "So was I. Different approaches for different people, I suppose."

"I still think you were wrong. Everything you said in your shop, when Cassandra was still here." Actaeon meandered along the perimeter of the room as he spoke. He brushed his fingers along the surfaces of random collectables.

Was there any significance to what caught his eye, or was it a random slip into the past with each item? "If you thought I was right, it might require some personal growth." Icarus couldn't help the edge that slid into his retort.

"I didn't track you down so we could argue." Actaeon picked up a porcelain statue of Athena. A gift from the goddess.

Bits of Icarus were raw from having pieces of his past so close to the surface. "Then change the subject."

"This thing with Zeus is bullshit." Actaeon looked at him.

Effective choice for a new topic. "I agree."

"What do we do?" Actaeon asked.

It was odd, being looped in on any hint of battle plans. At least these days. Icarus was a brilliant strategist, but there hadn't been much call for such a skill in a while. "Cross our fingers and pray?"

Actaeon chuckled dryly. "You're not funny. We have to make sure Lexi understands."

Icarus had that covered. He and Lexi had

exchanged thoughts about it while she was talking to Heracles. "She does."

"Right. You share dreams." The bitterness was back in Actaeon's reply.

"More than that. She tells me it's not like her servant's bond with Cerberus, but it's some sort of telepathy thing." Icarus didn't understand how it worked.

"That must drive you nuts—not knowing the details well enough to explain them. And before you ask, yes, I'm a teensy bit jealous."

Icarus turned and placed the puzzle box back on the mantle. Its stand was positioned so it would catch the light from multiple windows, depending on the season, and cast tiny rainbows on blank spots along the wall. "I'll figure it out, and so will you." He hoped both of those were true. "As for Zeus... You're a walking armory. There's no one else I'd pick to go with into a situation like that." Differences or not. Fractured past or not.

"I like the praise, but it's not reassuring. Zeus doesn't like having his authority challenged."

"He sent Clio into Lexi's thoughts, to inspire her to spill her secrets." Icarus didn't want to delve into the shared memories, but this was needed, to understand what they faced.

Actaeon raised his brows. "Morpheus said she was broadcasting on multiple channels, so it probably wasn't difficult for a muse to find her. He came to her as a dragon."

That must be an interesting story, and it probably

explained what happened in Icarus' shop. "Lexi is powerful. More than anyone realizes. Especially her. But I don't know if it's enough."

"She's young. She's impulsive. She irritates Zeus."

Icarus smiled. "I can't tell if you think those are good traits or bad."

"Both," Actaeon said.

"This is going to be on live TV, and Zeus has already told the world he wants to welcome Lexi into the fold."

Actaeon didn't look reassured. "You know as well as I do he'll twist that however he needs, to accomplish his goals."

Icarus did, and that was what worried him.

TWENTY-ONE

Actaeon should be grateful for the potential of two weeks of calm. But in the grand scheme of things, it was nothing. An insignificant blip on the radar.

When it came to life with Lexi, that much time with no looming threats sounded brilliant.

Rather, it had, five days ago. Watching her swap jokes and obscure references from fifty years ago with Icarus and Cerberus was grating.

Perhaps it was the fact Actaeon hadn't clicked with her like that, which gnawed on his nerves. He didn't know how to fix it, though. The night they spent with Cerberus in the underworld was brilliant. And Actaeon didn't know how to bring that back.

He sat in his study, trying to read, but his thoughts kept drifting back to her. What had he done in the past?

Nothing. Lexi's assessment of their relationship mirrored most of his that he examined. He'd had some things in common with Cassandra. They liked to go to the movies. Sort of.

She wanted high action, because the visuals made up for the fact she saw most movie endings coming a mile away. He preferred comedies. It was nice to laugh every once in a while.

With Morpheus, they people-watched. Which was always a little awkward when Morpheus could point out what most people's darkest hidden fantasies and dreams were.

Most of Actaeon's past connections weren't the kind of thing solid romance stories were built on.

With Icarus…

Actaeon tried to toe away from the thought before it formed. He didn't succeed. They used to chat long into the night, and into the next day. It didn't matter the topic—politics, religion, philosophy. Even when they didn't agree, they talked.

Why had he thought that was such a bad thing?

Because it terrified him. The way getting to know Lexi did.

Wow. That hit like Heracles' punching him in the gut.

"Do you have a minute?" Lexi's soft question was a welcome distraction from being stuck inside his own head. "I can come back later, if you're not done staring at that spot on the wall."

Actaeon blinked away the dryness in his eyes and dragged his gaze from the stucco. He turned to face her. "What's up?"

She stood in the doorway, one arm behind her back, hand grabbing the other elbow. "What are you worried about, with this Zeus thing? I'm not questioning your concern—the idea of this dinner makes my skin crawl—but I'd like to give a shape to my anxiety."

"I can't help you with that." He wished he could. "It doesn't feel right. It doesn't taste right. Every inch of me says to be prepared for *something*, but anticipating what Zeus is up to tends to lead to his doing an entirely different thing."

"You said you'd teach me to fight. Can you do that?"

"There's not a lot I can show you in the amount of time we have." Actaeon stood anyway. A little practice sparring was a welcome distraction.

Lexi relaxed. He actually felt the tension seep from her. That was interesting.

"You can't load up the right program and teach me kung fu?" Hesitant teasing lined her question.

He smiled. He got that reference. "Neo's got nothing on you. It took him a movie to figure out how to decompile the code. You built an entire town before I reached you in the underworld."

"I'm a fast learner." One corner of her mouth tugged up. "Which means you can teach me just enough to make me dangerous."

He hesitated, not sure if he should say what he was thinking. Fuck. It needed to be out there. "That's what I'm afraid of."

She slumped against the doorframe, tucking in on herself. "Why did I even bother?"

"I don't doubt that you learned amazing things from the sword master"—Actaeon wasn't handling this right —"but practiced forms aren't the same as the rhythm required in battle. You and I don't have that synchronicity."

Why not? The question blared in his thoughts. They should. The idea didn't make sense, but he couldn't shake it.

"Don't make me pout and whine that you promised. That's a cheap manipulation. We both deserve better," she said.

This wasn't the Lexi from the underworld. He saw now what was missing. In a way, it was a shame; being whole squashed some of her playful optimism. He hated knowing this version was more likely to survive. "You're right. I'll show you a few things, and we'll go from there."

A grin broke across her face. "Should we go somewhere? A dojo in Japan? A boxing ring in L.A.?"

"The beach behind the house." He pointed to the back door. "Save the travel for when we can enjoy it."

"Smart thinking." She fell into step beside him, and they made their way outside.

They walked barefoot onto the sand. "Do we need to change?" she asked.

He wore slacks and a button-down. She was in jeans and a T-shirt.

"Can you move in that?" He gestured at her clothing.

"Yes."

"Then no. This is fine. You've probably noticed, but the thing about the kind of fights I end up in is that there's not usually time for a wardrobe change."

"Okay." She shifted her weight from one foot to the other. Anxiety floated from her, like salt on tender skin.

Where to start? "Show me what you can do." He considered the request. "And if you're going to use the swords, can you make them intangible illusions?" "I can." She summoned the two swords. Sunlight glinted through them.

He was impressed she had that kind of control.

Lexi slid into a fighting stance, and then began a series of forms. She was graceful and fluid, dancing with her blades as if they were an extension of her. He recognized the fighting style—she didn't put much variance in it—but he still liked watching her move.

She paused after several minutes and met his gaze. "Are you actually observing, or just enjoying the show?" Her tone was light and playful.

"Both."

"Do you know what you need to? Or at least have an idea?" she asked. "You said we need a rhythm."

They did. It had been a long time since he was at a *training* stage in his development, and he'd never been much of a teacher. With Apollo, he learned because they hunted together. With Heracles, he did a lot of sparring.

Lexi watched him. "Well?"

"I… don't know." Why did he volunteer to do this?

She laughed. "At least you're willing to admit it. Any thoughts?"

One solution made more sense than the other. "With Heracles, we brawled a lot. It taught us each other's strengths and weaknesses. Let's try that first."

"Okay…"

"What's wrong?"

Her weapons flickered in and out of sight. "I only know how to fight with these. You're not that kind of fighter."

"I can do close combat. Your blades aren't real, and I promise to pull my punches but not my moves." Please don't let her be offended by that.

She looked at him with doubt. "Is that possible?"

"It is. We're both new to this, and I need to gauge how to ramp things up."

"I understand."

Thank Cronus for that. Actaeon put several paces between them. "Whenever you're ready, attack."

Lexi's movements were fluid, and she was fast. However, he was familiar with the fighting style. Experience told him where to step and how to dodge, to avoid each strike. He tagged her quickly, striking hard enough to knock her off-balance without doing damage.

She stumbled and caught herself on one knee, before spinning and darting back in.

"Do something unexpected." He dodged each swing. "Think outside the norms of what you were taught."

Her smile was tight. "All right."

He recognized her next move and slid to the left. She didn't follow-through the way he anticipated, and their feet tangled together. They tumbled to the ground.

"This sucks." Her frustration was tangible.

"We've only been going for a few minutes. How long did you say you trained in the underworld before I showed up?"

"A lot longer." She huffed but accepted a hand up, letting him tug her to her feet.

The next several hours were a series of rinse-and-repeat exchanges. Lexi's scowl was etched deeply in place, and she hadn't unclenched her jaw for a while.

Actaeon didn't know how to help her. Every instruction he gave resulted in a bigger complication.

"Why are you fighting this?" she asked.

He didn't understand the question. "This takes time. As in, much longer than an afternoon."

"No. We should be able to do this. We should just work together. That was how it happened with Icarus and Cerberus."

Wonderful. She'd set the bar too high. She hadn't asked them to teach her something so complicated.

"I'm not either one of them," he said.

"But we have a connection…"

"I don't know what you think that means, but it doesn't have anything to do with this."

Her scowl deepened—apparently that was possible. "But it should."

It was as though they were speaking two different languages. The words were there, and he understood them as individual components, but when he strung them together, Actaeon didn't know what she was getting at. "They're not me." The retort was like a lightbulb. "Your strengths aren't mine."

"What does that mean?" Her annoyance was directed as much at herself as outward.

He wished he knew the terminology from those

games she liked, with the quests. "Some people absorb the damage, and some people deal it."

"Like tanks and DPS."

"Yes." He would take her word for it.

"And you… multi-class?"

"I assume that means I do both." He could do this. "Yes, but I'd rather deal the damage and let Heracles absorb it." This was a conversation he understood. If he could put them in the same place, even if the terms were different, they could move forward. He could see clearly what she needed to be doing. The trick was explaining it. "You have magic-wielders in your games?"

"Yes. Mages. Illusionists. But you've seen my magic. I don't cast fireballs or anything. I suppose I could learn, but that's still going to get in your way."

She had a good point. He needed to backtrack a little. "Do you have a sneaky character?"

"An assassin? A thief."

"I like *assassin*. You don't have to stick yourself in the thick of the battle, because you're in the shadows, waiting for your chance to strike while your opponent is distracted."

"And that keeps me from being in the way?"

"It puts each of us where we're most effective. I can show you." They needed a third, though. They could practice with Cerberus, but the hellhound would hold back at the wrong times, and the connection between him and Lexi would be distracting. "Can you make me a practice dummy? A free-moving one?"

"Yes, but it won't fight any better than I do."

"You fight fine. I need you to understand that the

issue is about timing between us. It doesn't have to do with your skill level."

"I understand it, but I don't necessarily believe it." Her expression was softening, though.

"Make me a sparring partner that looks like Zeus."

Lexi furrowed her brow, and an unmoving Zeus stood next to her. "I don't know if I can control it and do what I'm supposed to at the same time. I don't even know what I'm supposed to do."

"One step at a time." He was making a lot of this up as he went along, but it felt right. "Make him fight."

The Zeus illusion fought identically to Lexi, but the visage freed a block for Actaeon. Apparently he wasn't capable of holding back strength without impacting skill. When he had an opening, he didn't hesitate to deal a mortally wounding blow.

They went several rounds, with the fake-Zeus' growing bolder each time, and Actaeon countering in kind.

"So you can beat up my illusions. Awesome." Lexi's tone was flat, but her disappointment had faded.

"Next step," Actaeon said. "You try to tag me while I'm fighting him. I'll keep the match going, to give you time to assess."

He expected another protest, for not giving her enough information.

"All right." Lexi nodded.

Another round started, and Actaeon fell into a simple sparring pattern with fake-Zeus. Minutes ticked away. Where was Lexi?

She kept him busy enough with the illusion that he couldn't afford to look around.

Something nudged the edge of his senses. It was her, behind him. The edges of her aura pressed into and mingled with his.

Even when he was engrossed in the fight, another part of him was tuned to her scent and sound.

She broke into his personal space, and he whirled to stop her.

She wasn't there. She had sidestepped, and she swept his ankle with her foot.

He rolled with the fall, to land on his back, and she straddled his waist.

"I win." She looked pleased with herself.

"You win." He liked having her this close. The pull had always been there, but this was more intense than in the past. It was similar to what he felt in the underworld, but in Super 16K HD.

Lexi rested a palm on his chest, over his heart. "Did you feel it?"

"Yes."

"I told you it was there."

"You were right."

Her smile grew. "Was that so hard to say?"

Not when her weight pressed down on him, and she studied him with those mischievous blue eyes. It was distinctly physical, but it wasn't all sexual. "Not when it comes to you." Because she was sexy and fun?

Because he trusted her.

He cupped a hand at the base of her neck, and another shock of energy twisted around them. He pulled her in for a kiss. Each new point of contact was another thread that wrapped them together. It had been there every time they had sex, but this was undiluted. Fine wine, as opposed to the smell of grapes.

Lexi broke away but stayed close, setting her hands on either side of his head in the sand. "I'm kind of surprised it didn't kill you."

"Admitting you were right?"

"Stooping to my level, to speak in RPG terms," she teased.

This was so much better than arguing. "It's a different language, but lucky for me, it's one I under-stand the concept of."

"I'm sure you'll pick up more of it, the longer you teach me."

He moved his hands to her hips, holding her in place. "I want something in return."

"Is this a barter?" She wrinkled her nose, but it didn't hide her good mood.

"No. I'll teach you more regardless. But you promised me a date."

"I did."

He knew the perfect place to take her. "I have a standing invitation from Athena, to visit the library."

"You're going to take me to a library?"

"*The* library. Alexandria."

"No. It was… Are you serious?" Her wide eyes and the awe radiating from her were worth the offer.

"I'll even read to you from one of my favorite books."

"It's not one with stories of the gods, is it?"

He rolled, eliciting a squeal, and pinned her to the sand, hands above her head. "It's not. It's about a submarine and a giant squid. And no, that's not a euphemism."

"It's a date. And I'm expecting it to be spectacular."

"You deserve no less." He kissed her again, falling into everything.

Her mood shifted. It wasn't good or bad—she was already happy—it was sideways. The others were home.

He wasn't sure how he felt it through her. The new sensation was strange, but he liked it.

"It takes some, getting used to," Lexi said, "but it's worth it."

"I believe it." It might have taken a lot of stress to get to this point, but it was all worth it.

If only dealing with Zeus was so easy.

TWENTY-TWO

Cerberus had spent his entire existence with Hades' emotions hovering at the edge of his mind. It was second nature for both of them to block those out or hide them, but the potential was always there for Cerberus to be dragged in.

Feeling Lexi's tension thrum under his skin was a different beast. It crawled through his veins and made him itch to act. To protect and shelter her. The problem was there was nothing more he could do. Not this time.

He was sitting on the couch, and she lay with her head in his lap. He trailed his fingers through her hair. The gesture comforted both of them, but stress still hummed in his thoughts.

"Why do you think she did it?" Lexi's question wasn't attached to anything—spoken or thought.

Cerberus backtracked through their conversation and couldn't find a point of reference. "I'm going to need more details."

"Aphrodite. Every time she hid snippets of my past

from me. I know what she said her reasons were, but they don't make sense."

Cerberus frowned. That was a good point. If the point was to keep the gods from knowing about Lexi, why take her memories of those events in her life? Why not take the thoughts of those people she'd interacted with, instead?

Especially with Aphrodite's comment to Lexi, that she'd done it too many times. That didn't sound safe. "I don't know," Cerberus said.

"You could ask her." Icarus' voice came from behind them.

Lexi sat up, and Cerberus looked over his shoulder, to see Icarus standing in the living room doorway, holding a piece of paper between his index and middle finger.

His presence didn't eliminate Lexi's stress, but it did add another thread of happiness to her mood.

Cerberus enjoyed seeing the way her mood changed when Icarus was around, and was happy she'd found the hero. He wouldn't have minded meeting Icarus a few centuries earlier, regardless. As they'd gotten to know each other, Cerberus was surprised they'd never met before.

"Asking Aphrodite for answers in the past hasn't gotten me very far," Lexi adjusted her position, so she could sit and see both men.

Since living Lexi's past through her memories, and coming back out, Cerberus had noticed a subtle change in their connection. Even when they weren't holding a mental conversation, he picked up on subtle things like her intent, unless she was blocking him out.

Icarus crossed the room to hand her the card, plus his phone. "Skip the temple. Give her a call. See if you can get a meeting in a neutral place. I have a feeling things have changed since the last time you spoke to her."

Lexi raised an eyebrow. *"Things have changed. That's an interesting way to say, the world is even more fucked up than I thought."* She dialed the number anyway, then set the phone on the back of the couch between all of them.

"Hello?" Aphrodite's lilting greeting filtered from the speaker.

Cerberus was surprised she'd handed out her direct number. From her tone, she didn't expect anyone to use it.

Lexi radiated trepidation. "Hi. It's Lexi."

"Good evening." Aphrodite's voice shifted in an instant. "I'm so glad you're all right."

"I understand you played a part in pointing Icarus toward an answer. Thank you." Lexi flexed her fingers, then wiggled them.

Cerberus grasped her hand and squeezed. She gave him a grateful smile.

"I'd do a lot for you, child." Aphrodite sounded sweet.

Lexi gripped Cerberus' hand tighter. "Because of fated love."

The pause was too long. "Because of fated love," Aphrodite said.

"And that's why you erased my memory at least half a dozen times over the course of my life?"

"Ah. You've remembered." Like that, the sugary tone was gone again.

Icarus knelt, to rest his folded arms on the back of the couch.

Lexi leaned her head into him for a moment, gathering her thoughts. "Hopefully everything, though I suppose only you know that for sure. Tell me the truth. Not this fluffy *for love* excuse that you gave Icarus. *I'll* know if you're lying."

"I wasn't lying. I meant everything I told him," Aphrodite said.

Now that Cerberus knew how dishonesty felt to Lexi, he recognized the faint traces of deception that she picked up on. Like a hint too much salt.

Lexi glanced between him and Icarus. "But you didn't tell him everything."

"Have lunch with me, and I'll give you those answers." There was that rub of friction that said Aphrodite was holding back.

"Try again."

Aphrodite sighed. "I'll tell you what I can."

"Closer." Warning crept into Lexi's reply.

"That gets irritating, child."

A smile flickered across Lexi's face, and she shook her head in amusement. "See, I believe that. Lunch sounds pleasant."

The exchanged details, then said their goodbyes. Lexi handed the phone back to Icarus.

The emotion that spilled from her was muddy,

making it difficult to choose which feeling to appeal to or soothe.

Icarus hopped the couch to settle behind her. She leaned into him and draped her legs over Cerberus'.

"Are you going alone?" Cerberus asked. Aphrodite wasn't a threat, unless she was the most twisted and manipulative god in history, and that was a high bar to reach.

Lexi nodded. "Something tells me I need to."

Cerberus rubbed her leg. "I hope she has satisfactory answers."

LEXI APPEARED in the location Aphrodite had given her. It was odd, getting used to traveling this way. Apparently, if she looked up an address and had an idea of where she was going in the world, she could get there, even if it was a new-to-her location.

She had no idea how that worked, but it was a neat trick.

It must not have worked this time, though. She stood on a patch of cracked asphalt. The building behind her was faced with warped wooden boards. The paint was fresh, though, and the curtains in the front window of the diner were clean and bright.

Painted in big blue letters, was the boast *$15 Steak and Eggs*. In the right corner of the glass was the pyramid-with-an-eye symbol that indicated they accepted barter.

"I hope I didn't keep you waiting." Aphrodite's voice startled her.

Lexi whirled, to see the goddess standing a few feet away. She wore a light sweater and a wrap-around skirt, and her hair was tucked under a scarf. If Lexi couldn't see her aura, she wouldn't have recognized her.

This was the right place after all.

"I never pictured you as a cheap-diner kind of individual," Lexi said.

Aphrodite pointed toward the door. "This is where Persephone met your stepfather."

Lexi faltered. It felt like a fist squeezed her heart. "Oh." Not the brightest thing she could have said. She recovered and headed inside with Aphrodite. The sign invited them to seat themselves, so they did.

Aphrodite sat with her back to the door. Lexi didn't understand it, but she wasn't going to argue. A lifetime of hiding had taught her the best place to be was where she could see the entire room and run quickly.

She probably didn't need to live that way, now that she was a goddess. How long before that impulse faded? Would it ever? That might not be a bad thing if Zeus decided he didn't like her.

"Order whatever you'd like." Aphrodite handed her a menu from the short stack tucked behind the salt and pepper. "I understand your stepdad was a fan of the grilled cheese, with fries and a side of ranch dressing."

"That does sound like Dad."

The waitress grabbed their orders. Lexi went with the recommendation, plus a strawberry milkshake. She didn't know if it was her imagination or not, but food here tasted better than in the underworld.

Someone else picking up the tab helped too.

Aphrodite asked for the same.

That was going to take some getting used to. Lexi might be a goddess, but she'd seen the entire pantheon believing they were above the *normal* people. Even Conner, back in high school, held himself in a way that said he knew he wasn't the same as everyone else.

"What do you remember?" Aphrodite asked when the waitress was gone.

"So much. The night with Conner, Poseidon's daughter turning me in, and Artemis talking to Actaeon in the back of Statesman's Deli."

Aphrodite frowned. "I didn't do that last one." She was telling the truth.

Was Actaeon so different back then that Lexi just didn't notice him? It was possible. She was glad he'd climbed out of that pit.

Lexi fiddled with a sweetener packet. "Why did you do any of it?"

"To protect you."

That was true as well, but it was missing some details. It would be nice if this gift for seeing the truth came with some pointer of which direction to look in when Lexi saw a lie. "To keep the gods from knowing about me? Because—"

"To keep you from knowing about them. I didn't want you to be a part of our world."

For the second time since she'd arrived, Lexi's heart stumbled. Why was she hurt by that? Because she'd thought Aphrodite's kindness meant something. For instance, that the goddess cared. Apparently not. "Why not?"

The waitress returned with their milkshakes. Aphrodite used her spoon to poke at the cherry on top, not looking at Lexi.

Should Lexi say something else?

"I loved your mother." Aphrodite finally spoke. "I'm not talking about the fleeting bullshit passion that movies and books portray as love, or the obsession Hades had for her. She was my best friend, sometimes my lover, and always a pillar of strength in my life."

Lexi had expected this meeting to be a strain, mostly as she tried to get answers. She didn't anticipate her emotions being yanked through the ringer. Cerberus had loved Persephone—as a queen. As a ruler. But this was so pure, it rolled over Lexi with its raw honesty.

Aphrodite pulled a napkin from the holder and draped it over her knees, then nibbled on a tiny spoonful of milkshake. "Persephone gave Hades everything, to keep him sane. Don't misunderstand—before time drove them apart, they were an incredible couple. The love flowed both ways."

Lexi didn't know what to say. This didn't answer her questions, but it was sincere, and a glimpse into her mother's past that she'd never had before.

"Cassandra saw your birth," Aphrodite said. "She didn't see beyond that, but she knew Persephone's daughter would be an oracle."

"Cassandra tried to kill me. Surrendered herself so that Hades could destroy me." Lexi forced her fist to unclench. Cassandra might have also sacrificed herself to save Lexi, but there was no way to know if that was intentional, or if she thought she was helping Hades.

"Immortality drives a lot of us off the deep end. I'm not making excuses for her. It is what it is, and you'll see more of it, the longer you live."

"None of this answers my question. And it's really a simple question," Lexi said.

"It's really not simple at all." Aphrodite shook her head. "You need context, to help you understand. I helped Persephone hide when she escaped. She had one wish for you—that you be kept from the world of the gods for as long as possible. When you were born, and I saw how intertwined with fate you were, I told her that wasn't an option. She made me promise to keep you away from everyone, including myself, until I couldn't anymore, and I did it without hesitation.

"At first, I did it for her. But I've watched you grow up. I've seen you struggle and overcome, time and again. You're so very strong, child. It may not make sense to you, but I see you as a daughter. So I hid your past from you, for Persephone. For me. I thought I was doing it for you, and I'll never know if I was right. However, I reached a point where I couldn't do it anymore."

As Aphrodite spoke, a rainbow of feelings flooded Lexi, but anger and frustration beat out gratitude. What gave this woman the right? "Why? What changed?" She couldn't keep the bitterness from her question.

"Things are unfolding. I don't know what exactly, but I knew you would be safer with Actaeon, Cerberus, and Icarus. I had to make one last tweak, to put you in their path—"

"You had to interfere again, to get me to where you wanted me." Lexi bit off the words. "You watched from afar for years, while I struggled and suffered. And then you decided it was time for me to fall in love, and that meant it was a good time to dig your fingers into my life."

The waitress returned with their sandwiches. Lexi hadn't touched her shake. Condensation dripped on the table, and ice cream had turned to liquid in the glass. She wasn't hungry.

"I'm sorry," Aphrodite said when the waitress was gone. Sincerity filled her apology. "I realize it doesn't help, but I hated watching you go through those things. I stepped in whenever I could."

"But not when Poseidon sacrificed Dad. Not when I was homeless and squatting in a run-down house with other abandoned immortals. Just when it was convenient for your plans."

"I can't say if my choices were right, and neither can you." Aphrodite spoke with kindness rather than reproach, and she believed what she was saying. "Conner grew up with the gods, and he sees the world differently than you do, and I realize some of that is nature versus nurture. I've always done what I thought was best, and I can't change the past. I can only help you now."

Could Lexi forgive this? She wasn't sure. It wouldn't happen here and now. Emotion lodged in her throat and squeezed the air from her lungs and clouded her thoughts. Learning more about her mother, and hearing the adoration in Aphrodite's voice, was so much to process.

"What's coming?" Lexi asked. It was easier than sifting through her feelings. "You said something is coming that's dangerous. That I'll be safer with my men when it arrives."

"I don't know. I'd tell you if I did, but I'm not part of the inner circle."

The deception was back. Not as blatant as before, but Aphrodite was leaving things out. "Tell me what you do know."

Aphrodite pushed her untouched food aside and leaned closer, locking her gaze on Lexi's. "Zeus and those who side with him have worked hard, to either align or kill any hero who's a threat."

Which was old news. "Does that include Artemis?"

"It's likely. She wears her neutrality like a badge, so I can't say for certain."

"What are they up to?" The story Charon told her flowed back. "Does it have to do with the promise Zeus made to his mother? That he wouldn't let Cronus, or anyone, step up and rule unreasonably again?"

Aphrodite gave her a dry smile. "He takes that promise very seriously. Zeus' interpretation of what's best for the world very likely doesn't match yours. If he feels this is his path to order—to ensuring mankind doesn't destroy themselves—he'll obliterate ten or twenty or thirty percent of humanity to save the rest. To ensure Olympians remain where he believes they belong —in power."

"Fuck. He really is a comic-book villain."

"No." Aphrodite's sigh carried centuries of exhaustion. "He's so much worse. Don't go to this gathering of his."

"You mean the one for me? If I tell you I am going, will you erase blocks of my memory again?" Lexi happily let the bitterness spill into her question.

"No. I'm here if you request my help. Otherwise, you're in much better hands now. I'm done interfering."

Too little, too late. But was it? Lexi couldn't say. Was anything in her life black and white? "And I'm done hiding. Hades dragged me into the open, and Zeus insists on keeping me here. I don't know how, but I'm going to make him regret that decision, and I won't be shoved aside again."

"I'll stand by you as you do whatever it is you do. I'm sorry for so much, but more than anything, that you didn't have more time with your mother. I promise you, she'd be proud of you."

"Thank you." Lexi choked on an abrupt surge of tears and blinked back the sting behind her eyelids.

She was still angry at Aphrodite for so much, but that wasn't a battle Lexi needed to fight right now. There was so much else at stake.

TWENTY-THREE

LEXI STOOD IN FRONT OF THE FULL-LENGTH MIRROR IN the back of a walk-in closet bigger than any room she'd called her own. Her dress hugged every curve, and the blue matched her eyes.

Cerberus had called a friend to tailor it for her, and Actaeon took care of the bill.

She looked incredible, down to the matching silk heels. She'd never dreamed of having access to a life like this. It was impossible to argue, when three wonderful men insisted this was the best way to meet tonight's challenge.

Her gut churned, as she smoothed the fabric down one more time. No illusions for this. She was going to be on camera and everything needed to be physical.

The tension flowing inside wasn't only hers. It weighed heavy in the house, threatening to suffocate her, depending on the mood of whoever she was near.

Lexi needed to learn to filter that. It would wait until she made it through tonight.

"*Fashionably late* has its limits," Actaeon called.

She rolled her eyes, but she appreciated the break from her thoughts. Considering it took a blink to travel to their destination, they had time.

She could do this, and she wouldn't be alone. The assurance was her armor for the evening.

Lexi stepped from the room and made her way to the stairs. Cerberus, Icarus, and Actaeon stood at the bottom, dressed in tuxes that let their personalities shine through.

Actaeon whistled when he saw her, and heat flooded her cheeks.

Cerberus met her halfway and offered his hand, then escorted her to the main floor. "You look incredible." He kissed her fingertips before letting go.

Icarus touched her cheek, drawing her attention. "Accessory for the evening." He held out a black velvet box.

She opened the lid, to reveal a thin gold chain with a lightning bolt charm. "I love it."

Icarus withdrew the necklace and hooked it around her neck. The pendant settled at the base of her throat, small but distinct.

"A symbol of Zeus?" Cerberus wasn't impressed.

Lexi traced her fingers along the design.

"Because it's amusing," Actaeon said.

It was subtle. Wearing another god's trinket as if it held no meaning beyond ornament.

Lexi managed a smile through her mounting tension. "Yes it is."

The event was being hosted in Las Vegas. Lexi had

no doubt Zeus picked the location for its various ties to her past.

"Here goes nothing." She hoped it was nothing, anyway.

In a heartbeat, the four stood in the lobby of the Las Vegas Parthenon. A string quartet sat in the corner, playing lilting music that wove into the quiet atmosphere. Everyone, from wait staff to the other guests, wore an aura.

"Look at you and your entourage." Conner joined them. "Way to make an entrance." He wasn't alone.

The woman with him wore a stunning silver gown that hugged her figure and sparkled in time with the vibrant red aura encircling her. That was a neat trick.

"Serenity, Lexi. Lexi, Serenity." Conner gestured.

Lexi knew the name. Serenity was Ares' daughter. One of the more prominent post-enlightenment heroes. "Pleasure to meet you." Lexi extended her hand.

"Same." Serenity's grip was firm, and her smile warm and genuine. "I've heard a lot about you. Don't worry. I only listened to the things he said." She nodded at Conner.

Something caught Lexi's attention. Serenity's aura had covered it, but now the red cord connecting her to Conner was distinct and stunning.

"Don't." Conner's sharp tone caught Lexi off guard.

She looked up, to find him watching her with warning in his gaze.

It made sense that he already knew the cord was there. She shrugged. "Not saying a word."

"Appreciate it." Serenity's expression never wavered.

They were both aware. And it was none of Lexi's business, as long as they were happy. "We should get to know each other better sometime."

"I'd love that." Serenity stepped into Conner's waiting arm. "We can swap stories."

"I'm sure yours are better than mine."

Conner chuckled. "Don't be so sure."

Lexi was grateful to start the evening this way. She'd take as many friendly faces as she could get. "Just tell me this. Did either of you get a coming-out party like this?"

"Nope. But I didn't kill a psychotic father and unintentionally assume his position in one of the three most coveted spots in the pantheon. So much for you steering clear of *our kind*." Conner kissed her on the cheek. "No one wants to talk to us; we're old news. But we'll be by the bar most of the night, if you need an excuse to retreat. Good luck. I'm rooting for you."

"Thanks." She didn't like the idea that she needed rooting for.

Actaeon settled a hand at the small of her back, and she focused on the energy wrapping around them, to help calm her. "Let's introduce you to everyone," he said.

They all stepped into the main hall. It was straight out of a movie. Lexi suspected that was for the cameras. Those probably wouldn't be on until later, based on what Actaeon and Icarus said, and what she'd seen on TV in the past.

"Small gathering. Good." Icarus' tense voice clashed with his words.

"This is small?" From here, she saw a couple dozen

of the major faces—gods and heroes alike—and that many more people she didn't recognize.

"I've never in my life felt like I was missing out by not attending one of these," Cerberus said in her head. *"Not expecting my opinion to change tonight."*

It was reassuring she wasn't the only person this didn't sit well with.

She was introduced to everyone in ones and twos. She was glad she knew most of them from history books, or she would have forgotten the first names by the time she reached the last introductions.

Even Apollo, whom she'd only seen in a tank-top and board-shorts before now, was dressed in the finest evening wear. She also owed him something.

"Do you want company?" Icarus asked in her head.

"No." Or rather, she did, but she had a feeling this was news best delivered with as few people around as possible.

She approached Apollo with hesitation, waiting a few feet away until he finished talking to Hera. He met Lexi's gaze and smiled. "Pleasure to see you again."

She stepped closer. "Same."

"Congratulations on your ascension. I wish we were running into each other under more pleasant circumstances."

He had no idea. But he was about to. It seemed half of the attendees didn't want to be here any more than Lexi did. "Thanks."

"I'd hoped to hear from you sooner. Though I understand why it took some time," Apollo said.

"Yeah. Finding myself after becoming one with an

entire plane of existence took some doing." She could have reached out any time in the past two weeks, and she hadn't. This was the biggest regret Lexi had about what happened to Cassandra. She'd promised Apollo to bring her back safe.

"Cassandra didn't make it back with you."

Lexi shook her head. "No. I'm sorry."

"It's all right. I'd already surrendered her a couple of times. All I hoped for her was a happy future."

She might be happier with no future. The thought didn't come with venom. It was based on what Lexi had seen of Cassandra's gift for seeing the future. "I'm sorry." She already said that.

"Did she at least… die well?"

Lexi didn't know what that meant. She should learn. "She saved us. She's the reason we made it out." There was no point in mentioning it might or might not have been intentional. Apollo had gone above and beyond to help Lexi. The least she could offer was comfort.

He gave her a sad smile. "Thank you." He grasped her fingers and kissed her knuckles. "Welcome to the pantheon."

She excused herself after a few more minutes of banter, to continue making her way around the room.

Aphrodite was sweet and apologetic.

Lexi was still working on forgiving her, but tonight she needed allies.

Artemis was polite, but the exchange made Lexi's skin crawl.

Lexi kept her reaction locked away from her

companions. *"I can't believe Zeus went to all of this effort for me."*

"Would it make you feel better or worse to know it's not for you—it's for show?" Icarus asked.

She wasn't sure. *"At least there are no sacrifices planned with the meal."*

"You're death. He doesn't want to feed your numbers," Cerberus replied.

She didn't care the reason, as long as the result was fewer people being killed.

"Hey," Actaeon whispered in her ear. "No leaving me out of the mental gossip."

"You probably know much better stories about any of them than I do."

They drank and chatted and worked the party, and none of it calmed Lexi. Zeus' presence was a constant reminder that her being here was a coerced choice at best.

The evening dragged on. The company wasn't bad. The tension was.

And then Zeus stepped to podium at the front of the room. "Let's get to the heart of tonight's affair."

"Cameras are rolling," Icarus said in her head.

Show time.

Lexi's heart lodged in her throat.

"As you all know, a new goddess has joined us recently. Born with the strength, but hidden from her birthright by a prejudiced and misguided stepfather." Zeus' voice boomed against walls without a microphone.

Lexi clenched her jaw at the reference to Dad. She

didn't want an excuse to lose her temper in here, but she'd take the risk if Zeus went too far.

He locked his gaze on her. "Ladies and gentlemen, I give you the new master of the underworld, the self-proclaimed goddess of truth, Alexandra."

A smattering of polite applause spread around the room.

She reluctantly left her dates behind and strode to the podium, prepared to make her first words a correction of her name.

Zeus stretched out an arm in greeting as she approached, and stepped to the side so she could join him. When she reached him, the air shifted, pressing in on her.

"This woman is an enemy of the state, and always has been." Zeus roared.

Lexi couldn't move. Cords of silver and sparks bound her.

Zeus looked over the room. "She freed Hades, and it wasn't enough. She slaughtered her father, to have his gift as her own."

This was so *so* bad. Lexi struggled against the bonds but couldn't break them. She tried to speak, but no sound came out. *"Help?"* She hated this. Where was Cerberus? Actaeon?

She looked over the room. They were out there, but similar bindings held them. Why wasn't anyone else stepping in? Panic surged inside.

Zeus radiated smugness. "This *child* will wreak havoc on this world if she's allowed. But I'm going to stop her before she reaches that point. Before she becomes an unstoppable force."

He tilted his head near hers, then grasped the gold chain around her neck and snapped it free. "How dare you come into my world and mock me? I'm waiting for one of those pithy comments of yours." His growl sank into her bones, leaving terror behind. "How's this for intimidating, little girl?"

"We're trying." Cerberus sent the mental thought. Reassurance traveled with it, but Lexi didn't buy the façade of comfort.

She wasn't waiting. She'd sworn *no more*. There had to be a way to snap these bonds. She reached deep inside and grasped a new thread of strength. It wasn't hers, but it was familiar and comforting. Moonlight wrapped in passion Actaeon couldn't hide even when he was fighting it.

Lexi let his power mingle with hers, until it crackled over her skin and pulsed in her veins. She strained against the bonds.

They still didn't give.

Could she push harder without hurting Actaeon?

"He'll be fine," Icarus said.

She hoped so. She tugged at more threads and forced the energy out. The bonds cracked and flexed but didn't give.

"What are you doing?" Zeus clenched his fist, and the restraints tightened.

Lexi clenched her jaw and forced out everything she could find. The aural ropes snapped. She allowed a grim smile to break through. "You want *pithy*?" She focused on Zeus. It didn't matter who was watching. They'd already formed their opinion, and getting out of here was more important than changing the general public's mind. "You want me to be intimidated? You win. I'm terrified. But I don't give a fuck if you're the king of gods. I write my own destiny."

"Stupid child." Zeus tried to trap her again, but she deflected the new bonds. "Hades wasn't the most powerful of us, and you're only a fraction of what your father was." He flicked his fingers, and she flew across the stage.

She landed on her feet.

"We need to go," Icarus said.

Cerberus was in her thoughts too. *"I second that. There's a time and a place to wage a battle, and this isn't either."*

Even the reluctance flowing from Actaeon agreed.

She hated the idea of running from Zeus, but if all her guys were on the same page, she needed to listen. She grasped the first setting that popped into her head, and they vanished from the party.

Lexi and the guys appeared in the middle of a city street. She leaned against a nearby building, needing the extra support. Her legs refused to hold her up, and her arms were rubber. She didn't know if it was the stress and terror pulsing inside, or because fighting Zeus took so much out of her.

Actaeon traced a thumb over her bottom lip, drawing her attention. A fresh surge of energy filled her, chasing away some of the weariness. "You were brilliant," he said.

She didn't feel brilliant. She felt stupid and naive and weak.

"Where are we?" Icarus asked.

She winced. "New Orleans." In the middle of the city, on a sidewalk packed with foot traffic. She probably could have picked a more discreet place to take them.

"This looks bad." Cerberus pointed her toward a TV visible through a restaurant window. It was the news, with a clip of the party broadcast in the upper left corner. The headline at the bottom of the screen said *Public Enemy Number One. Only Approach if You Can Kill.*

Zeus didn't waste any time in getting that up. He'd covered at least one contingency.

Icarus grabbed her elbow and turned her attention back to the street. "Zee."

People looked between them and their phones, and cut a wide berth around them. Something told her it wasn't because she and the guys were so well dressed.

"We need to be somewhere else," Actaeon said. "Now."

No fucking kidding.

TWENTY-FOUR

Cerberus smelled the fear and disdain radiating from the crowds that cut a wide path around them. Tension coiled inside, as she prepared for an attack. It didn't matter that Zeus had warned the world Lexi was a god. People did stupid things in the name of heroics.

Why had he supported this gathering idea?

"I have a place," Icarus said.

Understanding drifted from Lexi. "Is it still standing?"

"I couldn't bring myself to get rid of it."

Their surroundings were replaced with a stone, two-story house, with a field stretching in one direction and a forest in the other.

Cerberus had a good idea where they were; days ago, Lexi showed him what happened with Icarus. It was beautiful. He loved seeing her so happy, especially with a man who adored her.

There was a twinge of envy, but only because he

wanted the chance to experience similar, but unique to them, moments with her.

Then again, part of her trusted him enough to let him traipse through her past, including those bits that had been hidden from her. He couldn't ignore the kind of trust that took.

"I can't believe you still have this place." Actaeon's tone was subdued. He turned to Lexi. "How did you know about it?"

"Is this information he's not privy to?" Cerberus sent the mental question to Lexi.

"Probably. But in his case, it's not mine alone to share."

Icarus approached the front door and traced his fingers over the intricate carving before pushing the door open. "She and I spent longer here than you did."

Actaeon frowned. "She and I spent a day arguing about whether or not being stuck in the underworld was a quest, and the two of you lived a lifetime in our old house?"

"You do what you can with the time you're given." Icarus stepped inside.

Actaeon was irritated with the response. Cerberus felt it crawl along his skin. It was an interesting sort of feedback loop.

"I still have to focus, to stop you all from overlapping." Lexi's thought was apologetic.

"It's fine. There are many things worse than an intimate connection like this." The antagonism sparking between Icarus and Actaeon was one of them.

"The nostalgia is nice," Cerberus said aloud. "But if

Clio was poking around in your heads and reporting back to Zeus, we're not the only ones who know—"

Thunder clapped loud enough to drown out the rest of his thought. Lightning lit up an abruptly black sky. It struck various points in the house, in a succession of blinding flashes.

The stone didn't ignite, but the plants and aged interior sparked into a blazing inferno in an instant.

"No." Lexi breathed deep, waved her fingers, and extinguished most of the fire.

It didn't matter. Only the exterior of the structure remained.

"The earth is *my* realm." Zeus said from behind. "I'm tired of playing your games. There's nowhere you can go, no place to hide, where I can't find you."

"That's a bit super-villain-cliché." That didn't mean Cerberus had a reason to share his thought aloud and make things worse.

Lexi snorted. *"Right?"*

"Except your super villain is a lot smarter than Dr. Evil," Icarus joined in.

That was definitely weird. Kind of cool, though.

Actaeon cleared his throat. "You do know I can't hear the three of you?"

"Do you take anything seriously?" Every time Zeus spoke, thunder rumbled across the sky. "This is one of many reasons I won't allow you to assume Hades' role. I don't have a spare, but you'll be a lot easier to lock away than he was."

"My calendar's a little full right now. Can we get

back to you… never?" Lexi sounded flippant, but her terror radiated in suffocating waves.

"He can't find us in the underworld," Cerberus said.

"I'm trying. Something is keeping us from leaving." That explained parts of her terror.

Zeus strode across the scorched grass. "Don't go. We're just getting started. You and I need to talk. Alone."

Cerberus had half a blink to register Icarus and Actaeon had vanished, before he found himself on a street corner on Los Angeles.

"Lexi. Bring me back."

"I can't. He's stopping me."

It was good that the mental connection still existed. As her fear spiked through it, that wasn't as comforting as Cerberus wanted. If he ever got the chance, he was going to rip out Zeus' throat, watch him suffer and heal, and then start the process over again.

LEXI DIDN'T HAVE the ability to project false bravado at Zeus and dodge his attacks at the same time. After the first faux-smug smile, when a splash of lightning zinged through her, she dropped the masks.

It didn't matter if she vanished from one spot and reappeared in another, he struck her the instant she showed up. Whatever he'd put in place to keep her from bringing the men back, it also kept her from leaving.

She suspected she could keep blinking around the property for hours or days, but each time Zeus caught her—and it was impossible to avoid something that moved at the speed of light—another burst of pain speared through her.

"At any point in this entire affair, you only had to be less stubborn." Zeus' casual tone was far more intimidating than the one that shook the earth. He might as well be asking her for the time. "You've had your entire life to learn to stay in the shadows, and you were doing so well. Why did you think it was a good idea to step into the spotlight?"

"I didn't want the leave the shadows." That wasn't completely true. She'd be happy to still be an unknown face, but there were parts of this life she wouldn't surrender, in addition to the men she loved. "You and yours dragged me out."

"No. Your father dragged you out. You could have hidden again, once Hades was banished. I sent you and Actaeon to Greece. None of us cared if you lived that life, as long as you left us alone."

A bark of a laugh slipped out. "You realize Hades wasn't weaker at that point?"

With each question, he paused in the attacks, to allow her time to answer. If she didn't vanish the instant she finished her thought, he struck her again.

"I do. And another simple request. Get Icarus to build a new prison. Another thing you couldn't manage. Because… spite? Why?"

"You didn't even keep Hades locked away for half a century last time. What made you think—" She screamed in agony when a larger bolt seared through her. She dropped to one knee, needing to catch her breath.

Fuck this. She vanished, then reappeared behind Zeus, summoned swords in hand, and aimed at his head.

He blinked out of sight too, and lightning zinged through her body.

She couldn't do this alone. Desperation clawed at her senses.

"I'm not only speaking about recently." Zeus was near the house now. He wiggled his fingers, and one corner caved in. Rock tumbled to the ground, and ancient mortar floated into the air.

"Right. Because you've known where I was for years."

"Since you met Conner. It didn't matter that he kept most of the story to himself. Only one dead god could have had any children your age." He flicked a hand in her direction, and the electricity surged from the ground, zapping through her shoes and slicing like razors up her legs.

She was wrong. She couldn't keep this up for days. A few more minutes, if she was lucky. Weariness weighed down her limbs, and her head pounded with the over-load of pain. "It wasn't my decision. Not really. Aphrodite dumped me specifically where Actaeon would find me. She's the one pulling my strings."

"No," Zeus said plainly. "We like to play the *fate* card, but that's an excuse. I've spent centuries building up to this point, because I chose to. I struck Cronus down because I chose to. You walked into that maze, into the arena in Las Vegas, into the underworld, and into the celebration tonight because *you* chose it. If you do nothing else in your short time as a goddess, own your decisions."

Lexi could voice her agreement—everything he said fell in line with what she believed. She chose to keep the thoughts to herself. "What now? What's this great, grand plan of yours? This thing you've been building up to for so long?"

"I'm not a two-dimensional villain, who's going to tell you my entire plan, so you can foil me at the last minute. I don't have the kind of ego that requires your approval."

"You have a different kind of ego, but mostly because my approval doesn't grant you more power."

Zeus chuckled. "Clever. And true. What would you do with the information? Go on national TV and tell everyone my *evil* intentions? They tried that in the late twenty-teens, and it didn't work."

"Last time a god told me I couldn't do something, I used the information to destroy him." She'd like to believe she was keeping him talking so she could figure out an escape. Really, it was because he'd stopped zapping her so they could talk.

A bolt of lightning, larger than any of the previous ones, struck her where she stood, and she couldn't smother her scream.

"All you need to know is that we'll do this a little longer, until I believe you're battered, but not a babbling idiot, then we'll show the world what happens to a god who threatens me, as I bind you away more tightly than Hades ever was."

"You need Icarus, to do that. He's not going to help."

Zeus studied her for a moment. "He's not the only one who can do something like this. He was simply the easiest to convince. The first time for the challenge, and the second using you as a curiosity. I hope you're getting used to being the spectacle people want to stare at but not actually deal with. It's about to become your eternity."

Another attack stole her ability to respond and left her crumbled in a ball on the scorched earth, using the last of her strength not to dissolve into tears of agony.

TWENTY-FIVE

Lexi was out of ideas. She wanted to try a similar trick to what she'd done at the celebration, and share Actaeon's energy. What Zeus had done to keep her away from the men was also blocking her from that bond.

If she called out to Icarus or Cerberus, she'd hear their response, but they were gratefully silent. She didn't think she could handle the weight of their concern or the empty assurances of *you can do this. Get up*.

Her thoughts were giving her enough of that.

"Don't tell me you're already done." Zeus asked. He sounded haughty, but he kept his distance.

Actaeon was wrong. She didn't need to learn to fight in the shadows. She wanted to stab this asshole in the throat.

Part of that might be traces of what Cerberus was thinking.

What *would* Actaeon do? How had he dealt with Hades? She'd watched three of those fights. He always had someone else with him. Even for as strong as he was, he didn't tackle a god alone.

That didn't help.

A rapid-fire series of bolts struck her body at various points, until her skin felt like it would crackle and peel and fall off. There were no visible injuries, but she felt the pain to her bones.

"It's time to take you out of here, then," Zeus said.

No. If they left, if he locked her away, she might lose her last chance. Panic welled inside.

He's not killing you. You don't have to kill him.

The thought was hers, but not. She couldn't get away, though. Even if she could, he'd find her anywhere on the planet.

So go someplace else.

Where…?

Of course. She only needed enough of a break in Zeus' prison to leave. If she could get out of here, she could grab the guys and go home to regroup. *Her* home.

How?

It hurt to reach inside and access her power, but it was worth pushing past the pain. She vanished at the same time she created an illusion of herself, in the exact spot and pose she'd been in.

Zeus bound the illusion the way he had Lexi in the celebration, and she made it react accordingly. The instant he blinked out of sight, his shields dropped.

She extended her senses, grabbed three familiar forms, and brought them all back to the underworld.

Zeus should figure out her trick as she and the men landed on the other plane. In a way, it was a shame she couldn't watch the god's reaction through her illusion's eyes.

Not being dead or imprisoned was a better reward, though.

Cerberus wrapped her in a full hug, squeezing her tight. "Are you all right?"

"I'm better now." The energy of this place rushed into her, filling in cracks and soothing her from the inside out.

No wonder Hades was fine after the fight in Las Vegas.

Icarus and Actaeon joined in the group hug.

Then again, Hades didn't have this kind of love and support.

Mentally, Lexi wanted to curl up here and hide in this embrace forever. They could all live down here, in the land of the dead, for eternity, and Zeus would leave them alone.

In a lot of ways, it was tempting. Even with the warmth around her, despair hovered under the surface. "I keep getting us hurt. I don't know how to make it stop." She looked at Icarus. "You've lost two homes now, because of me."

"No. Not because of you. Don't think that ever for a heartbeat." His tone was firm. "Hades and Zeus did that. You didn't. Besides, those were just buildings. They can be repaired and replaced. Wherever we all are is home. And anyplace we've been, whether it's standing or not, we still have the memories. Those are worth more than anything."

She didn't expect the words to bring so much

comfort, but they wrapped around her, along with three pairs of loving arms, and chased away her sadness.

"What we do next is most important?" Icarus said.

"We go kick Zeus' ass." Actaeon's answer came easily.

Lexi couldn't argue. For all of Zeus' thoughts on choice, he actually meant there was no right choice except those that suited his purposes. And for as tired as she was after that fight, she was exhausted from a lifetime of watching him impose his will on the world.

"I want to take a nap, eat a really good sandwich, and then make a plan," she said

It was a next step. What worried her was she didn't even have a hint of the step the step after that.

***

Icarus was impressed with the saloon, but he wasn't surprised Lexi had figured all of this out—building the town, drawing in the lost souls, and making it her own.

When he found a set of stairs leading to the roof, he headed up. Taking a breather after what they'd experienced felt wrong. Zeus seemed focused on finding Lexi, though. If she wasn't there for him to pursue, he ceased to be a threat.

There were stars up here, bright and dotted across the black velvet of the sky. He recognized the constellations as the same ones that appeared above his house on summer nights.

Apparently she'd figured out how to cut a visible hole through to the sky without his help. Seeing all of this made his heart swell. He had such a wonderful woman, sexy and with brains.

It seemed selfish to want just a little more, but he did. Even spending a few weeks around Actaeon, after living another life in the home they'd shared, brought back a surge of emotion Icarus had denied for centuries. An empty longing. Were a couple of centuries enough to mature them, when millennia hadn't been?

"May we talk?" Actaeon's soft question wove into the stillness of the night.

Speak of the devil. Icarus could tell him *no* and walk away. But he'd been considering searching Actaeon out anyway. "Sure. What's up?"

"You were right," Actaeon said.

Icarus swallowed the impulse to say *was that so hard?* Something told him it was a good idea for this conversation to last longer than thirty seconds. He faced Actaeon.

Actaeon wore a tight smile. "I've spent a long time trying to go down in a blaze of glory. It's not a death wish, but it's..." He raked his fingers through his hair. "I'm one of the best hunters in history, because my mother raised me that way. I'm the child of the moon. I'm Apollo's bratty nephew. I'm the guy who helped Heracles destroy Las Vegas. The world knows about me, but after three-thousand years, you're about the only person who truly *knows* me. On one side of the coin, it's terrifying that someone does, and on the other side, I wish you weren't the only one."

"I know exactly what you mean. It's a tough place to

be." Icarus was sympathetic. He wasn't about to wreck this moment with a sarcastic retort.

Actaeon's body was tense. It was almost funny, how he could look so at ease walking into a fight but tonight he looked as though he might shatter if someone tapped him wrong. Regardless, he was a gorgeous specimen. In fact, the vulnerability added to his strength.

"I've been running from the wrong things," Actaeon said. "I belong with you. I've fought that for so long, because I'm fearless… except when it comes to you and me. I don't want to push you away again."

"No?" Icarus almost choked on the question. Experience said listening to this would end in heartbreak again. But it felt sincere this time. Was it possible to change after so long?

Actaeon closed the distance between them, until there were only a few inches. "I'm terrified of loving you, because you could break me. But I can't stop, and I won't keep running. I've loved you for centuries. Longer. I don't remember a time when I didn't."

That was almost poetic. But Actaeon had always been good with words… when he wanted to be.

"Well?" Actaeon watched him expectantly.

"I love you too." It felt incredible to finally say it. Such a simple thing, but Icarus had hidden it away forever. "And ditto all those sweet things you said. Except the part about being terrified. Nope. Not one little bit."

Actaeon smiled. "Liar."

"Maybe I'm a smidge scared." Icarus laughed. He

should be. Most of what he felt was relief. "Aphrodite was right."

"Not the best tangent."

"Love is worth jumping through a lot of hurdles for." Icarus understood why the goddess had done so much for Lexi and all of them. "Even the ones you put me through. I wouldn't surrender a single one of those memories, regardless of whether or not we reached this point. Though I'm glad this is where we go next."

Actaeon kissed him. So many emotions rushed through Icarus at the hungry touch, buoying him, exciting him, and filling his head with promises. He cupped Actaeon's face and returned the gesture, clinging for all he was worth. So many kisses over the years, and this was the best yet.

Perhaps he'd forgotten how good it was before, but he didn't think that was the case. Either way, it was all up from here.

"Oh." Lexi's surprise carried in her voice and thoughts. "I didn't mean to interrupt."

"Wait." Actaeon broke away, grasping Icarus' hand. He reached for Lexi as well. "I wanted to talk to you, too."

She paused near the doorway to the roof. Her mind was closed off, but hints of curiosity and hope flitted around her.

"Well, come here." Actaeon extended his free hand.

She drew near to grasp his fingers, and he tugged her closer.

"I don't know how much you heard," Actaeon said.

She shrugged. "I saw kissing. It was sweet. And kind of hot. I can infer a lot from that."

Icarus suspected she'd be right.

"I'd walk into any battle, physical or otherwise, by your side," Actaeon told her. "I worship you, and I'll even stop calling your gatekeeper *puppy*."

"That last one is between you and him, but I don't want you to strain yourself," Lexi teased.

Actaeon pressed his lips to her forehead. "Goddess, I love you. Those aren't just words, though they are a combination of words I never thought I'd say."

Lexi brushed her mouth over Actaeon's. "I love you too. And you." She turned to Icarus. "Though, you knew that."

Icarus' smile grew. "I'll never get tired of hearing it, though." This was what it should be. This circle—triangle? Square? Perfect shape of love. He couldn't see the thread the way Lexi did, but he felt the way it intertwined between the three of them, looped around Cerberus, made them a whole unit.

He rested a hand on the back of Lexi's neck and pulled her close for a kiss. He had his memories of the years they spent together—the wonderful nights and days and decades of life in their heads.

That was vivid and amazing, and this was better. It had that real spark he'd missed. The tingle of energy that raced between them. The taste of her kisses. The soft mewls that escaped her throat. He devoured her mouth and skated his hands up her back and memorized every sensation.

Actaeon cupped Icarus' cheek to turn his head and steal a kiss.

Icarus remembered this, too. Every other time he'd been with Actaeon, and the pain when it ended, over and over. The lies were gone this time. That insistence that there was nothing between them. That their intimacy was fleeting.

For as many times as they'd come together and fallen apart, this was different. It felt right. And incredible.

TWENTY-SIX

LEXI LOVED EVERYTHING ABOUT THIS UNION. SHE WAS caught between two other hungry mouths. On hers. On each other. She lost track of whose hands were where. A tug in her hair. A lick along her neck. A pinch on her nipple.

It was all delicious, and the adoration that enrobed them made her skin dance with desire.

A sliver of fear nudged her senses. What if she was coming between them? It was a silly concern, given all they'd been through, but the pit of doubt jarred her.

"Don't. You're not coming between us," Icarus said in her mind.

Actaeon bit her earlobe, and the sting made her gasp in delight. "You need to be here as much as we do."

She knew he hadn't heard the thoughts, the way Icarus did, but he had a sense… The pair of assurances chased away her uncertainty.

Icarus was kissing her again, his tongue dancing with hers, while Actaeon stroked him through his trousers.

She couldn't see it all, but she knew everything that was happening. Felt whispers of each touch.

"I could spend so much time exploring this. Discovering *us*," Icarus murmured against her lips.

"We have eternity. Or close enough," Actaeon said.

That sounded perfect. Lexi could snap her fingers and have all of their clothes fall away, but that removed the anticipation. The mingling of their auras was the perfect magical complement. The rest, she wanted to happen naturally.

Icarus tugged her shirt up, stopping when it was halfway off and trapping her arms. He swallowed her giggles with kisses while he held her captive. He finished pulling off her top, and tossed it aside..

Actaeon unhooked her bra, then slid the straps down her arms.

Being up here, under the night sky, surrounded by love and security, was incredible.

Icarus gliding his hands up her chest, to tease her nipples, made it even better.

She looked between the two men. "Why am I the only one who's topless?"

"Fair question. I can fix that." Actaeon grabbed Icarus' collar, yanked him closer, and tore as many buttons as he unhooked, in undoing Icarus' shirt.

Actaeon crushed their mouths together. Their groans mingled, as they roamed their hands over each other's bodies.

Lexi enjoyed watching them together as much as she liked being in the middle of them. Partly because it was hot as fuck, but also because she felt the adoration that flowed between them.

Actaeon broke away for the few seconds needed to take off his own shirt. He dropped his hand below Icarus' waist, to cup his clothed erection, then pulled down Icarus' zipper and worked his cock free.

Need pulsed between Lexi's legs, and heat raced over her skin. She wanted back in on the action. She freed Actaeon's dick and gripped Icarus', to tease them both.

Icarus kissed up the back of her neck, while Actaeon sucked on her nipples. She squirmed under the attention. Squeezing her thighs together didn't relieve the pressure.

Actaeon dragged her jeans down her legs, following the burn of denim on skin with a row of hungry sucks. He knelt in front of her and licked back up to her slit.

When he sucked on her clit, she moaned at the sensation that sparked along her senses.

Icarus slid two fingers inside her from behind. She rocked between his hand and Actaeon's face. Desire and climax built inside. Her breath tore from her throat in short gasps.

She knotted her fingers in Actaeon's hair, grinding into his attentions. Orgasm spilled through her. They continued to push her until she shuddered away from overstimulation.

Icarus withdrew as Actaeon stood. They pressed her between them. Icarus pulled Actaeon in for a deep kiss, sharing her taste.

She wanted more. Of this. Of them. Of everything.

Actaeon turned to her and rested his hands on her hips. He guided her back. When she bumped into something, he lifted her to sit on the ledge of the roof. The polished wood bit into her ass.

The two-story drop at her back was exhilarating, rather than terrifying. Actaeon had her, and she had no doubt she was safe in his arms.

He searched her eyes. "I can't say this enough." He looked between her and Icarus. "I love you both. If I were anyone else, I'd wonder what I'd done to deserve this."

Icarus laughed.

Lexi rolled her eyes, but she was grinning. "Definitely not *be humble*."

"I've got a few flaws, but that's not one of them." Actaeon nudged her knees apart with his own and slid between her legs. He teased her opening with the head of his cock.

She wrapped her legs around him and thrust her hips forward, driving him inside. This was better than the other times they'd fucked. This was more tangible. Instead of a swirl of auras, it was a smooth, sense-heightening blend. Like the buzz of fine whisky.

As Actaeon built to a steady thrust, she reached for Icarus. She knew exactly how he liked to be stroked.

She teased his shaft and glided her thumb over the head of his cock, in time to Actaeon's slamming against her.

Icarus cupped her cheek to kiss her. She tilted back her head when he nibbled down her neck, to suck on the tender skin. He dipped his hand between her legs, to tease her clit and brush Actaeon's cock at the same time.

Their desire mingled with her own, until she wasn't sure where hers stopped and theirs started. It blurred her senses in the most delicious way.

As climax built in Icarus, it swelled inside Lexi as well. He slowed in his attentions, but he didn't have to move, for her to feel him.

Icarus came hard, coating her hand with a sticky mess. His groans were as musical as any opera. Her pulse raced from the excitement. She *felt* it, and it pushed her to the edge of her own climax.

He resumed biting along her shoulder and stroking her swollen, tender sex. The onslaught of touches, combined with his pleasure lingering in her thoughts, pushed her over the edge again.

She screamed into the night when she came. Her orgasm drew out, as Actaeon hammered against her. She clenched around him.

When Actaeon spilled inside Lexi, it lit up her senses and sparked over her skin, until she swore she was glowing. She struggled to catch her breath. It was too much and not enough and the perfect balance of desire and satisfaction.

As the frantic moment ebbed, they all slowed to a stop and collapsed against each other in a breathless pile.

She couldn't say why sex exerted almost as heavy a toll as fighting, but she was grateful immortality didn't numb her senses. She loved the hum in her thoughts and veins.

Lexi was staying like this, wrapped in this moment, for as long as possible. When they broke apart, reality would burst in, reminding her that, despite how incredible love was, it didn't actually conquer all.

Cerberus felt the change in the air, as the four of them gathered around a table in the empty main room of the saloon.

It wasn't just the scent of sex, but also Lexi's glow of happiness. Her stress and worry were still there, but adoration and joy ran through it all. He'd granted her the privacy of staying out of her head while she was with Actaeon and Icarus. That may change in the future, but that could come later.

It was incredible to see. And he was going to have to either deal with the little threads of jealousy, or get good at hiding them and hope Lexi never asked him if he was one-hundred percent okay with things.

He didn't have an issue with her loving Icarus and Actaeon, but the connection between the three was different. Cerberus felt as though he was sitting on the outside looking in. He'd get over it. There were important things to deal with.

Lexi settled in Cerberus' lap, rather than taking a chair of her own. Her weight and heat and casual assumption helped quiet his irrational thoughts.

"What now?" he asked.

"We take the fight to Zeus' door. Off-camera." Actaeon didn't hesitate.

Icarus shook his head. "That almost killed us with Hades, and we had a way to bind him."

Cerberus didn't see the issue. "Unlike Hades, Zeus has children everywhere." The magic that bound a god required someone who shared their power—a servant or offspring.

"So, *one*, that killed Cassandra," Lexi ticked off a finger. "And while we could debate the highs and lows of her specific passing all night, I'm not doing that to a random stranger. Especially if we don't know that it will work."

She raised a second finger. "And *two*, we had him four-on-one in Germany. No, wait. It was just me, because he sent you guys away."

Fair point. "So we figure out how he did it," Cerberus said.

"We don't have to." Icarus leaned in, to rest his forearms on the table. "We only have to know how to stop it."

Lexi lit up. Literally. Her aura pulsed brighter. "Can you do that?"

Inspiration struck Cerberus. "The inverse of what you did with Hades. You bind people to a god like a magnet, using their energy."

"Yes." Lexi draped an arm around his neck. "Is he right?"

Icarus furrowed his brow in thought. "It's a sound theory. It needs to be a different kind of precise, sine we're all already bound. Something that forces proximity. I believe it's possible. That doesn't make it smart to go toe to toe with Zeus."

"You sure?" Actaeon asked. "We've got a lot more

unlocked firepower than we did with Hades. He may have ages of experience, but he hasn't fought for a long time, and he doesn't know what we can do together."

Cerberus agreed, except for any part of the plan that brought Lexi into the middle of a fight. Not that he had any delusions that he could stop her, but he didn't have to like it.

"Icarus is right." Lexi let out a long sigh and stood. "Zeus has fought his war in media and public perception for centuries. Plays. Movies. TV shows. Novels. Comics. Other names have risen and fallen in popularity, but Zeus and his pantheon have remained in people's minds since the beginning. He's pushed that. Sneaking off into some quiet corner to destroy him won't fix the overall issue. It won't tear down the structure he's created."

That was a lot bigger than a bit of pro-active self defense. Cerberus wasn't sure how he felt about it. "Is that the goal? Are you looking to destroy the establishment, or get them off your back?"

Lexi scrubbed her face. "Does it ever stop? Is there any reason to go after Zeus otherwise? Hades was killing people by the hundreds of thousands. Zeus is likely to slow down or stop the sacrifices now that I'm here, because he won't want to feed my numbers. He's not killing the masses to draw me out."

"No. He's killing the masses because he likes the fear it generates. I speak from experience—they ignore you if you don't stick your nose in their business," Actaeon said, "but their definition of *business* is volatile and probably not the same as yours. And you're not going to be happy, hiding down here."

Icarus stopped Lexi mid-pace and pointed her toward a chair. "You have to function within the system he built, at least until you can change it. This has been the ultimate slow burn for him. One hundred years ago, the gods never could have stepped in and demanded this level of faith. Forty years ago, registration wouldn't have stood."

"*We* have to do this," Lexi corrected him. "I can't do this alone."

Cerberus was drowning in her frustration and powerlessness. Why wasn't there a way to magically make this all better? "You don't have to. We're all by your side. We're in this together." He didn't question speaking for everyone. It was true. "What are we doing?"

"We're doing what Zeus wanted." Uncertainty hung in Lexi's tone. "I'd rather stay in the shadows for the rest of eternity, but Hades and Zeus took that from me. No more hiding." As she spoke, her confidence grew. "I'll tell the world my side of the story. They don't have to believe me, the same way they didn't have to listen to the other gods." She looked at Icarus. "Can you hook me into every streaming outlet and TV network, similar to what Zeus did?"

"I need access to a network. I can't do it without the connectivity already in place," Icarus said.

Cerberus had several contacts from when he'd been searching for Lexi. "I can get you into a hub. You should be able to hop everywhere else from there."

"Which is fantastic but isn't a real plan." Actaeon

didn't sound enthusiastic. "You can't just say, *I'm going to appear on TV.*"

"I'll have three great historical figures—"

"Two," Icarus cut her off. "I'm with you on this, but I have to stay with the electronics, to ensure you stay on the air."

A shadow of a frown passed over Lexi's face. "That makes sense. I'll have two of the most powerful non-gods from the history books with me. I'll tell the world my side of things... Yeah, I guess that is all there is to the plan. Zeus can come after me still, but the longer I keep out of his reach, the more people who step up with us, the greater discord it sews."

Cerberus would rather kill Zeus outright, but he saw the merits in the idea, and he was pro-keeping Lexi safe. "Next steps?"

"We need the bracelets to bind us all together, a location to film from, and something really compelling for me to say." Lexi listed off the items.

And they needed to pray that whatever Zeus still had up his sleeve wouldn't kill them.

TWENTY-SEVEN

ACTAEON SHOULD HAVE ASKED LEXI TO CONJURE HIM UP a book to read. He could give *Lord of the Rings* another try. Could she create entire books without knowing them word-for-word?

Pondering that was better than waiting while Icarus and Lexi created the bracelets to keep the four of them together.

Actaeon had tried watching Cerberus play something. It was a computer game with animated goblins and orcs. Watching someone else play was worse than trying to figure the game out on his own.

So he'd left them upstairs and was down in the saloon, observing people come and go. In addition to the stair troll, he'd met a pair of elves, a Sphinx, and a door-to-door milkshake-machine salesman from nineteen-fifty-two.

"Do you have a few minutes?" Lexi settled a hand on his shoulder.

Her touch didn't quiet his racing thoughts, but it did ease the tension coiling in his muscles. He intertwined his fingers with hers. "Sure."

She tugged him toward the kitchen. "Someplace more private?" Timidness leaked into her request.

That wasn't like her. His curiosity piqued, he followed her into the other room.

She was wearing the jeans and T-shirt she'd had on the first time he met her. It was both strange and comforting to see her like this, knowing she'd chosen it.

He leaned against a nearby counter. "What's up?"

"This is going to seem weird, and I don't want it to, but…" She jammed her hands into her pockets and stared at her feet.

This was definitely unusual. He placed a finger under her chin and raised her gaze to his. "What's going on?"

"The thing is, Icarus was thinking bracelets were too clunky, especially if fighting happens. Which, odds are good, regardless of what we plan for. And he figured out how to condense the magic, and it doesn't take the same kind, because we're strengthening an existing bond, not forcing one against our wills…"

"Lexi." He brushed his lips over hers. "It's okay. Whatever it is."

She pulled her hand from her pocket and opened her palm to display two thin rings—titanium with a gold hue. "There's one for each of you, and three for me. Rings, because they're unobtrusive. And symbolic. But they fit whatever finger you put them on, so you can wear yours however you'd like. You can put it on your toe if you want."

"Show me your left hand." He knew what he'd see. And there it was, on her ring finger, a thin band with a blueish sheen. Icarus would be wearing its mate. Cerberus' probably had a red tint, and he didn't have it yet.

Actaeon grasped the fingers on her left hand and kissed her knuckle over the ring. "Of course I'm going to wear it on my finger. I know I have a bit of proving myself to do, but I want to be by your side. We belong to each other. I'm not just giddy about that; I'm proud of it. Of you. I'll gladly bind myself to you, for today and tomorrow and eternity."

Pink spread across her cheeks. "I feel like we're exchanging vows."

"In a way, we are." He plucked the smaller ring from her palm and slid it onto her finger. "I'm not going to give you some cheesy TV-show line, like *heroes mate for life*, but I see us all together for that long." He pressed his lips to hers, memorizing the spark and sinking into the perfection of it.

When he broke away, she watched him with her bottom lip caught between her teeth. "I don't know if I can compete with something so heartfelt."

"It's not a competition. That's a component of what makes this work so well. It takes all of the parts to make the whole."

Lexi laughed. "That's the kind of thing I'm talking about. Here's the thing… My life has been a jumbled bundle of insanity since I met you. Not that you were the catalyst, but it feels like you were." She rolled his ring between her fingers, staring at it. "If that sounds like a bad thing, it's not. I can't say I'm happy with how Aphrodite interfered, but I'm pretty pleased with the results."

"Even with gods trying to kill you?"

"Even with. I figure they were working on it, regardless. This way, I don't have to face it alone, and I don't have to hide and hope it passes. I'm grateful I'm doing this with you. Not just fighting the gods, but also discovering this world I've hidden from for so long. And living life. And… everything."

He dipped his head to hover his lips near her ear. "Plus the sex is good."

"The sex is incredible." She slid the ring on his finger. "And I'd love you even if it weren't."

He wrapped his arms around her waist, and she leaned her face against his chest. "This entire thing terrifies me." Her voice was muffled.

"Me too. But I believe in what you stand for, and it's worth the risk."

TENSION RATCHETED through every inch of Lexi, as she stood in front of the house Dad was sacrificed in. It didn't matter how many reassuring touches or squeezes Actaeon and Cerberus gave her. Nervousness had latched on and wasn't going anywhere anytime soon.

Icarus had appropriated a camera across the street,

focused it on her, and given her a microphone. He'd done a little tweaking and assured her she'd be broadcast to everyone, in acceptable quality. He also promised that the rings would keep each of them rooted where they wanted to be, by strengthening the connection between them and her.

Actaeon suggested she wear the gown she'd worn to Zeus' gathering.

She wore her old clothing instead. It felt right, given the situation.

"You're live," Icarus said in her thoughts.

She took one more breath and focused on the camera. "Hey, all. Sorry to interrupt your evenings or days or mornings, depending on where you are. I promise not to take too much of your time." Despite her fear, she kept a confident mask in place. "Most of you have seen me before, courtesy of the other gods. You've heard their opinions of me, but none of it is true.

"The fact is, I'm not one of them. I was born postenlightenment. I grew up outside of the system, like so many of you with godly parents. I don't want to kill anyone or oppress anyo—"

Thunder boomed, drowning her out, and the sky went black.

Zeus was here.

"You're still broadcasting. He can't take this off the air. If he wants to confront you, he needs to attack you in front of the world." Icarus' words weren't reassuring. Zeus didn't seem to have any qualms about publicly executing her.

A sharp tug yanked Lexi's heart, and traveled to her

ring finger, aching through her entire body. Cerberus flickered to transparent, and then solidified.

Actaeon squeezed her hand, and the pain vanished. Warmth spread from her finger, and blossomed inside. The rings worked.

Another crack of lightning lit up the sky. Zeus appeared on the sidewalk, about fifteen feet away. And then Lexi was in front of him. Her heart dropped into her stomach at the unwilling relocation.

"I'm tired of your games." Zeus' voice rolled over her like a storm, crackling along every hair on her body.

An invisible hand gripped her throat and lifted her off the ground. She struggled to draw a breath. Every inch of her ached from being suspended by the neck. Would she suffocate before he popped her head off?

Where were Actaeon and Cerberus? She felt twin tugs focused on the rings, but they weren't by her side.

"We can't get to you," Cerberus said. *"He's doing that fucking forcefield thing he did at the banquet."*

Well, shit. Apparently keeping them nearby wasn't enough.

"I'm sorry." Worry and anger filled Icarus' response.

She didn't have enough mental capacity to talk to them and focus on getting away from Zeus at the same time. It wasn't anyone's fault but Zeus'.

Zeus studied her, brow furrowed but expression a blank mask otherwise. "You won't die like this. I can do it for hours. Days. Centuries. You'll suffer until you learn to ignore it, and then I'll switch to something else."

She tried to claw at the invisible force, but it was

intangible as well. She kicked her legs furiously. He held her just out of reach.

Pounding filled her eardrums. Her frantic pulse? No, it was more. Fists hammering on an invisible wall.

She couldn't talk. Couldn't think beyond panic.

What felt like fingers dug into her chest, and her heart constricted painfully. She screamed at the agony. It didn't matter that there was nothing to see. She fucking felt it.

"You can't stand against me." Zeus sounded matter-of-fact. "I've saved this world. I will *not* let you destroy all I've worked for."

And she refused to be steamrolled into submission. Defiance sparked inside, faint, but growing. It wasn't only her own. The glow spread through her limbs. The bright icy white that mingled with her power and enhanced it.

"And I won't let you take this world from its inhabitants." She forced the retort out.

The grips on her throat and heart tightened, and a new level of agony spiked through her. She tried to scream, but her voice was gone. Her air vanished.

Cerberus' worry blended with the pain. Icarus didn't speak in her thoughts, but she felt half-formed then rapidly rejected ideas for freeing her.

Lexi fought harder against nothing. She twisted and turned and punched, hoping to connect with anything.

Zeus gave a dry chuckle. "I don't need a specially crafted prison to lock you away. You're *nothing* compared to your father. I can bind you in power and pain for eternity. Your lovers will never find you, and you'll never be a hassle to me again."

"Fuck you." She forced out the gravelly retort.

Actaeon circled the forcefield, looking for a way in. She didn't need to see it, she could feel him hunting.

The sentiments were wonderful, but they didn't help. She needed them inside with her, not out there.

But they were here. It didn't matter that they couldn't reach her. She felt all three of them. She dove past the panic inside, forcing herself to ignore the pain and threats. She focused on the warm glow that ran between the rings and her heart, and dropped every barrier she kept in place between herself and the men.

The rush blinded her for an instant. Intelligence and love and strength surged, drowning her in the wash.

She refused to pluck a single strand, and let instinct take over instead.

"No more defiance? I find that hard to believe. You're not broken yet. But you will be." Zeus held up a clenched fist.

Now.

Lexi didn't know who spoke. She summoned her swords.

Zeus wide-eyed shock was priceless.

She swung in an *X* and cut off his extended hand in the middle of the forearm.

His fury erupted in an eardrum shattering roar. She dropped to the ground, landing in a half crouch.

A new hand appeared when the old one had been.

It didn't matter. The distraction was enough. Actaeon and Cerberus stood by her side— Actaeon with an arrow digging into Zeus' throat, and Cerberus in hellhound form, all three heads snarling.

Stop him. She felt Icarus' words as much as heard them.

Actaeon fired. His arrows struck a new invisible wall that only encircled Zeus.

They wouldn't have killed him anyway, but it would have been fun to use him as a pincushion.

"Play all the games you want." Zeus' cocky tone was gone. She swore fear flickered behind his eyes. "The four of you are nothing, compared to what I can do to you."

"Six." Serenity appeared behind Zeus, wielding a pike.

Conner stood next to her. "Us post-enlightenment kids have to stick together."

"Is that the only reason you're here?" Lexi's confidence was starting to feel real.

Conner shrugged. "I think it's a pretty good reason, but also because you're so much better than most of these assholes who think they should be in charge."

"This looks real good on camera," Icarus said.

Aphrodite appeared on the sidewalk, a few feet away. She smiled at Lexi as she strode toward them. When she was a few inches away, she said, "I'm so proud of you, child. And whatever it is you're doing here, I'm on your side."

No shit? Lexi choked back her disbelief. "Thank you."

The storm grew louder, and the sky darker. Large drops of rain struck the pavement, rapidly becoming a deluge. Icarus kept the cameras rolling, though Lexi had no idea what to say next.

A new figure appeared in the middle of the street, hidden by the sudden wrath of the weather. When Heracles stepped into view, her stomach dropped into her shoes. Of course Zeus would send his champion to do his dirty work.

Actaeon's tension rolled over Lexi. This was one of those variables they didn't plan for. But they should have.

Heracles strolled up to her, never glancing at Zeus, and knelt at her feet.

What the fuck?

"I've watched this madness for too long." Even on one knee, he didn't have to look up far, to meet her gaze. "I've been lied to. Manipulated. I was promised your safety at the celebration, and you deserved better. I won't serve Zeus any longer. Whatever you need, any of you"—he looked at each of the gods in turn—"I stand by you."

"No." Zeus' voice rolled with the thunder. "You can't make promises to these people."

"I'm not promising them anything but to do my best not to be an asshole," she said.

Zeus snarled. "Leaders aren't best friends. We drive civilization. We make the difficult decisions."

"*We* don't have that right." There was no reason for Lexi to hold back or filter her words. She hadn't yet, with Zeus. "People can make up their own minds." She tried not to hold her breath for his follow-up *people are too stupid for that.*

Instead, Zeus smiled condescendingly. "You know nothing about this world. About faith. About what it takes for a god to survive and thrive. Tonight's circus is proof of that."

"I've learned more in the last few decades than you have since the beginning of humanity." That wasn't completely true, but she didn't buy that Zeus had access to some great secret of godhood she wasn't privy to. Treating people right seemed like a decent bar for anyone, regardless of lineage.

"Do you think you're going to kill me?" Zeus asked. "You can't. Even if you could, the structure would crumble."

She didn't have the strength for that. Not here, and not now. "I'm not going to kill you. But the structure will find a way to become something new, with or without you. All of us are proof it can be done. But keep in mind," the words popped into her head, "I *am* death. You've destroyed hundreds of thousands of lives, and they live in my realm. I can give them the peace you never did. Not because I want their adoration, but because they deserve better than you offered."

Zeus shook his head, disgust distorting his features. "Enjoy your five minutes of fame. No one stands against me for long, and you'll have less time than most."

He vanished, and the storm went with him.

Lexi was at a loss. All the words and bravado were gone, and she didn't know where to turn or what to say.

"You don't need to say anything else. Feed cut when he left," Icarus told her. *"You were incredible."*

"Let's go home." Cerberus said as he grasped one of her hands, and Actaeon took her other.

Home. She loved the way that sounded. She grasped the mental thread that tied her to Icarus, and blinked them back to the beach house in Greece.

The four appeared in the living room, and Lexi dropped her façade. Adrenaline spilled through her veins, making her legs wobble. She gasped at the onslaught.

"Hey." Cerberus let go of her hand to wrap an arm around her waist, and slid behind her. Comfort flowed through their bond. "You were brilliant."

"I was terrified."

Icarus stood in front of her. He rested a hand on her cheek. "So were we. You handled it."

"You were incredible." Actaeon squeezed her hand. "But I knew you had it."

Icarus scrubbed his face. "You are such a liar. *You* wouldn't have had it."

"Yeah, but I'm not a god." Actaeon winked at her, the fell back onto the couch, pulling her with him.

Lexi landed in his lap with laugh. She heard the truth in his teasing, and it helped chase away her tension.

Icarus sat next to him, and pulled her legs to cover hers.

Cerberus sat on the floor. He turned so he could rest an arm on her leg and see everyone else.

This was good. Who the fuck was she kidding? This was amazing. But it didn't change what they'd done.

The world outside this house was going to suffer the backlash of tonight.

Over the next couple of days, she watched with her men while the consequences unfolded. TV news painted her as a deadly traitor. She wasn't surprised, since media was all god-moderated.

A lot of the internet didn't care for Lexi either. She was the very visible face of a position they'd all thought dead until Hades escaped. To them, she represented the loss of life, and now the loss of comfort as well. She was disrupting the status quo.

The overwhelming support caught her off-guard, though. People cheering her for taking a stand. The first rounds of comments were anonymous, but as hours ticked away, the cheers had faces and names.

She had a hard time looking away from the snowballing fallout. At one point, Icarus blocked all incoming internet and phone signals, and forced her to go outside to enjoy the sunshine.

Lexi couldn't do it. She spent the next few hours pacing the sand.

Actaeon assured her the world had survived with people in it for thousands of years. It wasn't going to crumble in the next sixty minutes.

Icarus finally relented and let her have access again.

Less than a week later, the protests began. Peaceful in those cities where Aphrodite and her family ruled. Small but fierce in those cities where Poseidon once reigned.

Then in Berlin. Las Vegas. Perth.

She sat at the dining room table, watching one shaky

phone-video after another, of a protest-turned-riot on Long Island. Half the signs people carried had her photo. Some were taken from the broadcast she'd done. Others had drawn horns on her, circles with a line through them over her face, or her bound by Zeus.

The slogans were catchy.

Nothingness is better than Death

Feed her to the gargoyles

Death… how do you like it, bitch?

Some of them, she didn't know if they were for or against her.

"How long have you been staring at it this time?" Cerberus took the seat next to her.

He already had his answer. He'd been nudging her thoughts for the last several hours.

She couldn't tear her gaze from the screen. "Zeus won't stand for this. Why hasn't he struck them down already?"

Flames licked at a building in the background. A temple of Poseidon. She'd turned the sound down already, and the silent fire was a new kind of disturbing.

"And send people who support you straight to their grave?" Cerberus covered her hand. The soothing that flowed from him was pleasant.

Icarus stepped behind her, and rested his hands on her shoulders.

Actaeon joined them too, taking the chair on her other side. "There are ways to destroy the soul, so they don't go to the afterlife."

Like what had happened to Dad and Persephone. She glared at Actaeon. "The reminder isn't helpful."

"It's true." He shrugged.

She couldn't argue that. "So, they'll cease to exist, just to make a stand?"

"You were willing to," Icarus said. He traced tiny circles along her neck with his thumb. "We all are. This is their choice, and they grew up in the same world you did. They know the consequences."

"So I should ignore it?" She couldn't do that. "They're dying in my name."

Icarus sighed. "You should be happy about that. But I know why you're not. And that's not all they're doing. They're taking their lives back. You've given them permission to do that."

"Being a god doesn't give you any more of a right to make decisions for them than you had before," Actaeon said.

She shut the lid on the laptop and leaned back into Icarus. Why did they have to make sense? "People are going to die. Cities will crumble. We started this."

Cerberus shook his head. "No. Zeus started it. Thousands of years ago. What he set into motion isn't going to be easy to undo. We knew that. All of those people, they want the same thing you've wanted your entire life. A chance to be themselves, outside the rule of the gods."

This shouldn't be comforting. Lexi supposed it wasn't. Not in an *it will be all right* kind of way. But it made sense. She understood why they protested. She wouldn't want that taken from her, and she wouldn't stop them.

"This is the opening salvo in a long war." Icarus

kissed the top of her head. Love and security flowed through all four of them. "We have allies. Those protestors out there have gods on their side. We won a battle, and as long as we're here to fight the rest, those people aren't protesting in vain."

"You're right," she admitted. Whatever happened next, humanity didn't have to face it alone. *She* didn't have to face it alone. That made it better. Still terrifying, but it left a light at the end of the tunnel, and she was going to focus on that for all she was worth.

EPILOGUE

Actaeon straightened the collar on his white button-down and smoothed an invisible crease on the leg of his trousers.

"I'm not used to seeing you nervous." Icarus' voice came from behind. The mirror showed him standing in the doorway to Actaeon's bedroom.

Actaeon gave their reflections a dry smile. "I'm not nervous." His pulse raced faster than normal, and his skin was hot, but that was anticipation of the best sort.

"Sure you're not. Tapping your thumb and forefinger together isn't a twitch at all."

Actaeon clenched his fist, but he didn't mind the teasing. "Nope. Not at all." Perhaps he was a teensy bit nervous.

Icarus crossed the room, grabbed a suit jacket from where it lay on the bed, and handed it over. "She's going to love it."

"Of course she will." Actaeon had been to hell and

back with Lexi. Twice. This was a date. There was nothing to get worked up over tonight.

This was different. The fate of humanity didn't hang in the balance, but he wanted her to have an incredible evening. Seeing Lexi happy, regardless of where that joy came from, lit up his world.

He draped the jacket over his arm and pushed away the flutters in his chest.

"See you in a few… days?" Icarus said.

"I think that's safe to assume."

Icarus brushed his lips over Actaeon's. "Have fun."

It felt wonderful, to have an exchange like this with love instead of antagonism behind it.

Actaeon walked across the hall to Lexi's room. That wasn't quite an accurate name. She didn't sleep much, but when she did, it tended to be in whichever bed was convenient. This room was more like Cerberus' at this point.

She kept her clothes in here, though. And the door was rarely closed, so he was surprised to see that tonight.

He knocked.

"Come in," Lexi called.

If it was that easy, it defeated the purpose of shutting the door in the first place. His curiosity was piqued.

He pushed into the room, to find Lexi sitting on the bed, her hair falling in a damp curtain around her shoulders. She was wearing a towel. Interesting choice, given they'd purchased her a closet-full of clothes. She'd protested at having the money spent on her.

Actaeon suspected it was years of habit—always

needing to travel light—as much as anything. He hoped that instinct would fade as time passed.

Cerberus sat in a nearby chair, his faint frown not hiding his underlying amusement.

"What's wrong?" Actaeon asked.

"The woman who insisted on wearing jeans and a T-shirt to speak to the entire world on camera can't figure out what to wear." Cerberus' tone was playful.

"I feel special," Actaeon teased. "You care more what I think than what the rest of the world does."

The furrow of Lexi's brow said she wasn't as amused as they were. "You doubted that?"

Not for a second. "I don't care what you wear. It can be the towel, if you want, and I'm fine with that."

She raked her fingers through her hair and puffed out a sigh. "I know you don't, and that makes this even tougher. Two months ago, the choice was simple—put on the outfit that was clean and wash the one that wasn't. I can't believe I'm letting a closet full of clothes trip me up, but it is."

"You're overthinking things." Cerberus stood to join them, and tugged Lexi to her feet. He moved behind her.

Actaeon didn't have the connection with Lexi that let them talk mentally, and he didn't suspect they'd ever share that. But his skin hummed when she was sharing thoughts with Cerberus or Icarus.

They'd cut back on it when he was around, and there was none of that now.

Cerberus glided his hands up Lexi's arms, leaving goosebumps in his wake. The parting of her lips was alluring. There was also an emotional energy loop that sent a wave of sensation through his veins.

The feeling was its own flavor of intoxicating.

"You could go naked, and no one would complain." Cerberus brushed his lips along the edge of her ear.

Lexi gave a half-sigh, half-whimper. "*You* wouldn't mind. Athena might."

"I doubt Athena cares what you wear. It doesn't matter. The library is your last stop, anyway." Cerberus kissed up the side of Lexi's neck.

Actaeon enjoyed watching, but he wanted a little hands-on time, too. He tugged the corner of the towel wrapped around her and let it fall to the ground. She stood naked between them. Her chest heaved, and pink flushed her smooth skin. The scent of desire filled the room.

Actaeon dragged his finger up her breastbone. "He's right. I'm prepared to spend weeks or months there, just letting you explore the books, if you want."

"Mmm… You say the sexiest things." Lexi licked her bottom lip.

Actaeon dipped his head, to nip along the same path her tongue took.

Everything about this was incredible. Not just the physical or the ethereal heat that wrapped around all three of them, but also the emotion. The intensity of the love flowing through the room.

He looked forward to an eternity of this.

Lexi pressed into Actaeon's kiss and Cerberus pressed into her back. The only thing wrong with this moment was that she wasn't dressed and they were. She needed to be closer. To feel skin on skin.

She trailed her fingers down the front of Actaeon's shirt, undoing buttons as she went. "I need to feel more of you." She said the words aloud and thought them at the same time, shoving Actaeon's shirt off his shoulders.

He wrapped an arm around her waist, and her body molded to his. Searing need flooded her. He tangled his fingers in her hair and found her mouth with his again.

Cerberus' chest heated her back. He glided his hand along the curve of her ass and between her legs.

There were times when a slow buildup and casual lovemaking that lasted an afternoon was exactly what she wanted. Tonight, fast and frantic suited her fine.

Cerberus teased her labia but didn't dip deeper.

Actaeon dragged a thumb over her nipple, then lowered his head to suck on the hard nub.

Fuck, this was incredible.

"You three make it hard to get anything done," Icarus said in her head.

She dropped the mental barrier, so he and Cerberus could hear each other. *"I won't apologize."*

"I can't hear you." Actaeon bit her breast hard enough to leave a tantalizing sting.

She pulled his head up, to devour his mouth. When they broke apart with hungry gasps, she said, "Your boyfriend's a voyeur and a pervert."

"I know." Actaeon smirked.

Icarus didn't say anything else, but he treated her to

images of him stroking himself while he watched and felt this through her.

Cerberus slid two fingers inside her, and she moaned at the penetration combined with the mental teasing.

"You don't have a problem with him sitting in the next room jerking off?" Lexi's question was breathless.

Actaeon dropped his hand, and desire sparked between them before skin met skin and he found her clit. "Nope." He pressed his lips to her collarbone. "I like the idea."

She fumbled with his zipper, but his touch made it difficult to focus. The wash of desire-filled auras surged inside. Cerberus' mouth on her shoulder and Actaeon's mouth on hers stole her thoughts.

Actaeon pressed harder against her sex, coaxing and coercing. Cerberus fucked her with his fingers. Icarus' building climax mingled with her own overloaded senses.

She spilled into orgasm, gasping and grinding and losing herself in the feeling.

Before she could slide back from the edge, Actaeon shoved his slacks to the ground, glided his hands over her ass, and lifted her to wrap her legs around his waist.

Fuck, she loved being in love with implausibly strong men.

Cerberus pulled his fingers out of her but stayed pressed against her back, acting as a support.

Actaeon adjusted her enough to slide inside her. *Goddess,* that felt amazing—being stretched out and impaled by his shaft.

She was surprised when Cerberus nudged her back

opening with his cock. She should have felt the warning in his thoughts, but she was too lost in everything.

Lexi wasn't a stranger to anal sex, but nothing about this position was typical.

Cerberus used her juices as lube, then penetrated her from behind, easing in slowly, an inch at a time, until he and Actaeon were both buried inside her.

Being filled from two sides... Being held up by two men... Feeling their need combine with hers and Icarus', as it spilled inside... Lexi tumbled into all of it. It was easier to let it run together in a single cloud of incredible sensation, than to try to process individual pieces.

She knew when Icarus came. The waves of pleasure that buoyed him filled her as well, tingling inside and sending her rushing toward a second climax of her own.

Cerberus and Actaeon built to a fast pace, slamming inside her. Friction sharpened her senses.

Cerberus tightened his grip on her hips. His grunts and free-flowing thoughts indicated he was close to orgasm. When he peaked, he didn't slow, but his ecstasy was another layer on top of hers.

The energy, adoration, and euphoria overwhelmed her, until orgasm engulfed her. She was wrapped in the waves when Cerberus slid out of her.

He didn't let her go, gripping her pelvis tight.

She clenched around Actaeon, until he spilled inside her. He pouded hard against her until he was spent.

He slowed to a breathless stop, and with Cerberus, helped Lexi stand on wobbly legs. Being pressed between them was the only thing holding her upright.

Cerberus brushed her hair aside, to lick along the back of her neck. The light touch tickled and enticed.

Actaeon hovered his lips over hers. "I think I made us late."

A grin spread across her face, goofy and unbreakable. "I'm willing to skip dinner in favor of this."

"But not the books part of the night," Cerberus said.

"Hmm… Books, or hot, sweaty sex with the men I love. You don't want to make me pick." Lexi scrunched her up face in thought.

Cerberus playfully slapped her ass. "I already know your answer. Fortunately, you don't have to choose."

She couldn't have said it better herself.

LEXI ENDED up grabbing something comfortable from her closet. A sweater and new dark jeans ensured she didn't feel out of place next to Actaeon.

He offered to take her someplace better than he'd ever taken Cassandra, like he'd promised weeks ago.

Lexi opted for familiar and low-key, and Statesman's Deli was still there.

After, Athena met them in front of the deli. "Hold out your hand," she said to Lexi.

Lexi did. Athena pressed her thumb into the fleshy bit of Lexi's palm. A current sped through Lexi, sharp and high-energy, before fading.

Athena let go and took a step back. "That's the key. You're welcome to come and go whenever you'd like."

"Are you serious?" She couldn't be. There was no

way Lexi had just been granted unlimited access to *the* library.

Athena smiled and nodded. "I am. It needs more than one god who will look after it, and I get the impression from Actaeon that you will."

"Thank you." Lexi wanted to gush, but she didn't want to make a fool of herself. So many books. Her mind was already running rampant at the idea.

Actaeon chuckled. "You realize that now we're never going to see her."

"I'll come out sometimes," Lexi said.

"I'm sure you'll figure it out." Athena held out her hand, and a book appeared in it. The cover was painted like a children's book, but the spine was bound with leather strips. The book looked ancient. She handed it to Lexi. "Feel free, always, to look at whatever you'd like. I ask you don't remove any of it from the grounds. And read this before you return it. You'll find others here." She handed Lexi a card with a row and shelf number written in neat script.

"I will." Lexi didn't see a reason to argue. It all sounded reasonable and wonderful. "Thank you again."

Athena vanished.

Lexi took Actaeon's hand and thought *Library*. She wasn't sure how she knew to do that, but it worked. Their surroundings vanished and were replaced with the most incredible sight she'd ever seen.

Several-story-high shelves of books surrounded them and stretched in all directions, spanning rows.

Lexi and Actaeon stood on a patch of marble

covered with a throw rug. There were several padded seats, some of them as big as beds.

"What did she give you?" Actaeon asked.

Lexi held out the book. The artwork was delicate and abstract, hand-brushed on smooth leather. She wasn't certain, but the picture almost looked like her. That was ridiculous. It was a woman with dark hair. It looked like a large portion of the population.

The title was in Greek, so it took Lexi a moment to translate. "*The Story of Truth?*"

"Do you want me to read it to you?"

She handed Actaeon the book. "You did promise me a story. Do you know this one?"

"If I have, it didn't have this title." He grasped her fingers and led her to one of the larger seats.

She sat next to him, her legs dangling over the edge.

He opened the book to the first page. The artwork inside was even more detailed than the cover. Stunning scenes, recreated with vibrant colors.

"There was once a girl, strong, smart, and defiant," Actaeon read. "She was born to powerful parents but taken from them as a baby." He turned the page. "She grew up poor and shunned, never daring to tell anyone the truth of her heritage. There was always the fear she'd meet the same fate as her parents."

Lexi wasn't sure she liked this story. A chill raced down her spine.

"One day, she met two great warriors and a wise-man," Actaeon turned the page.

She definitely recognized this painting. The three-headed dog by the brunette's side was a pretty good hint. "I think I know this one. Are you sure you're reading from the book?" The pictures made her think he was, but it was an odd coincidence.

Actaeon showed her the words, and she puzzled out enough that she couldn't deny he was delivering the story as it was written.

She rubbed her arms, but it didn't chase away the chill.

"Do you want me to keep reading?" he asked.

"Yes."

"She faced many trials with her companions. Battling a fierce warrior, a great wizard, and a powerful orator. A chimera and a dragon."

Sure enough, the picture was of the same dragon she'd created from thin air when she was younger. The same green-scaled lizard Morpheus appeared to them as. "Who wrote this?"

He flipped the book over. "There's no author name."

"Keep reading." Lexi had to know if there was more here than she'd lived. Athena must have known this was about her. Or the goddess had a really fucked-up sense of humor when it came to coincidences.

Actaeon nodded. "She and her companions faced each trial and triumphed, until only one was left. She had to confront the master of the realm. The beast who had taken her parents from her and had done the same to so many others. What she didn't realize…"

"What? What does it say?" She didn't care for the way his brow furrowed as he scanned the next page.

Actaeon cleared his throat. "What she didn't realize

was that the great master had been planning this for a very long time. As centuries passed, experience warped his perspective, but his goal was always the same—to save humanity from itself.

"The girl believed people should be allowed to decide their own fates, but the master felt they'd lost that opportunity. They needed those decisions made for them."

It wasn't identical to what she'd heard from Charon and Aphrodite, but it was close. "How old is this book?"

Actaeon shrugged. "I don't know. I've never heard this story before."

"What happens next?" Lexi wasn't sure she wanted to know, because they'd almost reached *now* as it corresponded to her life.

"The girl and her companions stood against the master, knowing that he had to be stopped. Her friends joined them, and their might was great. But the master had other plans. He and they retreated to regroup."

Actaeon turned the page, and was at the end of the book.

"No. It can't end there." Lexi needed to know what happened next. "There's no moral? No *happily ever after?*"

"It might be better that way." He closed the book and set it on the cushion next to them. "One thing I learned from Cassandra that was actually valuable—it's not always great to know what comes next."

Lexi didn't like hearing the other woman's name, regardless of context, but if she paused, she had to agree it was a good point. She had to sate her curiosity, though. "Athena said there were more." She was already on her feet and looking at the card Athena gave her.

There were no numbers on the rows. Where was she supposed to start?

"Lexi, are you sure you want to do this?"

"She wouldn't have given me the information if she didn't want me to look."

Lexi spun in a circle, scanning the stacks. There was a wider gap between two of them. Was she lucky enough that this was where Number One started? She counted until she reached the number on the card, and hurried down the row.

Actaeon followed, apprehension radiating from him.

"*Yes.*" Lexi let out a tiny *whoop* when she found more books like the one in her hand. There was even an empty space, about the width of the story she held. She pushed the row of books upright, and a note fell out.

The writing was in the same neat script as the card Athena gave her.

These were written by the first oracle. She spent years locked away, crafting these tales. When she finished, she gave them to me and asked me to keep them hidden from everyone, until the time was right.

Lexi was careful but anxious as she flipped through them. There was one for Clarity, Strife, and others, including another that said *Truth*.

She grabbed the next book in line, *Clarity,* and flipped to the first page. "This is Conner."

"You're going to read them all, aren't you?"

"They're not long, and it's not as though there are hundreds."

Actaeon grasped her fingers, drawing her attention. "What are you hoping to find?"

"Zeus being vanquished. The bad guy can't win. He can't." The insistence came out more desperately than she intended.

"Every villain is the hero in their own story."

Lexi clenched her jaw. "That's a shitty answer."

"I can't guarantee that we'll find an answer, one way or another, but we'll keep reading them. But remember—if you live your life based on what an oracle says, you won't ever have the whole picture. You'll spend all your time second-guessing your decisions, without having all the information."

"I understand that." Lexi didn't know why this was so important, but it was.

Actaeon took the book from her and tugged her back to the seats. "Let's read the next one, then."

She settled next to him on the cushion, anticipation spilling inside.

"What happens if we get to the end, and it says you lose?"

That was her fear, but when he asked the question, some of her tension evaporated. "We won't."

"Why are you so certain all of the sudden?"

"Because I have my loyal warrior and my wiseman and my broken-but-fixed guardian, and whatever the books say, we'll triumph."

"How do you know we're not the villains?" Actaeon asked.

"Because I know." She kissed him, then laid her head on his leg. "Because it doesn't matter what fate says or what any oracle says. I love you, and I know you feel the same, and it's real and strong and will withstand anything."

He trailed his fingers through her hair and leaned in to press his lips to her forehead. "But you still want to read these?"

"Yes."

Actaeon opened the book. "Once upon a time, there was a god. He wasn't a wrathful god. He preferred love and reason. But his best friend was war's champion…"

IF YOU'RE ENJOYING Allyson Lindt's suspenseful stories with a kick ass twist, check out VALKYRIE REBORN. Betrayal stole Kirby's past, across a dozen lives. Someone will pay the price. The only questions are how and where?

- Click here to start reading VALKYRIE REBORN